CRITIC
THE WORK

MW01092818

The Last to Fall
"Authors Jim Rada and Richard Fulton have done an outstanding job of researching and chronicling this little-known story of those Marines in 1922, marking it as a significant moment in Marine Corps history."
- *GySgt. Thomas Williams*
Executive Director
U.S. Marine Corps Historical Company

"Original, unique, profusely illustrated throughout, exceptionally well researched, informed, informative, and a bit iconoclastic, 'The Last to Fall: The 1922 March, Battles, & Deaths of U.S. Marines at Gettysburg' will prove to be of enormous interest to military buffs and historians."
- *Small Press Bookwatch*

Saving Shallmar
"But Saving Shallmar's Christmas story is a tale of compassion and charity, and the will to help fellow human beings not only survive, but also be ready to spring into action when a new opportunity presents itself. Bittersweet yet heartwarming, Saving Shallmar is a wonderful Christmas season story for readers of all ages and backgrounds, highly recommended."
- *Small Press Bookwatch*

Battlefield Angels
"Rada describes women religious who selflessly performed life-saving work in often miserable conditions and thereby gained the admiration and respect of countless contemporaries. In so doing, Rada offers an appealing narrative and an entry point into the wealth of sources kept by the sisters."

Continue your adventure in history with three FREE historical novels from James Rada, Jr.

STRIKE THE FUSE

Published by Legacy Publishing, a division of AIM Publishing Group.
Gettysburg, Pennsylvania.
Printed in the United States of America.
First printing: May 2020.

ISBN 978-1-7352890-0-7

Cover design by Grace Eyler.

315 Oak Lane • Gettysburg, Pennsylvania 17325

Black Fire, Book 2

STRIKE

THE FUSE

by
James Rada, Jr.

LEGACY
PUBLISHING

A division of AIM Publishing Group

Other books by James Rada, Jr.

Non-Fiction
- Battlefield Angels: The Daughters of Charity Work as Civil War Nurses
- Beyond the Battlefield: Stories from Gettysburg's Rich History
- Clay Soldiers: One Marine's Story of War, Art, & Atomic Energy
- Echoes of War Drums: The Civil War in Mountain Maryland
- The Last to Fall: The 1922 March, Battles & Deaths of U.S. Marines at Gettysburg
- Looking Back: True Stories of Mountain Maryland
- Looking Back II: More True Stories of Mountain Maryland
- No North, No South: The Grand Reunion at the 50th Anniversary of the Battle of Gettysburg
- Saving Shallmar: Christmas Spirit in a Coal Town

Black Fire Trilogy
- Smoldering Betrayal
- Strike the Fuse

Secrets Series
- Secrets of Catoctin Mountain: Little-Known Stories & Hidden History Along Catoctin Mountain
- Secrets of Garrett County: Little-Known Stories & Hidden History of Maryland's Westernmost County
- Secrets of the C&O Canal: Little-Known Stories & Hidden History Along the Potomac River
- Secrets of the Gettysburg Battlefield: Little-Known Stories & Hidden History from the Gettysburg Battlefield

Canawlers Series
- Between Rail and River
- Canawlers
- Lock Ready

Fiction
- October Mourning
- The Rain Man

Black Fire, Book 2

Strike

the Fuse

Chapter 1

May 1, 1922

David Lakehurst paced the small jail cell. First, back and forth, then in a circle and repeat. Each circuit covered thirty feet. Not challenging, but David limped with each step. The pacing wasn't the problem. It was the damned knife wound in his leg. Although the limp had nearly vanished, David could still feel the wound deep in the center of his thigh. When he paced, his leg throbbed and ached, and that pain kept him angry.

He passed the small window and glanced through the bars of the Frostburg jail, hoping to see something. The view of the soot-covered brick wall of the building across the alleyway never changed. Every once in a while, he placed his hand between the window bars and rested it on the glass. The temperature in the room was constant as long as the deputies kept the stove fed with coal. The temperature on the glass told him whether it was hot or cold or somewhere in between outside. It might be spring on the calendar, but the Western Maryland mornings could still be cool, especially since Frostburg sat on the top of a mountain 2,000 feet above sea level.

David stopped and punched at the thin mattress lying on the metal frame. The muffled sound and the creaking hinges weren't satisfying in the least. It was almost as if it was muffling the anger he felt. He had tried beating the wall to relieve his frustration. That idea didn't last very long once he split his knuckles open.

He hadn't shaved or changed his clothes in days. He knew he looked like a vagabond in the clothes his jailers gave him. Seeing his reflection was also something he hadn't done in a week. They were treating him like an animal not allowing him to bathe, shave, nor dress in real clothes every day. Having to wear jeans and a flannel shirt was punishment enough.

David shook the cell door, not because he thought it would swing open miraculously. He wanted to annoy whoever was on duty with the loud clanging of metal. During the week, he had been in the Frostburg jail; he met three of his jailers. Two of the police officers couldn't care less about the noise. But, David's annoying rattling interrupted the third officer's naps continually. David would shake the door viciously and yell. That caused Officer Parker to run back to David's cell yelling and cursing. David cursed him right back.

The silent voice in his brain repeated and repeated, "You do not deserve to be in here." What had he done wrong? Beat up a few whores? He had paid to use their bodies, and he had used them the way he wanted to use them. It was nothing more than a business transaction.

David was surprised to see the lean cop walk through the door from the front office. Officer Gaughran wasn't one of the police officers bothered by the noise.

"I hear you're up and about," Gaughran said. "I guess it's time to let you out."

David stopped pacing and moved up to the door of his cell. "What? Really?"

He expected the policeman to smile and laugh at his shock. Instead, Gaughran lifted his key ring and shook it. The keys rattled against each other. He flipped through the half a dozen keys on it until he found the right one. "Yeah, yeah, someone paid your bail a little bit ago. Believe me, I'm just as happy to see it come through as you are."

Who would have bothered to pay David's bail after leaving him to rot away in here for more than three weeks? Did he care? Hell no, he was getting out.

The jail had two cells that faced each other. David had shared his cell at times with drunks but, each them stayed usually for a night once their bail was posted. David was offered that option, but he couldn't afford it.

Officer Gaughran unlocked the cell door. It swung open for the first time in a week. David stepped into the hallway and all of a sudden his limp felt like a minor irritation. He felt an easing of pressure around him, as if the cell was releasing its hold on him.

"Where are my things?" David asked.

Gaughran jerked a thumb toward the front office. "I've got everything out front."

David started down the hall to the front room, and the cop followed him at a safe distance. David couldn't help but smile to himself as he thought Gaughran should be afraid. David towered over him by six inches. It was hard to think of him as a police officer, in fact, it was hard to think of him as a man.

David could have grabbed Gaughran by his belt and shirt collar, lifted him off the ground, and then slammed him into the bars of the cell. The thought brought a smile to his lips, but he decided not to follow through. He didn't know how many other cops were in the front room and whether they were armed. Besides, David was getting out of this hole. He just needed to stay calm for a little longer.

The only reason he was in a jail cell at all was that the police chief had been waiting for him when he limped out of Miner's Hospital a week ago. Despite still being bruised and having a knife wound, David might have taken the young chief on, but the man had been holding a pistol on him.

The man who put him in the hospital... now, that was a man who knew how to fight! He'd been a tough little bastard! A lot of these coal miners were strong and wiry. Their work digging coal gave them strong shoulders and arms, and their poor pay kept them lean because they couldn't afford large meals. David had been bigger than the man who had stabbed him, but that man had taken a beating and kept on coming, even after David hit him in the crotch with a rock.

David should have been able to beat a miner. He'd it before, but David's attacker knew how to fight. Not just rough-and-tumble bare knuckles like David. This man was trained in self-defense with his hands and a knife. He was probably a veteran, although plenty of vets lacked that man's grit.

The front room of the jail was empty when David and Gaughran entered. David sniffed.

"It smells like you all just piss on the floor when the urge takes you. I thought it was just that way in the back," he said.

Gaughran laughed. "It was fine until you walked in."

David raised his arm and inhaled. He blinked and lowered his arm. The cop was right. A breeze from an open window blew his stench back on him. How demeaning not to bathe except to use a damp rag to wipe off!

The deputy went to his desk and opened a drawer. He took out a billfold, key ring, bullets, and a pistol. David checked the billfold to make sure all of his money was still there. As he reached for his revolver, he noticed the officer's hand linger near his own pistol. David almost snorted. He could have used the pistol as a club and smashed it into Gaughran's face before the cop's pistol cleared the holster.

"So who posted my bail?" David asked.

"William Singletary with the Pinkertons. He left a note for you."

Why wouldn't Singletary stay and talk to David? He was here to post bail. It wouldn't be any trouble to just wait for a few minutes.

Gaughran picked up the note and handed it to David. It was short and to the point: "Meet me at your hotel."

David frowned. He wasn't out of a job or the agency wouldn't have posted bail, but his employers certainly wouldn't be thrilled that police had arrested one of their agents for beating a whore. The Pinkerton Detective Agency expected its employees to act with decorum. David wouldn't have even telegraphed the

Baltimore office, except he didn't have the money to pay the bail.

He'd been in town a few weeks–well, two months now and a quarter of that in jail or the hospital. He hadn't set up a local bank account, and he didn't keep much money on hand. He enjoyed drinking and women too much.

"You can't leave town," Gaughran reminded him. "You would forfeit the bail."

"Not my money," David said before he could stop himself.

Gaughran's eyes narrowed, and his hand moved back toward the pistol on his hip.

"Then you'd find yourself back in jail," the policeman said.

David ignored the comment. "Where's my bowler and clothes?"

The cop pointed to the coat rack. David's black bowler sat on a shelf above the coats on top of his folded clothes. He picked it up, brushed off some coal dust, and placed it on his head. It would hide his dirty hair. He debated changing into his clothes, but he didn't want them to smell as bad as he did. He settled for putting on his overcoat. The first thing he was going to do was check into the Hotel Gunter and then take a hot bath. His clothes had been folded, but he could see they hadn't been laundered.

"Since you don't live here, we need to know where to find you," Gaughran said.

He was probably worried David would bolt after his bail comment. The thought had crossed David's mind, but what would he do? Go to Baltimore? He'd have to find another job because the Pinkertons would certainly fire him then. He didn't have enough money to live on until he found another job.

"I'll be in the Hotel Gunter."

Gaughran nodded. "You need to let us know if you move to another hotel."

"That's the best one in town, isn't it?"

"Yes." The skepticism in the officer's voice said he doubted David could afford such a place. Who wouldn't be doubtful seeing David dressed as he was? He looked like one of the coal miners in Frostburg.

The Hotel Gunter had opened in 1897, built by one of Frostburg's wealthiest citizens. It had a restaurant, barber shop, petting zoo, and for those who enjoyed drinking, a speakeasy. When William Gunter purchased it in the early 20th century and named it the Hotel Gunter, he continued making improvements, such as electrical lighting, a larger dining room, and a pressed-tin ceiling. It was the premier place to stay along the National Road in Western Maryland, just the sort of place where David liked to stay.

"Then that's where I'll be."

David opened the door and stepped out into the warmth of the afternoon sunlight. He tilted his face up to enjoy the direct sun. He only had seen the sun for an hour or so each day in his cell because the alleyway had been so narrow. Sunlight only reached the ground in the alley during the noon hour. Even then, he had gotten no direct sunlight in the cell.

He thought about how much money he had in his wallet. Paying for the hotel room would take most of it. That was too bad. After a week without, he wanted a drink and a woman, but he needed a bath and a comfortable bed. He might have paychecks waiting for him at the hotel. He wasn't sure whether the Pinkerton Detective Agency had paid him during his time in jail.

David stepped onto the sidewalk and looked around. It was his first time outdoors in a week. The air was warming up. Spring was gradually coming to Frostburg. He started up Water Street toward Main Street. After three steps, he started to turn out of habit. He caught himself and continued forward.

Jenny Washington walked uphill along an alleyway between two buildings to reach Main Street. Why did it seem like all the streets in Frostburg go uphill? She guessed it was because she only remembered trudging uphill, especially when she carried groceries or other packages. She stopped at the Palmer Bakery to pick up day-old bread. Eloise Palmer sold the Bakery's day-old products for half price to anyone in need. Sometimes, if Eloise had any older baked goods in the store, she gave them away for free. However, it wasn't something the Palmers advertised to their paying customers, so people like Jenny had to come to the back door on First Street to get their breads and rolls.

Calista, the name she used when she was enticing men for sex, had no problem getting a man to buy her dinner. However, breakfasts and lunches were Jenny's responsibility. None of the men who knew Calista with her tight-fitting dresses and made-up face wanted to buy working woman Jenny Washington a meal.

Almost none. But Matt Ansaro was an exception.

Calista pretended with her fluttering eyelashes and sexually charged talk that she didn't care about money, but Jenny lived in a two-room shack and needed to buy day-old bread to get by. She could have lived better, but she religiously saved a fifth of the money she made. It was her safety net against the day that she could no longer turn men's heads.

She wasn't at that point now, but time was starting to show. She was thirty-five, and it took more and more make-up for her to look younger, although no amount of make-up would allow her to look as young and beautiful as Samantha Havencroft. She was Matt Ansaro's girlfriend and not yet twenty years old. Samantha lived an easy life that didn't pull her skin tight for lack of food or crease the corners of her eyes with lines caused by too much worry and sun.

Jenny reached into the basket and squeezed the loaf of rye bread Eloise had given her. It didn't feel that hard. She could warm it on her stove to soften, and slather the slices with jam, or maybe she would just dunk it in milk and eat it.

She stepped from between the buildings and started across Main Street, the heels of her leather t-strap shoes clicking on the brick-lined road.

She froze in the middle of the street and nearly screamed.

He was walking along Main Street. She recognized his bowler and coat, not to mention his size, especially his size. David Lakehurst was easily twice Jenny's size.

This was the man who had beaten and abused her. She had gone with him expecting sex in his hotel room. Instead, he had led her to the dark alley. She had joked about the cold affecting his performance, and he had slapped her across the face. When she cried out, he had just laughed. She trembled at the memory of his slaps and punches. His large hands had ripped her clothing as he savagely penetrated her. He'd left her bruised, bloodied, and unable to move in an alley on an icy, frigid February night.

Luckily, Matt Ansaro found her and took her to the hospital. He had also convinced her to swear out a complaint against Lakehurst. She believed he was supposed to be in jail until the trial, but now here he was free. He would know it was Calista who had told the police about him.

A horn beeped and Jenny jumped as a Hillman touring car approached her.

Lakehurst looked up. She saw his hard face, recognized the dark eyes, and his bisected eyebrow. She knew he also saw her. She hurried back to the side of the street where she had come from and disappeared down the alleyway.

She paused and leaned against the wall of a building. Maybe he hadn't recognized her. She wasn't wearing make-up or one of her fancy dresses. She wore a loose-fitting cotton dress that didn't hug her figure like her "work" dresses did. She looked like a different person, not someone who would attract his attention.

But she had caught his attention because of that car honking its horn. He had seen her.

Had he recognized her?

Jenny looked toward the entrance to the alley, half expecting to see his silhouette blocking out most of the light. She only saw cars and people moving past the opening between the brick buildings.

She walked rapidly down the alley and made a right on First Street, following it south. She kept looking over her shoulder, expecting to see the giant of a man running after her. When she realized she passed the alleyway where Lakehurst beat her and left her lying among the trash. She gasped for a breath and continued to walk at a rapid pace.

She slowed to a walk and turned down another alley and crossed Main Street, blocks below where she had seen Lakehurst. She hurried to her small two-room house. She fumbled to find her key in her pocket. She tugged it free from the folds in the cloth and unlocked her door. She rushed inside, slamming and locking the door behind her.

Jenny leaned against the door, breathing hard. Then she slowly slid down to the floor crying.

David walked under the triple arch entry into Hotel Gunter. The hotel sat near the northern end of Frostburg's business district along the National Road.

The lobby was a large room dominated by a grand staircase in the center that rose half a flight before turning left and right to continue to the second floor. Halls on either side of the staircase led back to the restaurant, ballroom, and barbershop. The basement held other things that one would not expect in a hotel. The fireplace off to the right was cold, although logs had been set for the next fire.

William Singletary sat in an armchair next to the fireplace reading a copy of the Cumberland *Evening Times*. David noticed a picture of a group of men on the front page. The headline noted that the jury had been selected for the West Virginia treason trial. This trial would determine whether labor leader Bill Blizzard had committed treason last year. His actions resulted in the Battle of Blair Mountain. It wasn't news that help calm tensions between coal companies and union miners during this current strike.

Singletary looked over the top rim of his glasses and saw David. Singletary folded the newspaper closed and stood up.

David walked over and said, "Good morning, Mr. Singletary. Pardon my appearance, but as you know, I've been in jail."

Singletary's nose wrinkled. He must have gotten a good whiff of David.

"Yes, you're the man who got himself thrown into prison for beating up a prostitute." Singletary said it with disdain, as if it was below him to deal with David.

David's jaw tightened. He needed to stay in control. He could have killed this bald little man with a single punch, but Singletary was his boss. If David wanted to be paid, it would come through

9

this man.

"It hasn't been proven," David said.

Singletary snorted. "That doesn't mean you're innocent."

David's fist clenched at his side, but he didn't raise it.

"Any other time, the company would have fired you and let you sit in jail," Singletary said. "Your actions reflect poorly on this company. Pinkerton agents protect the law. They don't break it."

David wondered how true that was. The Pinkerton Agency acted on behalf of whoever their client was, good or bad, as long as they paid.

David waited to hear why he still had a job. It was the only thing that would keep him from punching this man in his face.

Singletary looked around, his weak eyes squinting. "I would invite you for a drink so we could talk, but I doubt that it possible."

If there was one place in Maryland that ignored Prohibition more than Baltimore, it was Frostburg. It was said that six out of ten families in Frostburg made their own wine. That didn't include the dozens of stills hidden in basements, sheds, and barns dripping out gallons of harder liquor.

"I can help you there," David said. "Follow me."

David led his boss downstairs to the basement. They passed the holding cell where prisoners who were being transported between locations stayed the night. David followed the hall, making turn after turn until he came to a closed door. He rapped on it and a small panel at eye level opened up.

"We're thirsty," David said.

They knew him here. It wouldn't be a problem getting inside, but then, few people had that problem in Frostburg.

The door opened. A cloud of tobacco smoke wafted out, although only six people were inside. It wouldn't get crowded until later in the day. The room was small and an empty cockfighting pit dominated at a quarter of the space. Light came in through a small high window on one wall and a second window that looked out into an enclosed courtyard.

"Bourbon," David said to the bartender.

The bar ran along the wall to the left of the doorway, so people could order their drinks as soon as they walked through the door.

"Do you have real scotch?" Singletary asked.

"It's real enough, but I doubt you could count the age in years," the thick-chested man behind the bar said.

Singletary frowned. "I will try it."

David led his boss into the other room of the speakeasy. He wasn't sure why people bothered to call these illegal bars speakeasies. They were very noisy. It was hard to keep drunk people quiet. A more-appropriate name would have been payoffs, since generous payoffs to local police did more to keep these places open than quiet talk.

David and Singletary sat down at a small wooden table. Singletary dusted off his wooden chair before he sat down.

"Perhaps we should have stayed in the lobby," he said.

The bartender brought their drinks and left. Singletary lifted his glass toward the window to look at the copper-colored liquid. He swirled it a bit and sniffed at it.

"I notice he didn't ask what type of scotch I wanted," Singletary said as if it pained him to say the words.

"Beggars can't be choosers," David replied.

Singletary sipped the liquid and coughed. "Beggars wouldn't choose this."

David swallowed his drink in a gulp. It burned his throat, but he didn't care. It beat the dirty water and weak coffee he'd been drinking for the past week.

Singletary took another sip, winced, and set his glass on the table.

"Since you went into the hospital and jail, John Lewis called a national coal strike," he said. "Very few of the mines are working and none of the Consolidation Coal mines."

Consolidation Coal Company was a Pinkerton Detective Agency client. The coal company had started in the Georges Creek Region of Allegany County, of which Frostburg was a part, during the Civil War. The company continued buying mines throughout the late 1800s and early 1900s. It now operated eighty coal mines and was the largest supplier of coal on the East Coast. The

11

company's general offices were in New York, but it had a regional office in Cumberland.

David nodded. "I could read the newspapers in jail."

Reading every article in the newspaper, pacing, eating, and sleeping had made up his days. He had followed news of the strike, but he also paid attention to local news. Three men – John Anthony, Sylvester Shue, and Francis Grimes – of Midland, a town south of Frostburg had tried to rape a woman. Not only had the woman escaped them, they had only spent a night in jail because someone had posted their bail. Not like Singletary who had let David sit in jail for a week.

"What hasn't been in the newspapers yet is Consolidation Coal will start hiring strikebreakers and bringing them in to work their mines in this area."

David asked for another drink without asking whether Singletary was paying. Strikebreakers were expected during a strike. It wasn't a question of if, but when. "The miners who live here won't like that," David said.

"It is not expected that they will. The strikebreakers will need protection. Since the Pinkerton Agency already has agents and undercover detectives in the region collection information on union activities, we have been retained to provide that protection. It sounds like work made for you."

"Why?"

Singletary cocked his head to the side. "Because you are likely to have someone to hit, of course," he said without a trace of sarcasm.

So that's how it was. Singletary didn't like how David acted until he needed him to be brutal. David had no particular affection for strikebreakers, but then, he didn't care much for miners either. A job was a job.

"How should I go about protecting the strikebreakers?" David asked.

It didn't matter what Singletary said. David would do the job the way he saw fit. He just wanted to see how much he would have to hide from his employer. It was easier to ask forgiveness than permission, especially if he accomplished what was asked of him.

"You will have to decide that based on the situation," Singletary said. "We don't want another Matewan, but the company needs its mines to produce."

What had started with private detectives evicting union miners from their homes in Matewan, West Virginia, last fall had turned into a full-blown civil uprising. The fighting between miners and company men pulled in the police and U.S. Army. At its peak, about 40,000 people were fighting. About 130 people died. Although the Stone Mountain Coal Company had won the battle, it won no friends. Things in West Virginia were still tense; more so with the national coal strike ongoing.

"We have undercover agents still in place around the area," Singletary continued. "We need the information they are relaying to us as more miners seek to join the union for protection. They will be sending that information to you here at the hotel. The reason I'm here is to meet with our detectives and make sure they will protect the strikebreakers. I also need to contact our undercover agents and make sure they are still secure. Their positions are even more dangerous now because of the strike."

If coal miners discovered an undercover detective in their ranks, they might kill the man. At the very least, they would beat him so badly he'd be in the hospital a long time.

"My work also sounds more dangerous than what I was doing," David said, leaning back in his chair. He had been sent to Western Maryland to collect information about union activities and observe the miners to learn whom the leaders and troublemakers were.

The left side of Singletary's lips curled up. "Yes, it is more dangerous than beating up prostitutes."

David gritted his teeth, but kept his first reply to himself. Instead, he said, "I should get hazard pay."

Singletary's eyebrows rose. "Yes, you should, but you won't. Consider your hazard pay the cost of your bail and keeping your employment."

Singletary laid two dollar bills on the table and stood up. "I will contact you here if you need to know something. Try not to wind up in jail again. If that happens, the company won't help you."

He walked away, more than happy to get out of the speakeasy. David wondered if it had been the man's first time in one.

David relaxed in his chair. He picked up Singletary's scotch and finished it. It was horrible, but it was alcohol. At least he thought so. The way it tasted, it might be flavored turpentine.

When David walked back upstairs, he didn't see Singletary, not that he expected to see the man. The lobby was empty except for the desk clerk who stood at his post. It was too late for people checking out of their rooms and too early for those who would check in. The clerk was also a lookout for the speakeasy in case the police came to raid the speakeasy through the front entrance.

The hotel didn't appear large from the outside or even the lobby, but it had 100 guest rooms on three floors. It sat right on the National Road, and it was a popular stop for travelers on the highway.

The National Road had been the country's first national public works project started in 1811. It had started in Cumberland and ran to Vandalia, Illinois. Once built, it had gone through a period of deterioration because the federal government couldn't maintain it. Then, as the need for roads suitable for automobiles grew, states upgraded the National Road, added to it, and connected it to other roads. The National Road was now a major highway across the country, and it ran right through the middle of Frostburg, which brought a lot of tired travelers to the doors of the hotel.

David walked up to the front desk. The young desk clerk's eyes widened.

"Mr. Lakehurst, we didn't expect to see you." The clerk's voice quavered.

David leaned on the counter. "Why's that?"

The clerk blushed. "Well, uh, you hadn't been around for days and you had only paid for a week... so... well, we had no way to know."

David shook his head. His hand shot out, and he grabbed the man's tie, jerking the clerk closer.

"Spit it out, man, I don't have all day."

"We thought you left without paying." The clerk's lower lip trembled as he spoke.

"I'll be staying until I tell you otherwise." He let go of the clerk. "Do I have any mail?"

The clerk stepped back out of David's reach. "Sir, you don't have a room here any longer."

"What?"

The clerk jumped.

"You hadn't paid or said what your intent was," the clerk said. "We assumed you left without paying."

David's blue eyes narrowed. He had to make a conscious effort not to make a fist. He wanted to punch this fool, but that would only land him back in the jail, and Singletary made it clear he would be getting out a second time.

"Where. Are. My. Things?" he asked with forced calm.

"I... I believe most of them are in storage."

David's eyebrows shot up. "*Most* of them?" Now his fist did clench, but he didn't raise it off the counter.

"You've been gone a week, sir, and you left unpaid debts. The owners had the right to sell your goods to pay your bill."

A low growl escaped from David's chest, and the clerk pressed himself back against the far wall. Reminding himself that he wanted a bath and didn't want to go back to jail, David pulled out his wallet and slapped down most of the money he had.

"Here. Now get me my room, and bring me whatever is left of my luggage," David said.

The clerk reached forward and picked up the money. Then he quickly pulled his hand back. He looked over his shoulder.

"Do you still have your room key?" the clerk asked.

David nodded.

"We haven't changed the locks yet, so you can have your old room back. I'll have the bellboy go to the storage room to pick up your luggage."

"Then you will find out where my mail is since I was having it sent here." David needed the mail because he expected to find

15

the checks that would allow him to continue staying here among the letters.

David spun on his heels and walked upstairs to his empty room. He let himself in, and as the clerk had said, all of his things were missing.

He walked into the bathroom and started the tub filling with hot water. How he loved indoor plumbing. No more going to a washhouse or waiting for buckets of water to fill a small tub. He paid extra for a room with a private bathroom, but it was worth it. He didn't have to deal with anyone banging on the door as he relaxed in a hot tub.

David undressed and threw his dirty clothes into a corner of the bathroom. He'd send them out to be laundered later. He slid into the tub and sighed as the warmth of the water soaked into his muscles.

He lay against the back of the tub, allowing as much of his body to submerge as he could. The porcelain tub was large, but he was a tall man. He couldn't cram all of him into the space.

He was more than happy to stay in Frostburg. Yes, it meant he would continue getting paid, but he couldn't care less about protecting the strikebreakers. He would do it because of the money. The reason he wanted to stay in town was to find the man who had stabbed him. When David did, the two of them would settle who the best fighter was.

Chapter 2

May 2, 1922

Matt Ansaro couldn't sleep. Trouble was coming. It seemed odd to feel that way, given what had happened lately. He'd been trapped in a mine cave-in and seen a friend die before his eyes. How much more trouble was on the way? He lay in his bed staring at the plaster ceiling of the dark room, listening to the occasional creaking board or air popping in a radiator pipe. Other than that... silence.

It had been a calm night, and now it was a quiet morning. Since the coal strike began in April, men stayed up late drinking and yelling in the streets. Those disturbances had faded over the past month as the partiers realized that they would not be paid while on strike and that their cash would soon run out. The nights were peaceful again. Matt should have been lulled to sleep, but he could only catch brief naps often interrupted by an eerie sense of anticipation... foreboding... doom.

Ever since the Great War, Matt was a light sleeper. The sixth sense he, and so many other soldiers, developed made him feel like an enemy battalion stood outside his bedroom door ready to kill him. Some people called it paranoia or fear. Those words implied a weakness. Matt preferred sixth sense because he never saw it as a weakness. It had helped him survive the war.

Aunt Toni told him it was a fear of the dark. She said the mining accident that broke his leg and killed his friend Pete Spiker caused it. Then she said the painkillers Dr. Lund prescribed for him were a big part of his worry.

Matt knew neither was the case. Aunt Toni did, too. Matt knew she felt the same sense of dread. He wouldn't be surprised if most of the people in Eckhart Mines along Big Savage Mountain sensed it. Sometimes, it felt like such a looming presence he was surprised he couldn't see it. It was the way he felt in the coal mines when he was in the dark and could see absolutely nothing, but he could still sense the nearness of the tunnel walls. This time, it felt like the entire town of Eckhart Mines had been swallowed up by a coal mine.

Somewhere outside of the house, a cock crowed as the sun's rays crested Haystack Mountain, the dawn light dispelled his town-in-a-mine thought.

He made no move to get out of bed. He draped an arm across his forehead and inhaled, trying to calm himself. He was warm under the flannel blanket and down comforter his aunt had sewn. Besides, he had no reason to get out of bed. The coal mines in town were closed because of the strike.

True, the miners in Eckhart Mines and Western Maryland weren't unionized, but when United Mine Workers President John L. Lewis called for a national coal strike at the beginning of April, the Western Maryland miners walked out in sympathy with their union brothers. Lewis was a hard, forceful man from the coal mines in Lucas, just outside of Cleveland, and from a strict Mormon family. He was a man who shamed the rich and worked diligently to increase the wages of coal miners. And, the Maryland miners believed he would create a better living for them.

The strike had increased the tensions between miners and their employers. It struck a fuse that was bound to explode if the strike didn't end soon, which seemed unlikely. The question was when would the charge explode and how bad would it be? The trouble at Blair Mountain last year had been one such explosion. Over 100 people dead and tens of thousands fighting, and that had been in only a few West Virginia counties. This strike was national with lots of potential Blair Mountains just waiting to explode.

Matt thought he had returned home to prevent all of this from happening, at least in Eckhart Mines. That had been the foolish hope of a twenty-three-year-old who believed he understood the world because he had survived a war. He'd only ended up trapped in a mine and nearly dying.

He stared at the clock next to his bed. He could just see the hands in the near darkness. It was a quarter after six.

Typically, he would have been up, dressed, and eaten by now. The day shift started at 7 a.m. His headlamp would have been one light in the dozens of bobbing lights on the hard-hats of miners heading down the hill to the Consol No. 4 or No. 10 mine entrances.

Matt smelled the warm, yeasty scent of fresh-baked bread wafted through the house as his aunts prepared breakfast for the eight people in the boarding house. It mixed with the smell of burning coal from stoked furnaces. Outside, someone chopped at wood, swinging his axe in a steady rhythm. Each swing struck with a loud thud. The sound carried through the town. A car's engine rumbled as it made its way down a road. It didn't sound close enough to be in town, and few people here had a car. A screen door slammed somewhere as springs pulled it back into the frame.

Matt rolled out of bed and wobbled as he stood. The plaster cast around his lower right leg added at least five pounds to his weight and threw him off balance when he walked. He pulled a flannel shirt out of his dresser drawer and put it on over his long johns.

He caught sight of his reflection in the mirror above the dresser and rubbed his whisker stubble. He could go another day without shaving. He had considered growing a beard and mustache when he got out of the hospital during the Great War, but he realized a beard wouldn't cover the scar from his war wound on his neck. Whiskers wouldn't grow out from the scar tissue.

He rubbed the pink wound. It stood out against his dark skin. He thought, at times, it looked like a lighthouse beacon. Samantha

19

didn't mind it, though, which was the important thing.

Matt grabbed his jeans off the chair next to the bed. He'd had to slit part of the right leg to accommodate his cast. He'd take ruining a good pair of jeans over being dead. He'd already cut one leg off his long johns so he could wear them. Just five years ago, broken legs had been four times more likely to lead to death. If one good thing had come out of the Great War, it was advancements in medical care. They kept him alive after shrapnel tore up his neck during the fighting and after the mine cave-in had broken his leg.

Too bad medical care hadn't improved enough to save Pete Spiker. He'd been in the tunnel with Matt when the roof crashed down around them. Pete was injured, just as Matt was, and Pete held on the same as Matt. Right up until the rescuers found them. Pete was killed in an instant when a rock fell on his head.

It was rotten luck for sure, but it felt like something more, too. It was almost as if Matt was spared for a reason. What that reason was, he had no idea. He hadn't done any good in Eckhart Mines to give the Good Lord reason to spare him, and instead take a hard-working family man.

Matt opened the door to his room and hobbled out into the hall. He smelled breakfast cooking, but it wasn't ready yet, or Aunt Toni would have called everyone to the table. He grabbed his jacket off the coat rack near the front door and walked outside, catching the screen door before it slammed back against the frame. He didn't want to wake anyone who might still be sleeping.

It still wasn't full morning, but Matt could see things along Store Hill. It was one of the main streets in Eckhart Mines. His breath froze as he exhaled, but the cool temperatures didn't bother him. He had grown used to working in the mines where the temperature stayed in the low fifties. The miners only wore coveralls and thick shirts in the mines. As long as they worked, they stayed warm. It was sort of an incentive to keep moving.

Smoke poured out of the chimneys, marking the homes where the families were up and about. Usually, at this time of the morning, every home would have stoked their morning fires more for cooking than heat. Matt noticed a few of the chimneys were absent smoke, and he wondered whether the families had slept late or if the homes were empty.

He looked down Store Hill toward Beacher's Store. Plenty of people were out and about this morning, although not many of them seemed about anything in particular. The men he saw seemed at a loss for something to do. Most days, they would not be on the street at this time of day. If it were a Sunday, they would be walking toward either the Eckhart Methodist Church or St. Michael's Catholic Church in Frostburg.

Instead, they stood around in small groups, talking and lounging on porches in front of businesses. They were too far away from him to hear clearly, but he could hear the buzz of their conversation.

"It's a sad sight, isn't it?"

Matt jumped. It wasn't like him to be surprised like that. He was getting soft spending so much time around friends and family. He turned and saw Samuel Ansaro standing at the corner of the house. His shirt was sweat soaked, and he held an axe in one hand.

"Holy cow, Uncle Samuel, make a noise or something," Matt said.

"I thought I did."

Matt shook his head; surprised he hadn't heard his uncle chopping wood behind the house. Or maybe he had. He remembered hearing someone chopping wood while he lay in his bed.

Samuel was the tallest member of the family, standing a good four inches taller than Matt. While his height was a disadvantage in the low-ceiling tunnels in coal mines, Samuel still stood tall. He had not adopted the hunched-over posture some miners had.

"So what's so sad?" Matt asked.

Samuel pointed his axe toward the group of men talking on the store porch. "A town full of able-bodied men and so few of them working. They will find trouble."

"Trouble?"

Samuel lowered his arm, so the axe hung at his side. "Look at what happens on weekends when they are off work for a day and a half. Now they are off seven days a week. Combine that idleness with the tension from the strike, and you have a recipe for trouble."

Uncle Samuel might not be the most talkative of the Ansaros, but he saw more than most of them did.

The coal strike had been going on for a month now. That meant most of the men in town–and the country–had gone four weeks without a paycheck. They were feeling the pinch as their small savings disappeared. Some were buying on credit at the company store and other miner-friendly businesses, but that couldn't go on for too long if no one made payments on their accounts. The business owners had their own families for whom to care. Other men were leaving to look for work outside of the mines and outside of the county.

The four men on the porch walked up the road toward Matt and Samuel. They stopped in front of the Ansaros. Matt knew them from the mines, but he couldn't say that he was close to any of them. He only knew the names of two of them–Phil Kirk and Kenny Frenzel.

"Did you hear what the company is going to do?" Kenny Frenzel asked.

Matt looked at Samuel, who shrugged. Matt said, "No."

"They're bringing in scabs."

It surprised Matt. That seemed like something the Pinkertons should have informed their undercover agents of what was happening.

"Bringing them in? From where?" Matt asked.

"Pittsburgh and Baltimore probably."

It made sense. The strike wasn't settled, and John L. Lewis was flexing his muscle, keeping the miners out as long as possible to get what he wanted. The clash between the United Mine Workers and the coal companies had been brewing for years, and it had only grown worse since the Matewan Massacre in southern West Virginia last year. It was why the Pinkerton Detective Agency had sent Matt to Western Maryland undercover. Consolidation Coal Company, which ran the largest mines in the region, wanted to avoid being involved in a similar massacre.

"Are you surprised?" Samuel asked. "It happens during a lot of strikes. Miners stop working so the company gets people who will work."

"Well, it takes the pressure off the company to meet our demands," said one miner whose name Matt didn't know. He was a mousy man with a long nose and large ears.

Samuel rolled his eyes. "That's why the company does it, George, because they want us to meet their demands. We're each trying to financially pressure the other side into giving in."

George snorted. "Well then, we'll just have to run those scabs out of town."

"It won't just be scabs coming, not after last year. Either those scabs will be armed, or the company will hire guards to watch over them. If both sides aren't careful, we'll have Matewans all over this country."

Matt was about to say something similar, but he was glad his uncle said it first. Not only did Samuel command more respect in town, he had lived here all of his life. Matt had been away for five years. Most of this group knew him only as a boy. He had only returned in January.

"So be it then," Phil Kirk said.

Samuel shook his head and frowned. "Really? Who in this town do you want to see die? George? Kenny? John? Me? Matt? Once the shooting starts, both sides lose. Settling a strike is about negotiation and compromise if it is to work. Let John L. Lewis do his job."

"I'm about out of money, though," Phil said. "I need to work to feed my family, and the UMW isn't helping all that much."

The UMW had set up a headquarters of sorts in the Junior Mechanics Hall in Frostburg. The national union men were coordinating the regional strike efforts from there and providing support and food to the Western Maryland mining families. It helped, but it amounted to less than they had been making in the mines.

"Then find work," Samuel told him. "Who says that you have to sit around doing nothing until the strike ends?"

Phil waved a hand at him. "You just don't understand, Samuel. You and your family own this house. You're doing all right."

Samuel snorted. "You want to come around back and see all of the firewood I've been chopping? People are getting cold at night, but no one is mining coal. I've been selling firewood."

Phil looked at the ground and said nothing.

"We just wanted you to know about the strikebreakers," George said.

Samuel nodded. "It's not good news."

The men continued walking up the street. Matt turned to his uncle. "Selling firewood. Really?"

Samuel swung his axe up onto his shoulder. "We need money. I'm trying to get work in Frostburg, but there are a lot of men ready to fill any open jobs. They aren't all like that group."

Matt could have paid more money to his family, but that would have raised questions about where it came from, especially from Aunt Toni, who had already discovered he was a Pinkerton detective.

"I wonder if I'm disturbing anyone with all of my chopping," Samuel said more to himself than Matt.

Matt answered. "If it disturbed anyone, they aren't complaining."

"Well, who would argue with a man with an axe?" Samuel grinned and then headed around to the back of the house.

Matt hobbled down the road to the company store. It was awkward to move around, but he needed to exercise, especially now that he wasn't working in the mine. Besides, the store wasn't far away, and he wanted a newspaper. He also needed to pay on an account; otherwise, have gone to Beacher's or J. J. Carter's general stores for the newspaper.

The Consolidation Coal Company store and office for Eckhart Mines were in the same building. The office usually had some activity going on throughout the day, especially on Fridays when miners collected their pay. On those days, the connection between the office and store was important. As the miners collected their pay, they passed through the door into the store. Many of them paid on their accounts. Others were attracted to some items on display enough to purchase them.

Matt wondered if the office was now as quiet as the coal mines. He hadn't seen Joseph McCord, the mine superintendent, in three days. Given how the miners felt about the coal company right now, Joey might be keeping a low profile.

Matt limped up the wooden stairs onto the porch and then into the store through the double doors. It wasn't as large as many other company stores and nowhere near the size of the department stores in Frostburg. Other company stores were the only store in town, so they needed to be large enough to meet the needs of most residents in their towns. Eckhart Mines was close enough to Frostburg that department stores like Hitchins Brothers attracted many potential customers who wanted lower prices.

The Eckhart Mines Store carried the necessities, clothing, food, household goods, mining equipment, and more. If someone wanted to purchase something the store didn't stock, Portnoy could order it. That was rare, though, and only done by people who wanted to purchase on account.

No one was inside when Matt entered. Even Harry Portnoy, the part owner who ran the store, must have been in the back. The connecting door that led into the coal company office was closed. A large U-shaped counter ran along three walls. Portions of the counters had glass cases for displaying certain items like meat and jewelry. The shelves lining the walls were filled with package goods, mining equipment, seeds, and feed.

A large potbelly stove dominated one corner of the room. Matt could feel the heat coming off of it even from the door. He could also smell the coffee brewing in the pot on top of it.

The center of the room had two short aisles filled with clothing, toys, and housewares. Matt noticed quite a few empty spots on the shelves and counters. Because the store was small, Portnoy tried to use every bit of space he could, but now things were looking sparse.

"Mr. Portnoy!" Harry Portnoy had run this store for as long as Matt could remember. Besides the store's high prices, Portnoy was the other reason people didn't want to shop here.

"Just wait! I'll be out in a second," came the response from behind the curtained doorway that led into the stockroom.

Portnoy was a nearly bald man in his sixties. When he saw

Matt, he frowned.

"Oh, it's you. I suppose you'll just be wanting yesterday's *Evening Times*."

"Yes, but, I also want to pay off Pete Spiker's account," Matt said. He might not be able to help his family but he had made a promise to Pete to watch out for Laura and Jacob. He'd already made three payments on their account, but now it was time just to pay it off.

"Pete's? You mean Laura's."

"I mean I want to pay off the account," Matt said.

Matt took the bills out of his wallet and passed them to Portnoy.

Portnoy raised an eyebrow. "Her husband's barely been dead a month, and she's already got people paying off her bills."

"People?"

Who besides Matt had the money to do this?

Portnoy grinned. "Men."

Men? Meaning more than one? Pete's people were from down the creek, and they would be just as poor as every other miner in these parts.

"Someone besides me is paying off the Spikers' account?" Matt asked.

Portnoy counted out the money and then put it in the cash register drawer.

"Not for me to say, but it seems that that widow woman isn't grieving too much."

Matt clenched his jaw. He wanted to punch the old man in front of him, but that would just bring the sheriff down on him. Besides, he had a better idea.

"You know, Mr. Portnoy, while I'm here I ought to pick up a few things." Matt rattled off a dozen items that all just happened to be on the higher shelves. Portnoy climbed a ladder, collected the item, and then moved the ladder to get the next thing that Matt said he wanted. Portnoy grumbled and grunted, but he still collected all the items since Matt was his only customer.

When the clothing and food items were piled on the counter,

Matt said, "That should do it. How much is the total?" He took out his wallet and opened it so that Portnoy could see the bills inside.

Portnoy pulled out his pencil and started tallying up the prices. The smile on his mouth kept growing with each dollar increase. He finished adding and tapped the pencil on his pad, as he made sure he had included each item.

"That will be $27.15," Portnoy said, sounding a bit too anxious.

"$27.15! What kind of mark-up are you adding to those things?" Matt nearly shouted. He wished people had been in the store to hear him.

"The prices are clearly marked on these items," Portnoy said, indignant.

"Not when they are on the shelves behind the counter. That total is too much."

"It's not like you don't have the money." Portnoy said, pointing at Matt's wallet.

"That doesn't matter. It's whether they are worth the price. I can get these items for at least $5 cheaper in Frostburg."

Portnoy frowned and gestured to the large pile of items on the counter. "But I got all of these items down for you."

Matt nodded. "Yes, you did your job, but it is just too expensive. I'm going to go to Frostburg. Not only will I save money, but the clerks will be treat me nicer." Matt paused. "Oh, but I will take the newspaper."

Matt took out three pennies and laid them on the counter. He picked up the newspaper, turned and headed out of the store.

Chapter 3

May 4, 1922

Jack McCullough walked along the dirt road that led to the Penn Brothers Coal Company mine. His lunch pail swung from one hand. The water in the bottom compartment of the circular pail sloshed with each step he took.

Shadows on the dirt road retreated to the trees as the sun rose, but they didn't leave completely. Most days, Jack didn't see the sun until he came out of the mine to eat lunch with the other eleven miners with whom he worked. But, since the coal strike started, he chose to stay down in the mine to eat his sandwich and apple pie. It was easier that way. He didn't like to eat while striking miners – men he had gone drinking with a month ago – called him a scab and a traitor.

Despite that, he considered himself lucky. At least he still had a job. So many miners were sitting around Lonaconing, Eckhart, Mount Savage, and towns all over the country not working and not earning any money. Miners typically didn't have much in savings. Hard times were here with harder times to come. Jack had friends who were going deeper into debt just to feed their families during the strike. He wondered how they would ever be able to clear the books after this strike ended. That was another reason he considered himself lucky. He didn't have a family depending on him.

Penn Brothers was a small, family owned mine. It didn't pay as much as some mines, but neither were the conditions as bad as in some other mines. It was just large enough to support a dozen families. They didn't live in company housing because David and Richard Penn couldn't afford to run a town, and there was no need with only twelve employees. Everyone at the mine was a friend and half of them were related. They weren't members of the UMW because the mine was a family business. So when the UMW called for the strike, the Penn Brothers' miners hadn't walked out. Of course, most miners in Allegany County weren't union, but that didn't keep them from walking off the job.

For Jack, staying on the job was an easy decision to make. With most of the country's mines closed, the cost of coal was rising. David and Richard were talking about paying bonuses to thank everyone for working when it was easier to walk away like the other miners. That was another reason Jack liked working for the Penns. When was the last time, if ever, Consolidation Coal paid a bonus to its miners?

Jack had paid off all of his accounts at the stores in Lonaconing with his last pay. It was a weight off of his shoulders not having to worry about the debt. He could start squirreling away a bit of this week's pay. He might even save a decent amount of money for tight times.

The road curved to the left as it headed up Dans Mountain. When the mine entrance should have come into sight, Jack saw two men standing in the middle of the road. He recognized one of the men. Hank Gilroy worked in the Midland Mine when it was open. He'd walked away from his job along with the other miners.

"Morning, Hank," Jack said.

When Hank didn't reply, Jack slowed down. So things had moved from calling him names to not speaking to him at all. The men stared at him but said nothing. Then Jack noticed the thick stick in the other man's hand hanging down at his side.

"Who's your friend, Hank?" Jack asked.

Still no reply.

Jack stopped. Something didn't feel right. His skin tingled. Was Hank not speaking to him because Jack hadn't gone out on strike? Jack looked around and then turned to walk in the opposite direction toward Lonaconing. He'd walk back until he met another miner or two headed to the mine, and then he would come back. Safety in numbers.

As Jack moved back around the curve in the road, he saw two more men standing there. He didn't recognize them. They wore overalls, flannel shirts, and caps. They were miners but not at Penn Brothers. Jack doubted they were going to work at any mine because neither one carried a lunch pail. They walked toward Jack. He knew they were not walking behind him earlier. They must have been standing in the trees waiting for Jack to pass.

When Jack looked over his shoulder, he saw that Hank and the other man were also walking toward him.

Jack held up his hands. "Hey, I don't want any trouble fellows."

"Then you damn well shouldn't have crossed the picket line," Hank said.

"I didn't. No one at my mine is union, and we don't have any complaints with our pay. I mean I wouldn't mind it being more, but Dave and Richard Penn treat us right." Jack was starting to babble, but he couldn't think of what he should do.

He looked around wondering if he could find a thick limb he could use to defend himself. He realized he wasn't going to get out of this without a fight. Was anyone at the mine yet? If he yelled for help, was he close enough that someone at the mine could come help him out?

"Most of us aren't union either, but we walked out in support of our brothers. You should have, too. It would have kept you healthy," Hank said.

"I am healthy."

"Not for long."

The men rushed him. Jack swung his lunch pail; he heard a dull thud as it hit one man in the head. The man cursed and staggered, but he didn't fall. Then the man with the stick hit Jack across the back. Jack yelled. They were too close for him to swing

30

the lunch pail again. He dropped the metal bucket and struck at the men with short jabs. He wasn't the strongest man around, but he could hold his own in a fight.

The men swung back, and Jack felt at least one of them might have used a blackjack. He felt hard hits that were too small to be a fist.

The weight of the men carried him to the ground, and then they began kicking him. Jack gave up trying to fight and curled himself into a ball to protect his head and stomach. It did little good. It scared him that the men were quiet as they attacked him. They grunted with their efforts, but they didn't yell. They simply beat him until Jack thought he might die.

"Enough."

Jack wasn't sure he heard the voice at first, but the attack stopped.

Jack saw a pair of black oxfords in front of his face; too nice to be worn by a miner. He tried to look up, but his right eye was swollen shut, and his left eye didn't want to focus. The man standing next to him was dressed in a suit.

Who would dress like that and then walk on a dirt road?

The man shook his head slowly. "Jack, Jack, Jack. You brought this on yourself. Don't you see that?"

Jack recognized the man. It was Paul Tomlinson, the union organizer who traveled the area to keep the miners united and on strike. Jack had gone to Frostburg a couple weeks ago with some friends, and they listened to Tomlinson whip up a room full of miners into riotous excitement over what a coal miner could expect with the UMW in control. The miners whooped and yelled as Tomlison shouted above their roars how life would be like after the UMW won concessions from the coal companies. Jack had to admit it sounded good, but he felt a loyalty toward the Penns who had treated him right. He didn't join the union, but he held nothing against them... until now.

Even if Jack wanted to answer the man, he doubted that he could make a sound. His mouth tasted of blood and he was missing at least one tooth.

"Go home, Jack. Recover. Take all the time you need to get

well. Don't come back until the strike ends, or you might injure yourself again," Tomlinson said.

Then he turned and strutted away, followed by the four miners.

Chapter 4

May 4, 1922

Joseph McCord puffed on his cigar as he sat in his office next to the Eckhart Mines Store and stared at … nothing. The office walls were covered with charts and notices. It was all old news that he read many times over in the past month. He was normally busy going over reports from the previous day's work at the mine, but now with the coal miners on strike, there were no reports and nothing to supervise. He wasn't sure why he came in today, except he was bored stiff just sitting in his house.

Consolidation Coal had two mines located in Eckhart. The No. 4 Mine was a slope mine on the Big Vein Coal Seam. It used a room-and pillar system to get at the nine-foot-thick coal seam. The mine was entered on a slope and the miners worked the face in large rooms separated by thick pillars of coal that actually helped support the roof. It produced 40,000 or more tons of coal each year, but it was the more troublesome of the mines Joseph oversaw with drainage and ventilation issues. The coal was plentiful, enough so it usually kept nearly 100 miners working.

The No. 10 Mine, although on the same mountainside, tapped into the Tyson Coal Seam. It was only 30 to 48 inches thick. It was a drift mine that employed another 50 men. It was a simpler design that allowed miners to walk into the mine on a level plane. The mine also didn't cause as many problems.

Although Joseph knew the mining terms and how mines work, he had only been inside the coal mines just a few times. He couldn't say how tall the tunnels were, how many men worked in each room, what the air felt like in the mine, or dozens of other things. He never worked as a miner. He never wanted to, either. His father worked as a miner for a few years prior to his promotion to mine superintendent. Joseph was born later, so he was raised as a superintendent's son rather than a miner's boy.

The blackboard on the wall was usually covered with tonnage figures and notes on the changes in the Tyson and Big Vein seams' thickness. What did it matter if the seam in a tunnel was petering out? Or if the tonnage from the No. 10 Mine was outpacing the tonnage from the No. 4 Mine? Hell, nobody was working. It was all a zero. He wiped the board clean last week. He hated to be reminded of what should be happening beneath the town.

Joseph stood up and looked out the window that faced the No. 4 Mine entrance. Plenty of people on the street, but none of them were working. Actually, the town seemed quiet without the rumbling of explosions below ground as coal was ripped from the ground.

He picked up a chunk of bituminous coal from his desk and turned it over and over in his hand. He marveled at nature's process that took dead plants and pressed and cooked them over millions of years into a power source. Although bituminous coal was usually not as desirable as the harder anthracite coal, Western Maryland coal was highly sought after. It had powered many steamships during the Great War. Joseph nearly threw it at the wall, but he didn't want to give into the anger he felt. At least he didn't want to express it in such a useless way. He put the coal down, perhaps a little too hard.

Four weeks of no work. Three weeks with no coal being shipped from Eckhart Mines, and just about every other mine in the region. Some of the smaller mines managed to keep operating, probably because they were family operations with a daily tonnage that amounted to very little. They were starting to make a lot of money for mines their size because the cost of coal was rising. It was nearly double the cost per ton over what it was before the start of the strike. Even those mines were starting to run into some resistance from the miners who wanted to unionize. If only he could ship coal from his mines, at the current prices...

Joseph wished that he could find some way around the union strike. It didn't seem likely because his miners were united in solidarity with the national UMW. Some of them even joined the union. He guessed it was more for the benefits of being a union member, rather than the UMW's promises of high pay and low risk. Even so, how long could the UMW help support 600,000 striking coal miners across the nation? It had to be draining the union's resources, and for what benefit? Miners were permanently leaving the mines for other work while the miners who continued striking suffered from hunger and went deeper into debt.

Joseph looked over at the other desk in the office. Sidney Bloom, the paymaster, usually sat there. With no one to pay, Joseph had told him to stay home until the strike ended.

"But I need my pay, Mr. McCord, and I didn't go on strike," Sidney had told him.

"Then grab a pick and mine some coal. I don't have money to pay you to do nothing," Joseph had shouted. He'd been more frustrated than angry. Not that it mattered to Sidney.

That was three weeks ago. Joseph felt bad about it, but Sidney knew the situation better than Joseph because he kept the books. He missed the man.

Joseph walked around to the front of the counter. Just a short time ago, on every Friday afternoon, the office was filled with a line of miners wanting to get paid. He picked up the box he filled earlier with smoked ham, cheese, and canned goods from the store. He carried it with him into the company store. The stock on the shelves was looking thin and even empty in some places. With no money coming in, Portnoy couldn't afford to restock, not that any miners were buying anything from the store.

"Portnoy!" Joseph called.

The old man looked up from the newspaper and then went

back to reading.

"What are you doing?" Joseph asked.

"The same thing you are ... nothing," Portnoy said.

Joseph wished he could do something about Portnoy's disrespect, but even Joseph's father hadn't been able to do anything about the old man's attitude.

"How current are your accounts?" Joseph asked.

"I'd say they're about a month overdue."

"Nobody's paying anything?"

Portnoy shrugged. "A few, but no one's up to date, except for Laura Spiker. Between you and Matt Ansaro paying on her account, I'll be owing her money."

Joseph tried not to look surprised because he knew Portnoy was trying to get a rise out of him. Why was Matt Ansaro paying Laura's bills? Was he trying to seduce her? And where was Ansaro getting his money? He had to be the only miner in town not feeling the pinch of the strike.

"It's time to cut off the credit of everyone who is not current with their accounts," Joseph said.

Maryland law required company stores to be separate businesses from the coal mines operating in their towns. So, while Harry Portnoy owned the Eckhart Mines Store, Consolidation Coal Company still owned a stake in the operation. That gave Joseph a say in how things were run.

"I just told you that no one's current," Portnoy said as he kept reading his newspaper. Knowing him, Joseph suspected that when Portnoy finished, he would fold the newspaper up and sell it. That is, if anyone had enough spare change to buy a newspaper.

"Then we shouldn't be helping them get by during this strike." Joseph nodded as he puffed on his cigar. "Yes, that's the right thing to do. Make them get current before letting them borrow more. You should like that, Portnoy. It will bring in some money for you."

Portnoy snorted. "I doubt that."

"Why?"

The shopkeeper set the newspaper aside and stood up. "These

36

people don't have money coming in, so I'm not going to get money that's not there. At least not right now. As long as I keep their credit open and accumulating interest, they will owe me even more when they go back to work."

"And what will you use to pay for the goods to keep on the shelves while they dig themselves deeper in debt to you?"

"The strike won't last that much longer."

It had already lasted more than a month. Most everyone assumed it would be settled within ten days, two weeks at the most. Both sides dug in their heels, and the federal government supported the mine operators, which was not surprising since it had done the same thing at Blair Mountain.

"Cut them off, Portnoy. I plan on doing something. When their rents are due, I will have them over a barrel. Then they will go back to work if they want a place to live and credit at the store, otherwise they will be starving on the street."

Portnoy narrowed his eyes and stared at Joseph, but he didn't say anything.

Joseph had been thinking about this for a couple days now. He needed to put pressure on these people to get them back into the mines. Freezing their store credit would hurt, but most people had some canned goods they could rely on for a short time. It would put the most-desperate miners on notice.

Unlike the situation in many coal towns, the Consolidation Coal Company didn't have an iron grip on the businesses in Eckhart Mines. Where many mines were located in isolated areas, Eckhart Mines was close to Frostburg, which offered a variety of stores and didn't depend exclusively on coal miners for their business. People could ride the trolley from Eckhart to Frostburg or even walk.

Consolidation Coal Company didn't even have total control over the coal in Eckhart. Other small mines operated from time to time in the town. Since his miners could easily leave and find other work, it forced Joseph to be more creative in his dealings with them. Sometimes, though, situations required a firm hand.

When their rents came due, Joseph would deliver the

ultimatum. Work or leave the home built to house a working miner. Not all of the miners in Eckhart lived in company houses, but if only the miners in company housing went back to work, operations could be restarted on a small scale.

What Joseph needed was for the company to bring in strikebreakers. That would give him even greater reason to kick out the non-working miners. He had to be careful, though. Too many miners on the streets at once would create sympathy for them. Besides, if he did it gradually, he could have a family on the street every day. It would create more pressure on the remaining miners as they wondered when their time would come.

It would even help him with Laura. She lived in company housing and should have been evicted after her husband was killed. It was expected in a coal town. She already knew she was living on Joseph's goodwill. When she saw other families on the street, it would make her realize just how lucky she was to be in Joseph's favor.

He walked down the steps to the street and headed toward Laura's house. It was a small, square stone building like all of the company-owned houses in Eckhart. They were easily constructed and inexpensive. However, Eckhart's miner homes were sturdier than miner's houses in other towns because they were built from stone rather than wood.

Joseph balanced the box on one arm and used his free hand to rap on the door.

Laura Spiker answered wearing a threadbare green dress. Her blond hair poked wildly through gaps in the scarf that bound her hair atop her head. Joseph guessed she had been cleaning.

She smiled, and Joseph felt his cheeks flush.

"Hi, Joey." She was the only person he allowed to call him that. Not that others didn't do it behind his back, but no one else called him Joey to his face.

He pushed the box forward too quickly. It bumped the door, which threw Laura off balance. She staggered slightly and the smile left her face. It was back a moment later.

"I brought you something," Joseph said.

She saw the food in the box and her eyes widened slightly.

"Oh, Joseph, that's too much. You shouldn't have." Now she called him Joseph, to appeal to his manliness; something she did so well.

"It's all right. I wanted to help," Joseph said.

"But you've already given us so much."

Joey noticed her skirt rustling. He looked down and saw Jacob peering around his mother's legs. The little brat looked too much like his father.

"I put some candy in there for Jacob, too," Joseph said, smiling.

"Candy!" Jacob shouted.

Laura patted the top of his head. "Later, baby."

She stepped back and opened the door wider.

"Come in. Please," she said.

Joseph walked into the small house. The entire house could have fit in the dining room of his house on the hill. The bedroom took up the smaller room of the house. The larger room, which was about two-thirds of the space, was a combination kitchen and living room. Joseph had lived in Eckhart Mines all his life, but when he first visited Laura here, after Pete was killed, it marked his first time set foot in a miner's house.

He put the box on the table in the kitchen area, and lifted the items from the box to the table. He wanted Laura to see how much he was giving her.

Jacob caught sight of the rock candy and started bouncing up and down.

"Candy! Candy! Candy!"

Laura rolled her eyes. She took the smallest piece of the crystalized sugar and handed it to her son. The three-year-old popped it into his mouth and sucked furiously.

"Thank you again, Joseph, but you have to stop. You're spoiling us," Laura said with a slight, shy smile.

"I just want to do what I can to help."

"You've a big help."

Joseph smiled. "Can I help you put all of this away?"

Laura shook her head. "No, no. I will do it later. Won't you sit down?" She motioned toward the worn gray sofa.

"Well, I was thinking that it's such a nice day out...would you like to go for a drive through the country in my car? Maybe we could stop for lunch in Cumberland."

Laura laid a hand on his arm, and Joseph thought he felt tingling.

"That would be lovely," she said. "Jacob has never ridden in a car before."

Joseph tried not to frown. The last thing he wanted was for Jacob to come along. He would probably cry or do something just as annoying. This seed he planted was coming up a weed. He needed to pull it and plant again.

"Why don't you ask a neighbor to watch the little guy? I've heard that young children don't enjoy driving all that much, and we will be gone for hours. If he stays here, he can play."

Laura hesitated. Joseph could see in her eyes that she was on the verge of saying "no." He needed to shift things and make her feel like she was doing something to pay him back.

He took one of her hands in both of his. "Look, I will put the groceries away while you get someone to watch Jacob. Please, it would make my day to take you for a drive."

Her resistance faded, and she nodded. Joseph smiled. One just had to plant the right seed to get the desired flower.

Chapter 5

May 4, 1922

It was an early, overcast morning, Matt pulled on his plaid jacket and walked out to the mailbox to pick up the mail. The only thing in the mailbox was a single letter addressed to Matteo Ansaro. It had a Frostburg postmark, but no return address. He knew that Samantha didn't write it because it lacked her stylish, curving handwriting. She was the only person in town that Matt would expect to write to him.

He strolled back to his house, while he stared at the envelope for a clue to its sender or contents. He opened the envelope and paused, looking around the living room. Then he hurried down the hall to his room and shut the door. The letter was written on Pinkerton stationary, although it was in a plain envelope. A smart precaution because a coal miner would have no reason to receive mail from a detective agency. Matt unfolded the letter and read:

Mr. Ansaro,
I am staying in room 204 at Hotel Gunter in Frostburg. I will be here until the 6th. Please visit me at your earliest convenience. We have important matters to discuss, given the current state of affairs in the country.
Regards,

William Singletary

The language was vague enough not to give away dangerous specifics. If someone besides Matt read this letter, they wouldn't know what it was about, just that it was from the Pinkerton Detective Agency. Only the person to whom the letter was addressed would know what Singletary was talking about, and certainly Matt did.

Matt knew Singletary's name, but he had never met the man. William Singletary was one of the top men in the Baltimore office. Matt wondered what the devil was so important to bring him to Western Maryland. It must be related to the coal strike, although he could think of no new developments at least not around here. Had the Pinkerton Agency discovered Matt had family in Eckhart Mines? He hadn't told his bosses he had coal miners in his family and that they lived in Eckhart Mines.

Matt folded the letter and shoved it in his pocket. He didn't want to leave it lying around for someone to see. If anyone saw that letterhead, he would be in big trouble. He would burn it as soon as possible. Coal miners had no use for detectives after Matewan and Blair Mountain. Baldwin-Felts detectives were the ones usually blamed with striking the fuse that led to the Battle of Blair Mountain when they started evicting families from houses the coal company owned.

It was bad enough Aunt Toni knew his secret. No one was supposed to know he was here undercover. It was unfortunate that she discovered accidentally why he returned to Eckhart Mines. She was family at least, but Matt was still unsure if she would keep her information to herself. A stranger would have told everyone about him by now. Maybe someone did. No, if that was the case, someone would have confronted him. If his secret was out, it wasn't from general knowledge.

Matt went into the house and hobbled to the kitchen. It was the largest room in the house with plenty of work space. It was a bright room and always warm because either Aunt Toni or Aunt Myrna always seemed to be baking something. Antonietta had known she would be running a boarding house, so she had had her brothers install a six-burner coal stove and an oversized sink. The kitchen still had an icebox, though. Matt had talked to her about getting a refrigerator, but she said they couldn't afford it.

Aunt Myrna pulled a pan of biscuits out of the oven. Matt inhaled the warm scent. Antonietta was his aunt by blood while Myrna was related to Matt through her marriage to his Uncle Samuel.

"Can I help?" he asked.

Myrna looked up and frowned. His aunt was a warm woman, but her frown could freeze water. "You're wobbling around like a child's toy."

"I could set the table."

"And risk you stumbling and breaking all of our dishes? I think not. Go sit down. We'll have things ready in a minute."

When Myrna backed away from the oven, Toni slipped her tray into the oven. Myrna tipped her pan on end and knocked the biscuits into a basket. She set the hot pan down and draped a cloth napkin over the hot biscuits to keep them warm. Matt wondered if he could sneak one out when she wasn't looking.

Myrna walked into the mudroom next to the kitchen. She picked up a school bell from the shelf and gave it a few shakes. That was the signal for everyone to come down to eat whatever meal was prepared.

Matt heard rustling on the second floor. The out-of-work miners who were boarders rolled out of bed and dressed. They would not miss a meal.

Samuel walked through the back door with his shirt off and sweat glistening on his torso.

"Go wash up," Myrna told him. "It's time for breakfast."

"I know. That's why I came in."

He tried to give her a hug, but she jumped back and swatted him with a towel.

"Go wash," Myrna said.

Samuel laughed. He walked around her and headed upstairs to the bathroom. John Harper, Isaac Thompson, and Carter

Thomaselli came down dressed sloppily. Carter hadn't bothered to put on his shirt and was dressed only in an undershirt. With no work at the mine, these men spent most of their day wandering around town with nothing to do but talk to other miners.

The men sat on the bench along the dining room table as Myrna and Toni brought in plates filled with biscuits, bacon, and eggs.

Samuel walked down the stairs wearing clean clothes. Ever since he had been out of work, Myrna made sure he wore clean clothes, often making him change more than once in a day. Myrna said that since her husband couldn't use coal mining as an excuse to be filthy, she wouldn't allow him.

"Did you have a chance to look at the newspaper?" Samuel asked Matt. After Matt finished reading the newspaper, he set the copy of the *Evening Times* at Samuel's place at the table.

"I just glanced at the headlines on my way back to the house. It looks like some steel mills are feeling the pinch with no coal to run their furnaces. They might have to close up for a while." Not only were coal miners striking, but so were the railroad shopmen. To support the miners, the railroaders were refusing to haul coal being taken out of non-union mines.

Samuel nodded. "That's good news. People will see the value coal miners provide them."

Matt shrugged. "Or the steel workers might just get mad at the miners because they're out of work, because we wouldn't do our jobs."

"We are out of work, too."

"By choice."

Samuel shook his head. "They'll support us. Laborers have to stick together. Aren't the railroad men supporting us? That's the idea behind unions. United we are strong."

"You sound like a union organizer."

Samuel shoved a bacon strip into his mouth and spoke while he chewed. "Nothing wrong with that. They make a lot of sense."

Myrna laid a hand on his arm. "Don't talk with your mouth full, Samuel. It's rude, and you might choke."

Samuel glanced at his wife and nodded.

"If it's not a bad thing, why haven't you joined?" Matt asked his uncle.

Samuel looked down at his plate. "This smells delicious. I worked up an appetite outside." He used his fork to spear a piece of fried egg and eat it.

Matt glanced over at Aunt Toni and saw her frowning at him. She didn't like him taking any position she saw as supporting the coal companies. She hated the Consolidation Coal Company and blamed it for her husband's death. The black damp had killed Michael Starner while he was walking through the coal mine.

Mine fans kept air circulating through the mine, but occasionally methane released from mining found places to gather. A man walking through one of those dead areas would pass out unable to breathe. If no one was nearby to pull him away, he would suffocate. It was a major reason no one was supposed to be alone in the mine.

Enos staggered downstairs wearing jeans and an undershirt. He hadn't bothered to put on shoes and socks. His face was so stubble covered, Matt wondered if he had decided to grow a beard.

"Enos, I've told you to make sure you properly dress for breakfast," Myrna said.

Enos paused and looked at his sister-in-law. He shook his head. He walked into the kitchen and poured himself a mug of black coffee. Then he walked back upstairs with the mug saying nothing.

"I think he's only been home a couple hours," Toni said.

Everyone seemed to know that the reason Enos stayed was out so late was because he was out with the moonshiners. No doubt he was at one of the many stills in the county. Whether Enos helped brew the liquor or just drink it, Matt didn't know. His late nights had gotten later since the strike started and he didn't have to be up early in the morning.

After breakfast, Matt walked into the kitchen while Toni was washing dishes in the double sink.

"How is your leg feeling?" she asked when she saw Matt.

"It itches. I keep sticking twigs down the cast to scratch my leg. I have no clue if the bones are healing, though."

"You were lucky." She seemed to say that at least once a week, particularly when he was complaining about the cast.

Matt nodded. "I know." He paused for a moment and then said, "I noticed that the breakfast spread seemed a little lighter than usual."

Toni scrubbed at the biscuit pan until it was free from any crumbs. Then she set it on the drain board.

"I don't want you men to get fat," she said with a smile.

"Is that all?" Matt asked. "With the strike going on, no one is earning any money, so I doubt you're getting paid room and board."

Toni set the dish she was holding back into the sink. Then she wiped her hands dry on her apron.

"The running of this household is not your responsibility, Matteo." She hadn't raised her voice, but she had used his full first name, which meant that she was getting angry. She didn't want to talk about this subject.

"Let me give you some money."

She turned to face him with her hands on her hips. "Oh, and where are you getting money? It must be from your second job. I would rather go hungry than take money for being a spy."

Matt winced. He hoped no one was listening.

"I earn that money honestly."

Toni laughed. "Honestly? How can you say that? How honest are you spying on us?"

Matt glanced over his shoulder. When he looked back, he said, "You know why I am here."

"To protect us? Well, that hasn't worked out too well, has it? Your uncles are out of work, and we have no money coming in. We could lose the house if this goes on too long."

"Then take the money I'm offering," Matt said.

She looked away. "No, it's blood money."

"Blood money? I'm not a bounty hunter or an assassin, Aunt Toni."

She scrubbed hard at a frying pan that looked clean.

"You are helping a company that couldn't care less for the safety of its mines," she said. "If one miner gets killed, there's always another."

Matt nodded. "I know. I'm one of them."

"Not really." Her lips puckered as she thought for a moment, and she said, "You can always walk away from all this if you wanted. My Michael and Pete Spiker can't."

Matt closed his eyes and shook his head. That was a low blow from his aunt, more so, because it was true.

"I didn't report Uncle Enos when he joined the union," he said.

Toni's features softened. She reached out and patted his cheek. "That's true. I guess there's hope for you, after all, but I won't take your money."

Matt gave up. "I'm going into Frostburg. Do you need anything?"

"Does Samantha know?"

Matt thought for a moment she was talking about whether Samantha knew he was coming to town, assuming he was going to see her. Then he realized Toni meant did Samantha know Matt was an undercover Pinkerton detective?

Matt shook his head. "She has enough trouble dealing with what happened to me in the mine. Knowing the rest will only worry her more."

"She's tougher than she looks."

"I know that."

"Do you also know if you want to continue seeing her, you will need to tell her?" Toni told him.

"Why?"

"Because if you don't, she'll sense you're holding something back, and she'll imagine worse things than the truth."

Yes, Samantha probably would think that way.

"I'll think about it." He kissed his aunt on the cheek. "I love you."

"I know you do. I love you, too."

He headed out the front door toward the trolley stop on the

National Road. Which ran up the mountain alongside Eckhart to Frostburg.

Although Hotel Gunter was only two miles away on the far side of Frostburg, Matt couldn't make the walk in cast. The Westernport and Cumberland Electric Railway traveled from Cumberland to Frostburg and then to Westernport. It came through Eckhart Mines as it ran between Cumberland and Frostburg, connecting the small town with the larger towns in the county. This was another reason the Consolidation Coal didn't have sole control of Eckhart Mines. It was easy for people to leave and live and shop elsewhere if they wanted to. Matt took the trolley to Frostburg and got off at the hotel stop.

Frostburg was one-fifth the size of Cumberland and at a higher elevation. Being built on a mountain ridge, the wind blew through downtown Frostburg, bringing colder temperatures than were typical further down the mountain in Cumberland.

Although the town was named after the founding family, it also seemed an appropriate name because, on some winter days, an inch or two of snow covered the ground in Frostburg while Cumberland's streets were bare.

Matt liked Hotel Gunter and the restaurant on the first floor. He hadn't been in the hotel in weeks. It just didn't fit with his cover as a coal miner. Even Enos and his friends would be out of place in the speakeasy downstairs.

William Singletary had wisely given his room number to Matt. So, Matt didn't have to ask for Singletary's room and risk being remembered or questioned by the desk clerk.

He walked up the grand staircase to the second floor keeping a hand on the bannister to steady himself and take some weight off his leg. He didn't want to draw attention to himself. On the second floor, he turned left and started down the hallway looking for the room number he wanted. He found the door and knocked. A thin man with little brown hair left on his head opened it.

"Yes," he asked, staring over the top of his glasses.

"Mr. Singletary? I'm Matt Ansaro."

The man nodded and opened the door wider. "Yes, Mr.

Ansaro, come in, please."

It was one of the fancier rooms in the hotel, which had a private bathroom. The room itself was also larger with not only a bed but a table with two chairs, armoire, dresser, and sofa.

Singletary motioned to a chair next to a small round table.

"Sit down, please," he said.

Singletary sat on the chair next to the table. He leaned back in the chair and crossed his legs.

"I guess my letter was a surprise," Singletary said.

"Yes, sir, and a bit risky. I've been collecting my mail at the post office in town to help maintain my cover."

"I'm sorry about that. I was given a list of where our agents are in the area, but not how to contact them or in what capacity they are serving. I take it by your clothing that you are undercover."

Matt's jeans and plaid shirt were a contrast to Singletary's gray suit and black tie.

"Yes, sir," Matt replied.

Singletary motioned to the cast. "What happened there?"

"I was injured in a cave-in a few weeks ago."

"Really? Were you in danger?"

Matt nodded. "Yes, sir. The man who was with me died in the same accident."

Singletary nodded. "Will your injury interfere with your work?"

"To which work are you referring?"

Singletary held up his hands as if he was weighing something on a scale. "They are one and the same, aren't they? For you to do your work as a detective, you must maintain your appearances as a miner."

Matt shrugged, trying to seem nonchalant about the situation.

"Miners get injured. This injury will make me more convincing in my role as a coal miner. No one would expect a Pinkerton agent to have a cast on his leg."

Singletary sipped from a glass of iced tea and then nodded. "You have a point, and how are things in this region?"

"About as you might expect with a strike going on. The miners are supportive of the union, but they also have their doubts because of times in the past when promised help never came."

Unions had failed to unionize the Maryland mines in the past. Previous attempts were made in 1879, 1882, 1886, 1894, and 1900. They all failed because miners feared the coal companies more than they believed the unions could improve their way of life. During the 1882 strike, the National Knights of Labor didn't financially support striking miners, which weakened the miners' ability to continue striking.

"Things are going to get tense, I'm afraid," Singletary said.

"More tense?"

Singletary nodded. "Much more. The company is hiring strikebreakers to send here to work in the mines, and the Pinkerton National Detective Agency will have additional armed men on hand to protect the strikebreakers and company property."

Matt closed his eyes and sighed. "It will make things worse. If the miners see armed men, they will arm themselves, and then it is only a matter of time before shooting starts."

"I agree. But without armed guards, miners will attack the strikebreakers. The Consolidation Coal Company employs us, and this is what the company wants us to do."

"So did you come to tell me I've been recalled or reassigned?"

Singletary shook his head. "No, we are leaving our undercover operatives in place. They may be able to provide information to head off problems. We want to avoid shooting. Don't be afraid to join the union if you are asked to. With the miners on strike, it won't matter if the mine superintendent fires you, and it may help us because it will improve your credibility."

It would help, but Toni still knew that he was a Pinkerton.

"Do you think it will be a long strike?" Matt asked.

Singletary shrugged. "Long, I don't mind. It means more money for the company. I want it to be peaceful. Along that line, we will have a temporary office in Cumberland you can contact in case of emergency. Ask for the PND Agency on Baltimore Street. Even if a third party overhears, they won't hear Pinkerton mentioned."

Singletary held out a hand. "Good luck, Mr. Ansaro, and be

careful. We don't want another broken leg or worse to happen to you."

***

David Lakehurst stepped out of his room and shut the door behind him. He adjusted his tie and jacket. It felt good to take a bath when he wanted and to wear laundered clothes. This was a far cry from that hell-hole of a jail, where he hadn't belonged in the first place.

The desk clerk had found all of David's luggage. All he needed to do was hang the suits to get the wrinkles out. His mail was sent to his room as well, so now he had money in his pocket.

He walked down the hallway to the staircase. His plan was to hop on the streetcar and ride through the coal towns in Georges Creek. The coal field included Wellersburg in Pennsylvania, Frostburg, Lonaconing, Westernport, Barton and other small towns alongside Dans Mountain. He wanted to see where the mine entrances were and decide on where guards would be needed. He also wanted to gauge the number and attitude of miners in the towns. How likely were they to fight?

He didn't mind a good fight, but he wanted to avoid the towns where mobs would form. He needed to perform this assignment well to wipe away the black mark on his record of getting tossed in jail.

The stops would take up most of the day. Then he figured he might have dinner in Cumberland before taking the trolley back to Frostburg.

As he started down the stairs, he stopped and watched a man on the floor below him enter the stairs from the second floor. He wore a cast on his right leg that thumped with each step.

David shifted his position, trying to get a look at the man's face. He seemed familiar, but David didn't know many people in Frostburg except for the policemen. None of them wore a cast, nor did they dress in such rough clothes. This man wore coveralls and a flannel shirt. By God, he looked like a miner.

Why would a coal miner be in Hotel Gunter? It wasn't in the price range for most miners. Certainly he didn't live here. No

51

miner made enough to afford that.

The man in the cast reached the first floor and walked out of sight. David hurried to the second floor and looked down the hallway that the man came from. All the doors appeared closed, and no one was in the hallway.

William Singletary's room was along this hallway. Could the miner be an undercover Pinkerton? David knew of two undercover agents in this area, but there could be more. He remembered that Singletary said he wanted to meet with all the company's agents to assess the situation. It was certainly safer for the undercover men to come here to see Singletary than for him to go to the coal towns to meet with them.

The company wouldn't disclose the names of its undercover agents to David. The two he knew about he learned of from asking questions and watching groups of miners. He also staked out a message drop site one night to see who came to pick up messages.

David didn't like not knowing the agendas of everyone in the game. He wanted to know all the players in this strike, the company's men and the miners. In a situation like this, information was power, and above all, David wanted to be powerful.

Chapter 6

May 4, 1922

Matt stepped out of the hotel. He felt a bit self-conscious dressed below the hotel's standard. He glanced up the street for the Westernport and Cumberland Trolley. It was due in a few minutes. He really wanted to walk back to Eckhart. He needed the exercise, but he knew his broken leg would throb for the rest of the day.

A woman stood next to him as he leaned against the hotel wall. A gentle cool breeze stirred the air around them, and he thought he got a whiff of a flowery scent, maybe lavender. Matt took a side-long look at her and took a quick breath. She was tall, wore a long white manteaux that, buttoned tightly across her chest, her slim physique was emphasized by its chic design. The manteaux ended just below her knees, her shapely calves clearly visible. Her cloche hat was also white, adorned with an edelweiss hatpin, it was perfect for her shiny raven hair styled in a fashionable bob. She reminded Matt of Calista, or rather, Jenny. He hadn't seen her in days and he realized suddenly that he missed her. He should check in on her to see if she heard about a court date for the trial against David Lakehurst.

Forgetting about the trolley, he hobbled across the National Road and headed west on Water Street. Jenny's house was near the Linden Street intersection on the edge of town. It was a long walk for him, and his leg ached. It was good that he wasn't going to walk home if this short walk pained him.

Matt walked up to the ramshackle house and knocked on the door. The house was the size of a miner's house, but at least the miner houses in Eckhart were well kept and made of stone. This one had rotting pieces of wood that needed replacing. A fresh coat of paint wouldn't hurt either.

He heard a yelp from inside the house. He knocked again.

"Jenny. Jenny, it's me, Matt. Are you all right?"

He heard scurrying, and then not one, but two locks disengaged. What was the purpose? The door looked like it would give way if he pushed hard enough. The door opened slowly. A lot of security for a house that offered little in the way of wealth.

"Matt, it is you. Oh, Matt," Jenny said.

She was breathing hard. Her bloodshot eyes darted around. She opened the door a bit wider and waved him inside. He hesitated. He wouldn't have gone in, but she looked so panicked he felt he'd better. She might slam the door on him. Matt closed the door and locked it.

The inside of the room was about the size of a miner's cabin. Two rooms, one a bedroom. It was dark inside. She had drawn the curtains on all the windows.

"What's wrong?" Matt asked.

"He's out, Matt. I saw him. He's out."

"He?"

"David Lakehurst."

Matt paused, and his eyes widened. He hadn't expected Lakehurst to make bail. He thought he'd be in jail until the trial. He'd already been imprisoned for a more than week. It seemed late for someone to bail him out.

"Matt, what am I going to do? He knows it's me who said something. He'll be looking for me."

He put his hands on her shoulders. He felt her trembling. "It's all right. It's all right."

"But Matt, he'll be looking for me. He knows what I am. He'll know where to look for me. I can't work like that."

Matt rubbed the back of his neck. He paced a bit.

"He doesn't know your name, right?"

"He knows Calista. If he asks the right people, they'll be able to tell him about me. Oh, my God, Matt. What if he traces me to my house?"

Which is why she had the locks, but Matt wasn't about to tell her they would do no good. He wasn't sure how she would take that information in the state she was in, but he doubted it would be good.

"Maybe. I doubt he would know the right people to ask about you."

Jenny grabbed his shirt front. "He saw me, Matt. He saw me on the street," she said.

"Did he recognize you?"

"I don't know. I wasn't dressed up. I didn't even have make-up on. He might not have recognized me."

Matt sighed. "Okay. Well, he's not going to get himself into too much trouble if he's out on bail."

"Too much trouble? Too much trouble? What's that supposed to mean?"

"I mean he's not going to do anything in public against you. He can't afford any trouble, if he did anything with witnesses around, he would be thrown back in jail and no amount of bail would get him out."

She breathed a little easier. "But that's not where the problem will be. He wouldn't do something too over the top in public. He's smart enough not to."

She couldn't know how smart or not Lakehurst was. She was just afraid. Matt had no clue whether Lakehurst was smart, but he was dangerous.

"He'd want to find you in an alley alone or with somebody," Matt said. "He wouldn't care."

"Yeah, that's what I'm afraid of. I can't work. Even if I didn't go into an alley, he could follow me home. When I come home, the streets are mostly empty. Matt, I shouldn't have gone to the police. I shouldn't have said anything." She tapped her forehead with her palm. "Why did I say anything?"

She was beyond frantic and scared.

"You went because you deserve justice. You deserve not to be treated like that. Jenny, even if you had done nothing, how would you have felt when you if saw him? You know he still would have been in town. Everything you're worried about happening could have still happened."

Jenny sat down on a worn pink couch that sagged in the middle. She hugged her knees and rocked.

"But now I've given him more reason to come after me. You don't know how it felt to be beaten like that."

Matt laid a hand on her shoulder. "I found you. I saw you. I have an idea how it felt. Jenny, he doesn't need a reason to hurt you. He had no reason to treat you like he did that night. And, I am sure there are other women that he's beaten, or maybe worse. Probably other women right here in town."

"I don't know. He might have. It's not like we talk all the time about who to avoid and who not to."

"We need to find those women, Jenny."

"Why? They're not going to want to talk if they haven't talked already."

"I don't know. The police will be investigating it. Somebody will be investigating it because the case has to go to trial. We need the names of women who might have been attacked and give them to the district attorney. We should have a list ready when the DA comes to talk to you. The more women who are willing to come forward, the stronger the evidence will be against Lakehurst. It won't be just your word against his. It will be your word and their word against his word. Then the DA can show a pattern, and with a pattern, it's harder for him to play the innocent."

"You sound like a lawyer," Jenny said.

He wasn't, but Matt studied investigative techniques as a Pinkerton. His employer required him to learn some things, but how people think and act he learned on his own. Matt knew from his experience that when a man of Lakehurst's size beats a woman Calista's size, it's not out of a sexual need. It's because he wants to feel powerful, but he knows he's not.

Matt sat down beside Jenny, put his arm around her, and just let her cry into his shoulder. At some point, she slipped lower and fell asleep with her head in his lap. He wondered how long it had been since she'd slept. He thought about sliding out from under her and leaving, but that meant he would have to leave the door unlocked. It would upset her more when she woke up. So he sat there, gently stroked her hair and let her sleep.

He put his head back to nap for lack of anything else to do and thought about the situation.

When Jenny woke up, Matt made sure she was calm. He promised to check up on her. He also invited her to come to the boarding house to talk if she started feeling scared or overwhelmed. She reluctantly let him leave. As soon as her door closed, Matt heard both of the locks engage.

He walked across town wondering if Lakehurst could be brought to trial any quicker, and who would loan a woman beater the money to get him out of jail?

Matt knocked on the door to Samantha's house and was surprised when she answered it. She wore a light blue tiered summer dress with long sleeves like she wore to her classes.

"Oh, Matt!" she said, smiling. She stepped toward him, nearly knocking him off balance when she hugged him.

She kissed him, and he drew her closer, unconcerned about whether someone might see their embrace.

When Samantha pulled back, Matt said, "I guess your father isn't home."

She laughed. "No, he's still at the college. Can you come back?"

"Come back? Why? Do you want your father to catch us kissing? Because I'm happy to stay here doing that until he comes home."

Samantha ruffled his hair. "I want you to take me dancing tonight. I want to drink and dance until dawn." Matt wasn't sure if she meant it, but in Frostburg considering his leg was in a cast.

Matt put his hands on her shoulders and held her at arm's length. "What's with you? Have you been drinking?"

"No, I'm just happy. Happy to see you. Happy it's a nice day. Happy my classes are nearly done for the semester."

Matt grinned. "Just one of those days then?"

Samantha nodded. "Just one of those days. Come inside. I'll get you some iced tea, and we can sit on the back porch and talk."

She took his hand and pulled him into the house. They walked through the living room. Matt had grown up calling it a parlor. It was a room that used to be where funeral viewings were held in homes, but with so many deaths from the war and flu, people started relying more on professional funeral parlors. By the time Matt returned from Europe after the war, parlors in homes had been renamed living rooms to set them apart from the death rooms they used to be. Nothing came out of the Great War unchanged; not houses, not people.

They walked around the dining room table, through the swinging door into the kitchen.

Mrs. Fratelli stood at the table in the center of the room chopping cooked chicken into pieces for a potpie. She was a tall, sturdy woman with graying hair, although her face showed little signs of her age.

"Mrs. Fratelli, we will drink tea on the back porch," Samantha said.

The cook put her cleaver down and wiped her hands on her apron. "I'll get it for you."

Samantha patted her shoulder. "That's all right. You're busy. I can get it."

Samantha opened the cupboard and took out two glasses. Then she opened the icebox and took out a pitcher of cold tea. They carried the glasses and pitcher to the side porch, which wrapped around the back of the house.

They sat on the porch swing, and Samantha leaned against Matt.

"So will you go dancing with me tonight?" she asked coyly.

Matt tapped his cast against the wooden porch as he moved the swing back and forth.

"I'm not that good a dancer even without a cast," Matt said.

"Don't be a wet blanket."

"That's what you will think if you see me dance."

"Well, I am a great dancer. You should see me fox trot."

"I have, and you are great at... more things than just dancing."

Samantha hugged him. "You just want me to let you out of taking me dancing."

"How about I take you to dinner?"

"At a club?"

Matt raised an eyebrow. "If you want, but I'm still not dancing." He decided to change the subject before she changed his mind. "Are you still collecting stories about pioneering women?"

Samantha had a scrapbook filled with clippings and pictures of women who were leaders in different fields and who made notable contributions to the world.

"You know I am," Samantha said.

He pulled a folded clipping from his shirt pocket and handed it to her. Samantha scanned the article Matt had circled and smiled. It was about Coco Chanel, a French fashion designer and businesswoman. The article was a short item about Chanel at the Longchamp Racecourse in Bois de Boulogne in Paris, France. It mentioned how her clothing designs were becoming more popular in the United States. Most popular with women was the sporty, casual classic look.

"I found this in a Baltimore newspaper I was reading."

"Why were you reading a Baltimore paper?"

"I like to read them when I can find them to see what is happening in the city where I used to live."

He also found it an excellent way to follow world events and other things that might involve his Pinkerton office.

"Thank you, Matt. This is a wonderful addition to my collection," she said and kissed him on the cheek.

"You're welcome."

"Do you ever think about going back to Baltimore?"

He shrugged. "Sure. I used to like to sit on Federal Hill and watch the ships come into the harbor."

"So why stay here? You're not working with the strike ongoing. Why not move back to Baltimore and get a new job?"

He could have told Samantha he was a Pinkerton detective right then. He wanted to. He truly did. He may have even opened his mouth to say the words, but he couldn't bring himself to do it. It was bad enough that Toni knew. He couldn't risk more people finding out. Even if the ones who knew were people Matt trusted, just the fact more people knew increased the chance the wrong person would find out.

"Well for one thing, you're here and so is my family," he said. "Now that I've reconnected with them, I'm not sure I want to give it up."

"And what happens when I graduate next year and get a job somewhere away from here?"

He'd thought about that from time to time. He wavered over what to do. He was willing to leave Eckhart Mines to be with Samantha, but what would happen when he got an assignment in another state while Samantha was teaching at a school? She wouldn't be able to leave. Was he willing to give up being a detective?

"Maybe I'll be ready to leave by then," he answered weakly.

"And leave your family?"

"Maybe you'll be my family."

"Matt…"

He put a finger on her lips. "I know it's too soon to talk about marriage, but I wanted to throw it out there."

Surprisingly, Samantha said nothing. She just rested her head on his shoulder and clung to his arm.

David Lakehurst stood at the bar in Hotel Gunter's speakeasy. Despite it being a small place, people gave Lakehurst a wide berth. His size and frown intimidated them. David nursed the bourbon in front of him, partly because it tasted lousy, obviously a poor batch of moonshine colored to look aged. The other reason was he was thinking about the miner he had seen on the stairs.

The man looked familiar, and David had a good recall of faces, so why didn't he remember this man?

He looked around the bar. Maybe he had seen him down here, although none of these men looked like miners.

Although David might have come across the man at a bar where miners frequented, he didn't think so. It wasn't the man's face that was familiar, it was his size and something about the way he moved. He didn't walk hunched over or slump shouldered like most miners. That cast, though, it was a giveaway. If David had seen someone with a broken leg, he would have remembered him.

And what was the man been doing upstairs among the hotel rooms? A miner wouldn't be staying at the hotel.

David downed his drink, dropped a dollar on the bar and headed up to the lobby. He saw the clerk at the front desk.

"You were working this morning, right" David said.

The man stepped back from the desk remembering how David had treated him earlier in the week.

"Yes, Mr. Lakehurst," the clerk said.

"I saw a miner upstairs today. I think he was a guest."

"We don't have any miners who are long-term guests, and I don't remember any staying here recently."

"This man was wearing a cast on his leg."

"Oh, I do remember someone like that." The clerk perked up, glad that he might have information David wanted. "He wasn't a guest. He was here visiting someone."

"Do you know the miner's name?"

"No, sir."

David sighed. "Then who was he visiting?"

"He didn't say. He knew the room because he went directly upstairs. He didn't stop and ask about a guest."

A coal miner in Frostburg wasn't that unusual. A coal miner with a broken leg was more uncommon, but there were still a dozen towns the man could be from, and David wasn't even sure it was worth knowing the man's name.

However, he now had another question that puzzled him. Who was the man been visiting? David didn't like unanswered questions.

"How many people are staying on the second floor?" David

asked.

"I can't..."

David leaned over the desk. The clerk pressed himself against the wall.

"I'll have to check."

"You do that."

Still, the thought gnawed at David, and David wasn't one to ignore his instincts. However, he wasn't going to travel from town to town looking for a miner in a cast.

The strikebreakers would start arriving next month. He would be busy getting them settled and watching over them.

The clerk scanned the pages of the register. After a minute or two, he said, "It looks like forty-nine."

That narrowed things down.

"How many of them were in front rooms to the right of the stairs?"

The clerk looked again.

"Sixteen, although it looks like one gentleman checked out earlier than I remember seeing the man in the cast."

"Who were in the other fifteen rooms?"

The clerk hesitated.

"If I have to look it up, you will regret it," David said.

The clerk sighed. He flipped through the pages and read off the names of guests and their hometowns as he found them among the signatures. One name stood out.

Mr. William Singletary of Baltimore.

That had to be the connection and why the man looked familiar. None of the other names sparked anything in him, although that meant nothing. Singletary was here because of the coal strike, and the unknown person was a miner. The miner was a Pinkerton. He had to be. It made sense. Singletary had said he would be meeting with the other agents in the area.

David slammed his hand against the desktop. The clerk jumped back and raised his hands over his head.

David ignored the clerk and rubbed his chin.

The connection was Singletary. Since the Consolidation Coal

Company was paying the Pinkertons, their agents would be in town with the Consolidation Coal mines. Around here, that meant more than a dozen of these little coal towns.

That was a workable number, and they were towns David would visit during the next week. He would find out who the miner was and why it bothered him so much.

Chapter 7

May 4, 1922

Samantha lifted a sweater from the coat rack. It was warm outside, but the breeze was blowing across the top of Big Savage Mountain, so it would feel at least five degrees cooler out on the street. It was warmer yesterday. This weather reminded everyone winter was not finished with Frostburg even if it was May. She opened her canvas bag and laid the sweater on top of her textbooks. Then she headed out for the brief walk to the State Normal School campus. She always enjoyed the approach to the campus along the tree-lined paved sidewalk. There was something so calming and reassuring about the solid brick Old Main and the wooden benches that dotted the grounds. It was how she thought life should be – calming and reassuring.

Classes were winding down for most of the students. She would only have a short break at the end of the spring semester then the summer classes would start. She was registered for advanced rhetoric and modern teaching methods.

Her father insisted she attend classes year round because he wanted her to develop a habit of learning. She suspected part of his reason was to keep her busy and hopefully out of trouble. He didn't like it when she stood on the streets promoting women's rights, and he hated when she went dancing and drinking in speakeasies.

As she walked, she noticed the streets were busier than usual, or at least what was usual before the strike. Since then, a lot of men who would normally be underground during the day were out on the street lounging around and talking with other striking miners. The industrious ones looked for work; either short-term to get by until the strike ended or long-term to get out of the coal mines.

Samantha had a science class first thing this morning. This semester she was studying natural and physical sciences with Professor McTeague. He was sick last month, and Professor Billingsley took over his classes temporarily. It was only a short-term solution since the college had only four instructors. Her father told her Professor McTeague had a heart attack and wouldn't be returning to the classroom. Her father hired a new professor to relieve Professor Billingsley and finish out the semester.

The State Normal School No. 2 opened in 1902, and since then had gone through five presidents in sixteen years. Her father was the sixth. He first came to the school in 1919. Samantha had attended the local high school, Beall High School, and she was a member of the Class of 1921. She heard a lot about the college during her high school years because the townspeople raised the money to buy the original two-acre park where Old Main was built.

The first students graduated from the school in 1904, and a lot of the students in Beall saw it as a way to avoid the coal mines, if they could afford the tuition. The college was small, but it was growing. Samantha liked the Model School because it offered hands-on teaching. It had opened in 1913. Student teachers worked with young students there and gained practical knowledge. A college gymnasium opened in 1914, and the first dormitory building, Frost Hall, had opened in 1919.

The two-year course work consisting of Latin, mathematics, history, rhetoric and literature, natural and physical sciences, drawing, music, calisthenics, psychology, philosophy of education, philosophy of school management, pedagogy, observation, practice work and primary manual training. The college, with great pride, graduated more than a dozen teachers each spring.

Natural and physical sciences was on the second floor of Old Main. Unlike most classrooms that had lines of desks where students sat, this room had large tables where students could conduct experiments, not that they did much experimental work in natural and physical sciences.

When she entered the room heading toward her seat, she saw a man in tan trousers and a white shirt writing on the blackboard. He was detailing methods of testing a mineral's hardness. When he finished, he stepped back from the blackboard and read his work. Satisfied, he set the chalk down on the tray under the blackboard.

He turned to pull his jacket off the chair, and Samantha saw he was young. He couldn't be much older than she. He was a bit taller than Matt with sandy colored wavy hair and yes, a neatly trimmed moustache. So very Philadelphia.

He glanced at the clock on the wall. "Well, it's time to get started. As you can see, I'm not Professor Billingsley. My name is Professor Williamson. I'll be your instructor for the rest of this semester."

Jane Paulson leaned near Samantha and whispered, "Well now, he's handsome."

Leave it to Jane to notice that first. Her main reason for coming to college was to find a husband. Her family owned warehouses in the Baltimore harbor district. They were well off and sent their daughter to school so she could become a proper young lady who would make a suitable wife to someone in her social class.

With her long face and wide nose, Jane wasn't attractive. She had little luck with the male students at the school. If they had any interest in her it was because of her family money, or they needed a last-minute date.

It didn't seem to matter to Jane. She carried on with mild enthusiasm. Samantha figured her friend would go through a lot of men in her life.

Jane wasn't wrong, though. The new professor was handsome with his attractive hair that verged on curly and light brown eyes and chisled profile.

"I know you all are adults, but I will call roll until I learn your names. Hopefully, I can do that before the semester ends," Professor Williamson said.

He picked up a sheet of paper from the desk and started reading through the list of eleven names.

When he got to Samantha's name and read it, he paused. "Havencroft? Are you related to President Havencroft?"

"He's my father," Samantha answered.

The professor pressed his lips together in a tight line. "Well, I hope that you don't think that will help you get a better grade in this course."

How could he assume she would use her name to get a good grade? He was the one who had called the roll. She had just answered his question.

Samantha felt herself blush. "I'm offended that you would even mention it. You brought up the family relationship, not me."

Professor Williamson stared at her, saying nothing. Suddenly, he smiled.

"You are right. I guess that was rude of me, but I was surprised and more than a bit nervous for my first class."

Luckily, the class got better from there. Professor Williamson knew his subject and enjoyed talking about it.

Matt knocked on the door to Laura Spiker's house. He carried an extra loaf of white bread Aunt Toni had baked, still warm and smelling delicious. He also had a quart of milk from their cow and a toy gun for Jacob. He bought the gun while he was in Frostburg checking his post office box for mail from the Pinkerton office.

Laura answered the door in bare feet and wearing her everyday red-checkered dress.

"Good morning, Laura."

"Hi, Matt, what brings you by?" she asked.

"Aunt Toni made an extra loaf of bread for you. I also snatched a quart of milk on my way out the door, and I brought something for Jacob."

Laura smiled, lighting her face up. "That's really nice of you. You didn't have to do it."

"I wanted to. I know this must be a hard time for you with a child and no husband." They might not be dating any longer, but Matt still considered her a friend.

Laura sniffled, and Matt hoped he hadn't upset her so much that she would start crying. She held back the tears and invited Matt inside.

He walked across the room and set the bread and toy on the table. He opened the icebox and set glass milk bottle inside. He noticed that the icebox was nearly empty. She had few fresh goods. He hoped that her pantry wasn't as bad off.

"I appreciate it, but you don't have to," she said. "I know things must be tough in your house, too, with the strike going on."

"Laura, I've been holding off saying anything because I know your whole life has been turned upside down since Pete died, but it's been more than a month since the cave-in."

She sighed and nodded. "What do you want to say?"

"Well, when we–Pete and I–were in the tunnel before we knew help was coming, Pete asked me to look out for you and Jake if something happened."

Laura gulped. Matt saw tears form in her eyes. He knew how she felt. When Priscilla Bankert called off their marriage last year, it had torn Matt apart. And Priscilla hadn't been killed, nor had they been married. Pete and Laura had been married four years.

"The food can help you some, but it's only a temporary help," Matt said. "At some point, you've got to move forward. I don't know how much money Pete left behind, but I have a friend who works in the bank in Frostburg. He can help you figure out your finances."

"That's nice, but we didn't have much savings. We owe even more to the store," she said.

Matt frowned. The Eckhart Mines Store allowed miners to purchase overpriced goods on credit and then charged them a high interest rate. It was easy to buy, but hard to get out of debt to the company store. And the Eckhart Mines Store wasn't the worst type of company store.

"Your account at the store has been paid off," Matt said.

Laura's face brightened. "That was nice of Joey."

Matt's mouth fell open a bit. "Joey? What makes you think Joseph paid off your bill?"

Well, Matt could guess why Joseph might do it, although it angered him to think about it.

"Who else would?" Laura asked.

"Why would he?" Matt asked.

Matt even had doubts whether Joseph felt any guilt over Pete's death. He and Pete shouldn't have been working that section of tunnel when it collapsed. Tom Giaconne, the shift foreman, had reported safety issues with it, but he had told Matt that Joseph insisted that Pete and Matt work it.

"He's been a friend to me and Jacob," Laura said.

Matt had a few things to say on that, but he kept his mouth shut. He had other things to talk with Laura about, and he didn't want to get himself worked up.

"Another thing is, you have to start looking for work. Aunt Toni and Aunt Myrna volunteered to watch Jake for you while you are working. They're at the house all day, so he can stay with them."

"Oh, that's very nice of them," Laura said. "I have been thinking about what I need to do."

"You might find a clerk job here in town, but you would have a better chance in Frostburg."

"I've never worked before, Matt. I'm not sure I'd know what to do."

"You're smart, Laura. You could learn just about any job."

It wasn't flattery. She had been one of the smartest people in their class at the Eckhart School. He also heard she had done well at Beall High School in Frostburg, although Matt, like most of the Eckhart Mines boys, had gone to work after the eighth grade.

Jacob waddled out of the bedroom wearing his night shirt. He rubbed his eyes. He was a thin child. Most miner's children were rarely chubby.

"Did you have a good nap, Baby?" Laura said.

She bent over, and Jacob walked to her. She scooped her son up and hugged him. Jacob squirmed until she put him down.

Matt walked over to the table and picked up the toy gun.

"Hey, Jake, look at what I got for you."

Matt held up the sheet metal pistol. Jacob squealed and ran over to Matt. Matt handed him the toy.

"What do you say, Jacob?" Laura said.

"Thank you," the little boy said as his eyes grew in size.

Jacob pointed the gun and pulled the trigger. There was a slight click as the hammer pulled back and dropped.

"You know he'll go around trying to shoot everything he sees," Laura said.

Matt grinned. "Every boy needs a gun, and I figured you wouldn't want him to have a real one for a while yet."

Laura smiled as she watched her son fire the gun. "It's very nice. I'm sure he'll enjoy it."

"I saw it in Frostburg and thought he might like it. It wasn't expensive."

Laura laid a hand on his arm. "Matt, just because Pete asked you to look after us doesn't mean you have to."

Matt nodded. "I know, but even if he hadn't asked, I would do this. We've known each other for years. We're friends. I can't watch you going through this and not try to help."

He only wished he could help his own family with their money problems.

Then Laura cried and hugged him.

"Oh, Matt, everything is wrong. It wasn't supposed to be this way," she said.

He thought about all his expectations that had turned out differently than they should have. His injury. His friends dying in Europe. Priscilla dumping him. His parents dying. Him not being with Laura.

"Life is never what you expect it to be," he said.

Laura sniffled and nodded.

"You paid, didn't you?" she asked, drawing back from him.

"What?"

"You knew the bill had been paid, but you were upset I thought it was Joey," Laura said.

Matt nodded. "See? I knew you were smart."

"You shouldn't have done that, Matt."

He shrugged. "You didn't need that debt hovering over your head with everything else you have to deal with right now."

She hugged him tighter. "Thank you."

"You're welcome."

"What about you?"

"What about me?"

"You're not working now with the strike and your broken leg. Are you able to make ends meet?"

He almost laughed to see her concerned about his well-being.

"I have some money saved up. Plus, my family owns our house. It gives us breathing room until the strike ends." He didn't tell her that the boarders hadn't paid in weeks. She didn't need to know that. No need to upset her. She didn't need to know he was earning a paycheck from the Pinkerton National Detectives.

Samantha walked downstairs and seated herself at the dining room table. Her father sat at the head of the table. Once she sat down, Mrs. Fratelli brought out the salads. Although Mrs. Fratelli was the cook, she also had been called on to serve since the maid, Pauline Hopkins, had quit to move to Hagerstown with her husband.

John Havencroft poured a few tablespoons of dressing on his salad and then cut it up.

"So, my dear, how was your day? Have you heard of any problems with the striking miners?" her father asked.

Samantha stopped eating.

"Why would I know something like that?" she asked.

"I thought Matt might be keeping you up to date on the situation." He said it casually, without anger or even disappointment.

Samantha rolled her eyes. "Father, we don't talk of mining when we are together. We have more pleasant things to do."

Her father started coughing, and she realized how what she said had sounded.

"Father! It's nothing like that." She laughed at her father's foolishness, but she could feel herself blushing. Not that she hadn't imagined being intimate with Matt. They just didn't seem to be at that point in their relationship, although he had mentioned marriage.

"I didn't say anything."

"You didn't have to. The fact that you nearly spewed your salad across the table said plenty. You don't trust Matt."

Her father shook his head. "You are wrong. I trust him, perhaps more than you realize, but I know he is not the one for you."

More than she realized? What did he mean by that?

"Why isn't he the one for me?" Samantha asked.

"You will become a teacher next year, and that position will most likely be in a city. Matt is a coal miner. You don't find coal mines in cities."

She knew her father was right. Hadn't she suggested the same thing to Matt? What did the future hold for her and Matt? She loved him, but they lived in two different worlds that would most likely soon come apart. Would he follow her to the city and find work other than as a miner? Could she stand to remain here and settle for a job as a teacher in some small one-room school? And marriage? That wasn't for her, at least not now.

"Why did you ask about the strike?" Samantha asked.

Her father shrugged. "I heard things, and if they are correct, they are worrisome. It could be dangerous for students to be on the streets."

Samantha had already run into such situations before the strike started. It wasn't the striking miners who caused the problem; it was the drunk people and too little law enforcement who caused the problems.

"The female students are already cautious," Samantha said. "We generally are if we are alone on the street. The boys will be careless no matter what you say."

Her father raised an eyebrow. "I see that you have moved past seeking equality and homed in on the superiority of women."

He blew on a spoonful of soup before swallowing it.

"I'm simply stating what I've seen."

Her father nodded. "Perhaps you are correct in this instance."

"No, perhaps about it, Father."

"How was your day?" her father said, changing the subject to avoid an argument.

"I met the new science professor," Samantha said as she cut her ham into bite-size pieces.

"Professor Williamson."

Samantha nodded.

"So what did you think about him? I grabbed him right out of Princeton."

Samantha paused a moment before she answered. She definitely would not repeat Jane Paulson's comment on the professor's attractiveness.

Instead she said, "He is direct and confident and seems to know his subject." She thought about mentioning the professor's paranoia with nepotism, but he had apologized for that mistake.

"He should."

"Are you not worried he is too young?"

"What does that have to do with anything if he knows his material?" her father said as he sipped his tea.

Now she didn't have a choice but to go where she didn't want to. "He is good looking, Father, which can be distracting for some students."

"You, for instance?" he asked, raising an eyebrow.

Not her. Her issues with Professor Williamson stemmed from his attitude, not his blue eyes and wavy hair.

"I won't deny he's easier to look at than Professor McTeague, but I already have someone to distract me."

"For now."

Samantha stared at her father, wondering what he was thinking or planning.

Enos walked around the black Duesenberg Model A, letting

his fingertips trace its edge as he did. It was a gorgeous vehicle made in Minnesota. Some police were still using horses, and the ones who had cars were driving Ford Model Ts. This car could reach eighty-five miles per hour, which would leave any horse easily behind. If only it was his car. Someday it would be.

It wasn't the taxi Enos wanted. This car sat only two people, which meant it had more places to hide moonshine. He needed a touring car to run a taxi, and then he could drive it around town like Joseph McCord did with his Renault GS.

A small car company in Luke had manufactured steamer runabouts at the turn of the century. He had seen one of the Maryland Automobile Manufacturing Company's steamers when he was a boy. It was the first car he had ever seen. It hadn't been impressive by today's standards. It used a vertical two-cylinder steam engine and chain drive for power. The body was made of wood and it had large wooden-spoke wheels with solid rubber tires. It didn't matter to Enos. It moved on its own. It was magic. He had fallen in love with automobiles and had wanted one ever since.

"You know what you have to do?" Vincent Gambrill asked.

Enos stopped walking and looked up, although his fingertips remained on the car. Vincent stared at him from the other side of the car.

"I've been on runs before," Enos said.

"But not by yourself."

Vincent was the highest-ranking person in the moonshining operation who Enos knew. He wasn't sure if Vincent owned the operation, but it didn't matter to him. Vincent paid him. That was what mattered to Enos.

"I had to learn to drive first before I could do my own runs," Enos said.

Vincent grinned. "I have to admit you learned quick enough. You've got skills, Enos. I may have you teach our other drivers if you prove yourself."

Vincent slid a list of names and addresses across the roof of the car. The names were the only persons he could ask for or leave the moonshine. Enos scanned the half dozen addresses. They ranged from Grantsville to Lonaconing. Besides learning how to drive during the past month, Enos had also learned all the back roads in this area. Some of them were little dirt tracks, rutted and barely wide enough for a car. They might be bad, but they could get him from town to town if he needed to outrun the police. His goal was not to attract their attention, though. He was an excellent driver, but he wasn't sure how well he would do on some of those back roads without headlights on a moonless night.

Vincent opened the back door and showed Enos how to trigger the hidden switch that unlocked the back compartment in the car. He lifted the panel and showed Enos the sixteen one-gallon jugs hidden beneath. The thick sides on the ceramic jugs held up to what could sometimes be a jostling ride.

"Make sure you get the money first," Vincent Gambrill said. "And don't let anyone see where you hide the shine or how much you have."

"I won't. It's not my first time.

"But it could be your last time if you aren't careful."

Vincent reattached the panel on the car. Enos climbed into the front seat, inserted the key and started the engine. Vincent stepped back.

"I'll see you in the morning," he said.

Enos released the clutch and pressed the gas. The car started down the dirt road with a hidden entrance. Guards near the entrance moved the brush away so Enos could pass. He waved to them as he pulled onto the National Road heading into Frostburg.

The names on the list were organized in the order that Enos should deliver them. The closest places were first so he could get rid of his product as quickly as possible. Then he would drive on the road the longest from his last drop, but he wouldn't have any hidden moonshine that could get him arrested. Enos had memorized the first name and address. The first stop tonight was a bar in Frostburg that supposedly only sold near-beer now, or beer that had an alcoholic content of 2.75 percent. It tasted nastier than the worst moonshine Enos had ever tried.

Now, Vincent Gambrill made good shine. He didn't cut any corners like using tobacco to make the moonshine look aged or labeling double runs as triple runs. Because of that, his shine tasted decent, although Enos still preferred the real thing. His good quality moonshine was in demand even where people were closer to a still for their purchases.

Vincent's shine cost more than most. People paid five dollars a pint for it, but they got their money's worth. Stuff selling for four dollars a pint around here tasted terrible, and the two dollar a pint shine had barely more kick than water. Enos paid only a fraction of that since he worked for Vincent.

Enos drove the car north along the National Road. He drove carefully and within the speed limit. He definitely did not want to get stopped. The bar was on the northern end of town, a block past the Hotel Gunter. Frostburg was busy, which wasn't unusual. It was early enough that people other than drunks, prostitutes, and rowdies were on the street. It would switch over in another hour.

He parked behind the bar. Actually, it was a two-story brick home with a small bar in the basement, which was still open. Enos knocked on the back door until a tall, thin man answered.

"Are you Randy Pfaff?" Enos asked.

"Yeah, who are you?"

"I have your delivery from Vincent Gambrill."

The man's eyebrows rose. He stepped onto the back porch and closed the door behind him.

"You're new."

"Not really. I just haven't been here before."

Randy looked around. "Well, where's the stuff?"

"Money first. You know the rule."

Randy scowled. Enos didn't know if the man was trying to pull something on him, but Enos wasn't taking a chance, especially on his first night making deliveries.

Randy reached into his pocket and took out some folded bills. Enos took the money and counted it.

"Be right back," he said.

He ran over to the car and opened the panel furthest away from

Randy. He pulled three jugs out of the hidden compartment. He closed up the hidden compartment and carried the moonshine jugs back to Randy. Randy lifted the lid on a trash can.

"Put them in there. I'll come back for them later."

He wanted to hide them in case police raided his speakeasy.

Enos set the jugs in the can. Randy set a brown bag full of trash on top of the jugs and put the lid back on.

Enos walked back to the car to head to his next delivery. The next three stops were in Grantsville. Then he traveled south to Jennings and Bloomington.

The evening's work went smoothly. At one point, he thought he noticed a car following him for a long stretch. He turned off on a side road and drove a couple of miles. The car didn't follow him.

He finished up his route around 4 a.m. and drove back to Eckhart. He dropped the car off and handed the money to Vincent, who worked through the night. Vincent counted the money, nodded, and handed Enos his earnings for the evening. He made more in one night than he made for a week of working in the mines. This is what Enos called a job.

77

Chapter 8

May 6, 1922

Joseph waited on his front porch and watched as Winston McCord, his father, parked the Ford sedan in front of the house. The older man climbed out wearing his best gray suit. Although it was a business meeting, Joseph had thought it might be casual since his father had wanted to meet at the house rather than the mine office. Joseph suspected Winston McCord wanted to see exactly what Joseph had done with the house, especially since he lived in the house before Joseph became the superintendent for Consol No. 4 and No. 10 mines. Winston was the superintendent before Joseph. His father was critical of Joseph's management style, always comparing it to his own and finding Joseph's lacking.

Get ready for it, this is another of "when I ran things…" sessions.

They sat in the den next to the fireplace. Although his father had been a coal miner and the Consolidation Coal mine superintendent in Eckhart, he rarely ventured down into the mines nowadays. He worked in the Consolidation Coal Company office in Cumberland. Originally, the company started in Western Maryland, but now its national office was in New York City. However, the company maintained several regional offices in order to deal with local mines issues.

Joseph poured his father a glass of brandy and passed it to him. Winston McCord sniffed it and swirled it around in the glass.

"Don't worry, it's not moonshine," Joseph said.

Fortunately, he had stocked up on wine and liquors before Prohibition started. He kept his stock in a small wine cellar in the basement. He planned to use his stock for special occasions, but he had few gatherings at his home. He would have preferred not to waste excellent brandy on his father's visit, but Winston McCord would certainly not drink moonshine. He hated the taste and didn't trust the ingredients.

His father sipped at it tentatively.

"So, I see the mines have produced nothing," his father said.

Joseph shook his head. As if just about every other mine in the country wasn't shut down, he thought.

He sighed and sipped his drink. He only wished it wasn't his first today. He had finished two drinks earlier to prepare for his father's visit. "It's not my fault if the company can't negotiate a good contract with the UMW."

His father scowled. "Those miners don't want to negotiate. They want to be paid to do nothing."

Coal companies across the country were negotiating with the UMW and getting nowhere. John L. Lewis was determined to win this battle and cement his authority in the union. He had started his association with the UMW back in 1906 when he was elected a delegate to the UMW national convention. Five years later, Samuel Gompers hired him as a full-time union organizer. He became the acting president on November 1, 1919, and soon thereafter called his first major coal union strike. During that strike, 400,000 miners walked off their jobs. Since becoming president of the UMW in 1920, he had been aggressive in asserting the power of unionized coal miners.

"Nothing? It hasn't been that many years since you worked here. You know those miners work hard down there. We had two men killed in a cave-in last month."

"And I suppose that is the company's fault?"

Actually, it was Joseph's fault. He had insisted that the men work in the tunnel that collapsed, even though he knew it wasn't safe. He had wanted Pete Spiker and Matt Ansaro to be the ones killed. He had needed Pete out of the way in order to have a chance with Laura. And as for Matt, he had ignored Joseph since they were kids. Joseph got half his wish, and it was the best part.

"Too bad you're not negotiating with the UMW for the coal companies," Joseph said, trying to hide his sarcasm.

Winston nodded. "It is too bad because now the company has hired strikebreakers. They will arrive next week earlier than we planned. We'll bring the workers in on the Cumberland and Pennsylvania spur."

It was not an unexpected reaction. Joseph would have actually brought them in weeks ago.

The Cumberland and Pennsylvania Railroad ran a spur to Eckhart Mines, which the company used to ship out its coal. The town didn't have a station nor platform for passengers. By bringing in the men this way, Eckhart's strikebreakers wouldn't come through Frostburg. The less time they were in the public eye, the less likely people were to get worked up about them.

"We'll start with about fifty men," Winston said. "That will be enough to get the mines reopened."

"Barely. That's about one-third of our normal workforce."

Winston shrugged. "It can't be helped. Finding workers willing to cross the strike line is not easy. Where are you going to house them?"

Joseph had been raising his glass to his mouth. He stopped. "House them?"

"Of course. If they work here, they need a place to stay. You're the superintendent. It's what you do for your miners."

"I thought the company would be making arrangements."

"Do you expect us to do everything? We found the workers so you can open your mine here, and we've arranged for their protection. You need to find a place for them to stay."

The company-owned houses, but all of them had striking miners living in them.

"We have a few vacant houses, probably enough for half of the

80

number you're talking about bringing in."

"And the other half?"

Joseph rubbed his chin. "I could evict striking miners who are in company housing. They rent their homes month to month, and they know the houses are for company men. We evict families if a miner dies or can no longer work, why not evict them now? I read that some companies are doing that, and the courts are backing them."

"And those companies will regret it when the strike ends," his father said, making Joseph squirm under his stare.

"Why? It will show the company's strength and help show the miners that the UMW can't be everything for them."

His father did not understand what it took to run a coal mine in this day and age. He hadn't worked as a superintendent for years.

"And what will happen when the strike ends? The strikebreakers will leave, and you won't have most of your miners. I've already seen reports of miners leaving the area. At this rate, miners' wages will increase simply because we will be competing for the remaining miners with other companies. Once coal prices drop again after the strike ends, we don't want to be paying high wages."

Joseph knew his father was right on that point. It was simple supply and demand. The same supply and demand also guided the price of the coal the company mined.

Joseph poured himself another glass of brandy. "Where are those miners going? It's a national strike."

"But not all the non-union mines were shut down like they were here. Some miners are finding work in the Somerset coal field. Those mines aren't union, and the miners are working. Some miners are finding different work altogether."

"All the more reason for us to do something now to stop the company from bleeding miners. This will force the union to the bargaining table. The union doesn't care about our miners because they aren't members of the union."

"The UMW won't give in. They will only dig in more, and in the meantime, you will turn the public against the company because you will be hurting women and children."

Joseph thought of Laura and Jacob. He didn't want to hurt them, well, at least not Laura, but Joseph didn't have to treat her and Jacob like other miners' families.

"It's not my fault their husbands and fathers are union miners or sympathize with the union," Joseph snapped.

"Of course they sympathize with the union," Winston said. "The union promises what it can't deliver and then blames the company for its failure to deliver on its promise."

"Then why not show them what the union costs them?"

"The public won't see that. They will only hear about women and children on the street. It will be just as bad as Matewan, if not worse."

Joseph slammed his tumbler down too hard on the table. If there had been any brandy left in it, it would have sloshed out.

"Then what should I do? You want the mine to operate and then tie my hands over what I can do."

"That's why we pay you, Joseph. You figure it out." His father set his glass down and stood up. "Your mother asked about you. She wants you to come to Sunday dinner."

He walked out of the room to the front door.

Since the coal strike started, dinner at the Starner Boarding House was as important a meal as breakfast. No one had money to go elsewhere for dinner, and no one wanted to miss a meal.

The conversation around the dinner table centered on the progress or lack of progress in the settlement talks. The rumors, the stories of violence, and the truth were all debated back and forth. Matt didn't share everything he knew because he didn't want to be pressed on how he learned it.

After dinner, everyone separated and went their own way. The boarders and Enos went to their rooms. Everyone else sat in the living room and continued talking. Matt listened for a while, but he decided he needed some air and left after about fifteen minutes.

He left the house and walked down the hill to the No. 10 Mine entrance.

He studied the dark entrance, placement of the buildings, the surrounding hills, and where the nearest homes were located. The No. 4 mine entrance was on the side of the mountain. Anyone going into the mine wouldn't be seen from town. It was deep in the shadows, so all Matt saw was a black pit. If the mine was operating, lights would have burned, illuminating the company's property.

This mine would be open again soon with strikebreakers heading inside. That was asking for trouble because the regular miners wouldn't stand for it. Most people would simply complain, but he knew from past strikes, even here in Allegany County, frustration could push miners to violence. Matt had already heard reports of miners sabotaging coal company equipment and fights among bored miners. He also heard that union miners set fire to the home of a miner who kept working, and that was just against other local miners who dug coal for small family businesses.

Matt watched as a few people walked by the entrance. They didn't pay any attention to it. The mine was closed, and that was all that concerned them.

He sat on a hillside in the shadows and pulled his coat tight around him. The days might be warming up, but the nights were still cold.

He looked up at the stars shining brightly in the night sky and wondered if they were really so far away. Astronomers talked of planets that couldn't be seen with the naked eye and stars like the sun, some even larger, were small specks of light. He read Jules Verne's *A Trip to the Moon*, and it seemed impossible to think of traveling so far away. However, a scientist Robert Goddard was experimenting with rockets and publishing his results. Some people thought his rockets might eventually reach outer space.

Matt watched Enos walk down the Store Hill road, moving fast. He carried a lantern and crossed the National Road and disappeared into the woods and brush on the other side.

No need to wonder where he was going. Samuel and Matt fetched Enos from the still operating on the mountainside last month. It was well hidden and protected with armed guards. But,

Samuel knew where to go, and the guards knew him.

Allegany County had hundreds of small stills making bathtub gin in every other basement, it seemed.

This one was a larger operation, producing 200 gallons a day. It supplied a lot of the moonshine to the private businesses in both Allegany and Garrett counties. It was a good income for the shiners, but the operation had to be paying off the police to stay away. Too many people knew about it for the police not to know what was going on in the woods.

A car drove up the National Road and turned onto Porter Road. It drove past the company store and stopped in front of Laura's house.

Matt watched as Joey climbed out and walked around the car to open the passenger door. It surprised him to see Laura step out. She wore her Sunday dress. It was bright yellow and white. She seemed to glow in the night.

She took Joey's arm as he led her to the front door. What was she doing with him? She was dressed so nicely it appeared they had been on a date.

That couldn't be. Pete had been dead barely a month. She wouldn't be dating yet.

Joey led her to her door. Matt braced himself, expecting them to kiss, but hoping beyond hope it wouldn't happen.

They talked for a few moments and then Laura walked into the house. Joey stared at the door. Then he turned and headed back to his car.

Matt was tempted to walk down and talk to Laura, but it was none of his business.

Hadn't he promised Pete to look after Laura and Jacob, though?

Matt shook his head. What was Joseph up to? Was he courting the widow of one of his miners? Had they been having an affair? No, that couldn't be. Laura had more sense than that. Still, some coal company men got sexual favors in exchange for extending credit or keeping an injured miner on the payroll. Matt hadn't heard of it happening in Eckhart Mines, but he had met one woman

84

in that situation. He'd been too young to realize it at the time, but one of his friend's mother had been terrified to enter the company store in another town where his friend lived. She cried and muttered, "He'll make me go upstairs." Matt had gone into the store for her to get what she needed. He had asked the man behind the counter, "What's upstairs?" The man's face went pale and then he turned red. "Get out!" the man had yelled.

It was only years later before he left for the war that he realized what the woman had been talking about. Not that the women would want to talk about it. The company men might, but if they did, and it got back to the wrong ears, those men wouldn't be around long. If miners knew about it, at least one of them would have taken action.

Had Laura gotten herself into trouble since Pete died?

Samantha came off the small dance floor in the night club on the first floor of Hotel Gunter in a room behind the restaurant. She fanned herself because it was hot in the small night club. Ceiling fans spun quickly, but there were just too many people here tonight and the room was too small. Plus, the windows and doors had to stay shut to not be blatant about breaking the law. It kept the temperature high. Although dancing and serving food was legal, the drinks most people had in front of them weren't. The speakeasy in the basement supplied them.

She ordered a gin and tonic and sipped it as she looked around for a place to sit. The waiters served alcohol if they knew the customer, and the customer was discreet. Too bad Matt wasn't here with her, but even if he had been, he wouldn't have wanted to dance.

She saw Matt's friend, Calista, across the room. Samantha was still unsure of how the two of them were friends. Calista was obviously a prostitute. Samantha had seen the woman in the club before. No one could mistake her as a flapper. She dressed in tight dresses, caressed men's faces, whispering in their ears, and walked off with them to transact her business.

When Samantha saw to whom Calista was speaking, she

85

choked on her drink. It was Professor Williamson. Samantha wasn't sure what surprised her more that he was here in the Hotel Gunter or that he was speaking with a prostitute.

He must have turned down her offer because Calista smiled and moved off, letting her hand trail across his shoulders. Samantha couldn't tell whether he looked disappointed or relieved.

Samantha walked over to his table. He glanced up at her and then did a double take.

"Miss. Havencroft, I'm surprised to see you here," he said.

"I can say the same thing about you," Samantha replied. "It didn't take you long to find this place."

"It wasn't that hard. I have to say I am surprised at how few precautions are taken to hide all the alcohol in this town."

Samantha had nothing to compare it to. This was the only town she had been in since Prohibition had started. It was a stupid law no one except her father obeyed. Matt said the moonshiners paid the police to ignore their activities.

"I come for the dancing," she said. When Professor Williamson pointed to the drink in her hand, she added, "I didn't say that was the only reason I came."

He laughed. It was the first time she had heard it. He was always very serious in class.

"Please don't tell my father you saw me here should the topic come up," Samantha asked. "He suspects I visit these places, but I would rather not confirm things for him."

Samantha suspected her father knew a lot more that he let on. She wasn't sure how he found out things about her. He never seemed to meet with anyone outside of school, and Samantha saw no faculty off campus, except, of course now, Professor Williamson.

"Yes, fine," the professor said. "I agree if you reciprocate. I doubt your father would like to know his staff likes to drink from time to time."

He held out his hand and Samantha shook it.

"You are probably right. I know my father isn't a teetotaler, but he has become one simply because of that law. What if the law had been that we couldn't eat meat or had to walk backwards? I've never understood why he is so quick to obey even bad laws like a sheep, but he is in charge of a college."

Samantha saw Calista across the room running to get out of the dining room. She bumped into a man seated at a table, causing him to spill his drink on himself. Her face was so pale that even her make-up couldn't hide it. A big man with a scowl on his face rushed after her.

Had someone taken more than offense at her offers?

Samantha laid a hand on the professor's arm. "Please excuse me."

She stepped around him and hurried after Calista. She stepped into the hallway and heard footsteps pounding down the stairs. She followed as quickly as she could. She saw the two holding cells at the bottom of the stairs where police traveling with prisoners along the National Road used to leave their prisoners when they stayed overnight. She turned to the left and then followed the hall in a half circle.

She turned a second corner and saw Calista cowering against a wall. The big man had his fist raised.

"Stop that!" Samantha shouted.

The man looked over his shoulder. He had piercing green eyes wide with anger. His nostrils flared.

"Go away, or you'll get what I'm going to give her," he said.

"Don't Samantha," Calista said. "Help me! He'll kill me."

Samantha wasn't sure what she could do to help. This man was bigger than both she and Calista put together.

Samantha moved forward, not sure what to do. The man shoved her. She staggered backwards in her high heels and fell against the opposite wall.

"Samantha!" Calista cried.

The man smacked her across the cheek. Calista shouted.

"You need to learn to shut your mouth!" the man said.

"What's going on here?"

Samantha turned and saw that Professor Williamson had followed her out of the club. The big man looked back and forth between Samantha and the professor. The man growled like a

87

JAMES RADA, JR.

cornered dog.

"This isn't over," he told Calista.

Then he stormed down the hallway and out the back door that opened onto First Street.

Professor Williamson held out his hand and helped Samantha to her feet.

"Are you all right? I still don't know what was happening," the professor said.

Calista hurried over and hugged Samantha and then the professor. "Thank you, both of you. He would have killed me."

"I think you might be exaggerating things," the professor said.

Samantha wasn't so sure. She had seen the anger in the man's face.

"No, he was in jail because of me. He wants revenge," Calista said.

"Why?" Samantha asked.

Calista glanced at the professor. "I really can't say."

"Should I call the police?" Professor Williamson asked.

"It wouldn't help," Samantha said. "He's gone."

The professor must have understood because he said, "I'm going to follow that man and make sure he doesn't come back."

"Thank you, but be careful," Calista said.

When he left, Samantha said, "Now, can you tell me why you think that man wanted to kill you?"

"He beat me up one evening rather than..." She looked at the ground. "... rather than pay me. He left me in an alley in the middle of winter. Matt found me and helped me. He also convinced me to press charges."

Matt had told Samantha some of this story, enough to keep her from being jealous of Calista. He hadn't told Samantha about being a hero, which was just like him.

Samantha nodded. "Matt was right. You can't let that man get away with that."

"He was in jail, but he made bail, and now he's out looking for me because he knows I'm the reason he was in jail. He doesn't want a trial to happen that could send him to the penitentiary."

88

Samantha hugged Calista to calm her down. She was shaking.

"You'll just have to be careful," Samantha said.

"I can only be so careful. I still need to work. All he has to do is look for me in places like this."

"Then go to different places."

Samantha couldn't believe she was encouraging Calista to continue to prostitute herself, but she needed to be safe. Now that she saw Calista up close, Samantha saw the woman was older than she and Matt. She was still beautiful, but for how much longer could she remain so doing this work?

"He may watch those places, too," Calista said.

"Can you leave town?" Samantha asked.

"And go where? I am alone."

Calista sunk down to sit on the floor. Her dress was so tight it stained at the seams.

Samantha leaned against the wall and stood next to her. She fancied herself as someone who was helping women get ahead, but this woman who really needed her help, and all Samantha could do was suggest she find a different place to be a prostitute. There had to be a better answer.

"What if you found other work?" Samantha asked.

"Like what? Matt thought I should be a clerk in a store, but no merchant would hire someone like me, let alone keep me on when he found out what I did."

Samantha nodded. "That makes sense. Such work would also place you in full sight of that man. You do need other work, but it needs to be where he won't find you."

"I just want him to go away."

Samantha patted her shoulder. "I'm sure you do, but the problem is when he is gone, another one might take his place. He can't be the first person you have run into who mistreated you."

What a sad way to live, to think being treated poorly was normal. No wonder she was attached to Matt. He had shown her kindness.

"He's the only one I thought might kill me," Calista said.

"Can you wash, polish, and clean?" Samantha asked suddenly.

Calista stared at her. "I have to. I can't afford a maid."

"But can you be a maid?"

Calista paused and then said, "Who would hire me? It's the same problem with merchants, maybe worse, because people might think I did other things in the house where I worked."

"But could you do it?"

Calista shrugged. "Yes. I imagine anyone could."

Samantha smiled and pushed herself to her feet. "Then I have a job for you. Our maid quit last week, and my father hasn't hired a new woman yet. Do you want the job?"

"What's your father going to say?"

"He'll be happy to have the help so our cook will stop complaining about having two jobs and getting paid for one."

"And if he finds out about me?" Calista asked.

"Let's cross that bridge when we come to it. At the very least, if you do a good job, I can give you a reference that should help you get work someplace else."

Samantha held out her hand to Calista. Calista shook it.

"Now I think you should go home and get some sleep. You start work at seven in the morning."

Chapter 9

May 8, 1922

Jenny Washington left her home at six in the morning when the sky was just beginning to lighten. It was cold, but spring was here, and soon even the mornings would be warm. Working days would take some getting used to. Not many days ago, she would have been home for just a few hours at this time of the morning.

She paused at the gate and stared at the house. It was a three-story brick Georgian home with six bedrooms. She'd never been in a house so large. Her small house wouldn't even take up one floor. It looked new, at least the paint wasn't peeling and the mortar in the bricks gleamed white.

She smoothed down her dress. It was her everyday dress, not fancy at all, but it would be a suitable work dress for her.

Did she want to do this? Could she do it? She hadn't worked an actual job since she was Samantha's age. That had been years ago, before she married and moved to Frostburg. It was before her loneliness and need to earn money drove her to prostitution.

Jenny closed her eyes and took a deep breath. Then she walked up to the door and knocked. Samantha answered quickly and waved her inside.

"Try not to make any noise," she said. "My father is still asleep."

Jenny looked at the well-kept furniture, art on the walls, and area rugs on the hardwood floors. This might be the nicest house she had ever seen.

"I didn't know college presidents made so much money," Jenny whispered.

Samantha looked confused for a moment. "Oh, my father makes a good living, but it wouldn't pay for all this. His family has money."

Jenny nodded and followed Samantha down the hallway to the back of the house. They went into a room that appeared to be a washing room. It had a washing machine, sewing machine, and armoire in it. The servants' staircase to the second floor ended here.

"We have a maid's dress in the armoire. If it doesn't fit, we'll get you one that does this afternoon."

"Yes, Sam... ma'am," Jenny said.

Samantha smiled. "I don't care if you call me, Samantha, but don't do it around my father or guests. He won't like it. Also, always call him, sir. Now try on the dress while I explain your duties."

Samantha shoved a black and white dress in her direction. When Jenny took the dress, Samantha picked up a piece of paper off a table and read a list she had written up. Jenny changed. The dress fit her, although it was a little high. The former maid must have been a shorter woman. The duties wouldn't be hard, but learning the rules of conduct might. She needed to be quieter and more unassuming than she was normally.

"Oh, wonderful, it fits," Samantha said when she saw Jenny in the uniform.

Jenny looked at herself in the mirror on the wall. She looked like a maid. She had worn very little make-up to reduce the chance of anyone who visited recognizing her.

Samantha then took Jenny into the kitchen to introduce her to Mrs. Fratelli, the cook. The woman was older than Jenny, but she still had flaming red hair that she wore tucked up beneath a cap.

"How do you do?" Jenny said, shaking the woman's hand.

"Jenny is new to this type of service," Samantha said. "I want to see her succeed, though."

The woman paused and stared at Jenny and then shook her hand. "If you're willing to work hard and help when needed, you won't hear a complaint from me. I'm happy not to have to do the work of two. It was wearing me down. I'm not Miss Samantha's age anymore."

"I will do my best," Jenny told her.

Mrs. Fratelli nodded. "I'm getting breakfast ready now. The family eats at 7:30 a.m. I will have everything ready by then. You just take it out and serve them and stay in the dining room in case they need something else. When they leave the table, bring the dishes back to me, and I'll take care of them."

Samantha clapped her hands together. "Great! I need to go upstairs to finish getting ready. I have afternoon classes today so I will be around after breakfast to help you get settled in, Jenny."

"Thank you."

Samantha left and Jenny looked around. "Is the table set? Is that part of my duties?"

"Yes and yes. You set the table and clear the dishes, but you don't have to wash them. I set the table this morning so you could ease into how things work. Lord knows, I don't want to scare off someone who can help me."

Jenny smiled. "Thank you. Can I do anything to help you now?"

Mrs. Fratelli shook her head. "No, I'm fine, dear."

A few minutes later, Jenny heard movement in the dining room. She poked her head through the swinging door and saw Samantha and another man sitting at the table and talking.

"They're seated," Jenny said.

Mrs. Fratelli pointed to the cups of fruit. "Take those out first. It is usually all Miss. Samantha eats for breakfast. Mr. Havencroft will eat eggs and bacon after his fruit. It will be ready soon. I like to make sure it is hot for him."

Jenny put the two glass cups of sliced fruit on a small platter and carried them out into the dining room.

The man looked up, surprised. "Who is this?"

Samantha said, "This is Jenny Washington, our new maid. I told you I hired her. Jenny, this is my father, Mr. Havencroft."

"How do you do, sir?" Jenny said.

She set the fruit cups in front of Samantha and her father.

"Mrs. Fratelli is preparing eggs and bacon this morning. What would you like to drink?" Jenny asked.

Her heart pounded so fast she hoped she didn't appear flushed.

"I just take a glass of milk in the mornings," Samantha said.

"I like juice with my meal and coffee at the end," Mr. Havencroft said.

Jenny nodded. "Very good. I will bring the juice and milk out."

She walked into the kitchen and brought the drinks out. As she set the glass of milk in front of Samantha, she smiled an approving smile at Jenny.

This would work. Not only was David Lakehurst never likely to step foot inside this house and find her working, but one benefit of the job was it included live-in quarters. Even if Lakehurst found her Water Street house, Jenny wouldn't be living there any longer. Samantha promised to help her move her belongings from her home to her room on the third floor once Samantha could borrow her father's car.

Joseph read down the list of names that Sidney Bloom, the paymaster, handed him. He was happy to have work to do even if didn't involve coal mined from below the town.

The names on the list didn't matter. All Joseph noted was that most of them looked Italian and Irish with some German thrown in. Joseph made a silent count in his head. Twenty-five.

Twenty-five tomorrow and twenty-five next week with more planned to arrive depending on how negotiations went. Joseph was thrilled he'd be able to reopen his mines, if only partially, but he had to find a place to house these people.

"We'll put them all working in No. 4," Joseph said. Better to have only one site to protect, and the No. 4 mine was the most productive.

Eckhart Mines could soon start cashing in on the high cost of coal.

"That's fine, but where will we house them?" Sidney asked.

"How many empty houses do we have?"

"Three and two rooms in the single men's boarding house. Plus, the Widow Spiker is still in her house."

Joseph's head snapped up, and he glared at Sidney. "Leave her out of this."

"But the policy with company housing is that it's for company employees, and her husband…"

"I know the policy, dammit, and I told you to take her off the list."

"Fine."

Sidney scratched a name off of the list.

"We can put four men in each house," Joseph said. "It's temporary."

"We'll need more beds."

"Get them out of storage." The company had cots and temporary bedding for emergencies and overcrowding situations, which hadn't happened in years. "We'll double up in all the single men's rooms."

"All? The miners won't like it."

"Nuts to them," Joey said. "They haven't paid rent in weeks. I hope they do complain." Evicting single men wouldn't be as bad as evicting families.

"That gives us nineteen spots."

"And if we evict the single miners from the company boarding house?"

"Then we've got twenty-two."

"There's got to be three more spaces somewhere."

"There are, but you don't want to hear it."

Joseph glared at the paymaster.

"We could find three spots in the other boarding houses in town," Sidney suggested.

"I won't pay people to house miners when we have the space."

"Then you'll have to evict someone." Sidney wisely kept silent on who he thought should be included. "Also, this only solves the immediate problem. Next week, we'll have twenty-five more miners coming in and no empty spaces."

Joseph shook his head. His father was going to be angry with him, but what else was new? "Who is the most overdue on rent?"

"They were all up to date at the end of March." Not surprising, since rent was a payroll deduction. "No one has paid since then."

"Is there a family that's just a husband and wife?" Joseph asked.

"Yes."

"Start with them. Tell them they need to pay April's back rent and this week's rent today or be out tomorrow morning. If they pay, they can stay for now, and the company gets some money. If they don't, then we gave them a chance and out they go."

"If they pay, we're still short three spaces."

"Then work your way down the list; should be at least one of them not able to pay. Get going."

"Alone?"

Joseph shook his head. "No. There are two guards at each mine. Take one of them with you. Let me know by noon where these men will stay," Joseph said, as he shook the list of strikebreakers at Sidney.

David walked into the mine office and saw the two men seated at desks on the other side of the counter. The office was small but not as small as some offices in other mining towns he was in over the past week. This office was quieter, though. The men weren't speaking or paying much attention to each other.

"I'm looking for Joseph McCord," David said.

The larger of the two men looked up from whatever he'd been writing.

"I'm Joseph McCord."

David was struck by his soft features. He expected miners to be lean men with hard angles in their face, but then he remembered McCord wasn't a miner. He was the mine superintendent.

96

"My name is David Lakehurst. I'm with the Pinkerton Detective Agency."

Joseph stood up and walked to the counter. He didn't bother to shake David's hand.

"What can I do for you?" Joseph asked.

"I am here to protect the workers your company is hiring and the company property."

Joseph's eyebrows rose. "One man? We have over two dozen workers coming in tomorrow and more the following week."

David pulled out his pistol and laid it on the counter. Joseph glanced at it and shrugged.

"Three out of four men in this town own guns," Joseph said.

David nodded. "Maybe, but many of them will hesitate to use them against another person. I won't, and I have the authority to defend your strikebreakers. I will do whatever it takes to do my job."

David could bring in Pinkerton detectives to guard company property as needed. He didn't tell Joseph that, though. David would rather let the mine superintendent think David could handle everything himself.

Joseph rubbed his chin and stared at David. David didn't like the man. McCord was weak, but his arrogance wouldn't allow him to see that. He thought because he had power in this small town, he was strong.

"Fine, just make sure that my mines stay open," Joseph said.

"I will post guards at each mine entrance, and I will oversee the men as they go to and from the mine. Any efforts to hinder the mine operations will be met with force and overcome," David explained.

"We already have two men at each mine."

"That might not be enough or too many. I have to see how things are in this town when the strikebreakers arrive."

Joseph smiled. "Good, then do your job, and you'll get no complaint from me."

Joseph turned to head back to his desk, but he noticed David Lakehurst didn't move.

"Is there something else?" Joseph asked.

"I am looking for someone who might live in this town. His leg is in a cast."

Joseph frowned and nodded. "Yeah, that's Matt Ansaro. He is one of my ungrateful miners." He said it like he tasted a piece of rotten meat.

"When did he break his leg?"

"He was caught in a cave-in, at the end of last month, for which he was probably responsible."

A miner. Just as David thought. Miners could fight, but David never met a miner he couldn't beat.

"Is he much of a fighter?" David asked.

"I wouldn't know. I'm the mine superintendent. I don't make a habit of brawling with my miners."

David seemed on the verge of saying something else, but then he turned and left.

He stood on the porch of the store and pulled a Camel cigarette from his pocket. He lit it and took a puff as his eyes took in the street.

This was the town. Now, he had found the man.

David let his gaze wander up and down Store Hill. This was the main street in town, at least as far as local business went. From here, most of the businesses and houses moved north, staying below Frostburg. David was surprised more houses were not built on the southern side of the National Road, since it was the major road for travelers who passed through town.

He watched the people moving along the streets. They walked in clusters. The women traveled with other women. Having not been in Eckhart Mines before, he wasn't sure whether that was common or because too many miners with nothing to do were on the streets. The miners sat around in large groups of about a half a dozen men.

He felt the eyes of people seen and unseen watch him as he walked. Good. He walked a little taller and strode with purpose. Let them see me, and more importantly, let them fear me, he thought. Their fear would make his job easier because if they tried to interfere with him and his work, they would suffer the consequences.

The No. 10 mine entrance was near the top of the mountain. Miners could walk into it without the need of an elevator lowered into the shaft. It led to the smaller Tyson Coal Seam. Below the No. 10 was the No. 4 mine that tapped into the much larger Big Seam Coal Vein. According to David's research, the No. 4 mine yielded more than No. 10, but it was plagued with drainage and ventilation problems.

Not that David had gone into either of the mines or any coal mine, for that matter. He enjoyed being able to see the sun and not have a mountain sitting over his head ready to drop down and kill him, all of which depended on the whims of fate.

David walked around both entrances on his way to the company store. The No. 10 entrance was easy to defend. It was the high ground. A guard there would see anyone approaching. All of the equipment was still intact. The tool shed was locked. If black powder was still stored inside, it would need to be moved. Someone intent on causing problems could break in and have enough powder to close a mine, blow up a building, or spray shrapnel in a crowd.

It needed to be moved someplace else that was safe and unknown to the miners. Maybe the store had a basement where it could be hidden. It might not be too safe for the store, but it would be much safer for the company.

The No. 4 could cause problems. Not that anyone had destroyed anything at the site. Far from it. Everything had been in order, just like at the No. 10. It was the mine's location that bothered David. It was on the slope below the roadway, which meant anyone who wanted to cause trouble would have some cover approaching the mine. He would have to set a guard high enough to watch the approaches to the mine and another guard on site to watch for anyone who might sneak in close enough to cause problems.

As he walked to the top of the hill, he saw a group of four miners watching him. David drew his shoulders back and approached them.

"You need to move off company property," he said.

The largest of the four miners was still three inches shorter and twenty pounds lighter than David. He stood in front of the other three men and said, "This isn't company property."

David raised an eyebrow. "I've been hired to protect company property, and I will determine where it starts and ends in this town. This is a Consolidation Coal town."

"That doesn't make everything Consolidation Coal property."

David stepped closer to emphasize the height advantage he had.

The miner didn't back off, although he gulped. "There's four of us and one of you. I think maybe you better listen when we tell you this isn't company property, and maybe you ought not to be so bossy."

David's fist shot out, striking the man hard across the jaw. He dropped to the ground, stunned. The other three men closed on David. He swung back the side of his coat so they could see the pistol hanging on his hip.

"This gives me my authority to be bossy. Now, I suggest you get off company property or you'll wind up with more than broken bones like your friend."

The other men hesitated, staring back and forth between David's face and his pistol. The man on the ground started moaning. They grabbed him under the arms, helped him to his feet and walked away. They mumbled and looked over their shoulders, but they left.

David had sent his message.

Chapter 10

May 9, 1922

Samantha sat on a bench outside of Old Main, the college classroom building enjoying the warmth of the sun while munching on an apple. The trees were filling in with leaves, and she saw some students walking about without coats or sweaters. Even she was without her cardigan.

"May I join you?"

She turned around and saw Professor Williamson. He wore a charcoal gray suit with a tailored cut and pinched waist. Quite dapper, she thought. He looked like a professor and at the same time looked like a handsome dandy ready for dancing, in his jazz suit. She hadn't spoken to him outside of his class since he had helped her and Jenny at the Hotel Gunter.

"I suppose," Samantha said. "After all, we are each other's secret keepers."

"That was a bit of an adventure the other evening," he said as he sat down on the bench beside her.

Samantha tried to wipe the apple juice she felt escaping from the corner of her mouth without appearing obvious.

"Welcome to Frostburg. I've had more than one unexpected experience in the past year!"

He crossed his long legs and braced himself with one arm on

the bench. "Such as?"

"Well for instance, nearly being knocked off an apple box and onto the National Road; pursued by two drunk miners up the street; and, sitting outside a coal mine wondering if someone I care for was dead."

Professor Williamson's eyes widened, and then he smirked.

"Yes, I can see those are things one would not expect the daughter of a college president to deal with such instances, but then, you do not live that life."

He leaned back on the bench and lifted his chin toward the sun.

"You don't believe me?" she asked in surprise.

"If I hadn't been part of what happened, I would say no, but that not being the case, I have to say I do believe you."

Silence fell between them. Samantha knew what he wanted to ask, but she would not bring up the subject.

Finally, he asked, "How is your... friend from the other night?"

"Jenny?"

"I thought she said her name was Calista?"

"That is a name she uses... when she is working." Samantha felt herself blushing, but she couldn't stop it.

"Working? What she offered is far from work or at least not unpleasant work."

"Professor!"

He chuckled. "I did not take her up on the offer as you saw, but she is an attractive woman. I am surprised she is a friend of yours."

"Oh, I would not call her that, although we may become so. She is a friend of a friend, and I felt I owed her a debt."

The professor lit a cigarette and inhaled it. "You are quite an interesting woman, Miss. Havencroft. Far from what I expected of a college president's daughter."

Samantha liked that she was more than a submissive woman. She had dreams and goals she hoped to achieve. They were a bit vague now, but she knew she was destined as more than a teacher or as an ordinary wife.

"That's your problem, professor," Samantha said. "You look at people as a group rather than individuals. There is more than one type of college president's daughter, or professor, or coal miner, or prostitute."

"I know three of those people, if I am to look at them as individuals as you say, then who is the coal miner?"

Samantha hesitated, not sure how personal she wanted to get with this man. "He is someone I am seeing."

"And what makes him more than your typical coal miner?" Williamson asked.

"He grew up here, but he has been a Marine in the war, and he lived in Baltimore afterwards. I don't know whether it's all that or something else, but he seems more worldly and knowledgeable than other miners I have met."

"Like the two drunk miners you said chased you on the street."

He was paying attention to what Samantha said and remembering. Often, her father would seem to be listening, nodding and saying "Yes, yes" or "Interesting." Even Matt sometimes got a faraway look while they were speaking.

"Yes, in fact, that is when I first met Matt. He's the coal miner who helped me," Samantha said.

"He wasn't one of the ones chasing you?"

Samantha laughed. "No, he thought I needed saving, and he stepped in to help."

The professor raised an eyebrow. "Did you?"

Samantha exhaled softly. "I'd like to think not."

"Which means you needed help and don't want to admit it."

Samantha gave him a knowing smile.

"It's sort of like what happened in the hotel," the professor said.

Samantha hadn't considered that. She didn't want to be a damsel in distress, but it seemed like she got herself into a lot of tough situations.

"I suppose."

"Who was that man... the one in the hotel?"

"Someone Jenny put in prison for a while and will hopefully send back."

The professor puffed on his cigarette. "What did he do?"

Samantha hesitated. Jenny's secrets were hers to share or not. "That's not for me to say, but once I heard what happened, I agreed. He belonged in prison."

"So how serious are you and Matt?" Professor Williamson asked, switching directions.

"I like him a lot. My father doesn't approve, of course." She had to admit that was part of Matt's attraction. He was strong, and his scar made him mysterious. He was funny and intelligent, although it was more common sense than book smart. He cared about his friends, family, and her.

"I think you enjoy taking a contrary opinion to your father's," the professor said.

"That's rather impertinent."

"Is it? You go to speakeasies. You date coal miners and make friends with prostitutes. A prim and proper college president's daughter would do none of those things."

Samantha never considered what she did as an act of defiance against her father. Well, except for the drinking. She did what she did because it was who she was.

"It is not, and you must think me a shallow person, if you think I lead my life that way," Samantha told the professor.

The professor drew back. "Oh, I'm sorry if I misread things, but I assure you, I don't consider you shallow. Now, Jane Paulson, she is shallow and very obvious in her intentions."

"Which are?"

"To find herself a husband to take care of her. I met women like her at Princeton. They were hard to escape at times, at least the persistent ones."

It hadn't taken him long to get Jane's measure, and while true, Jane was a friend. Samantha felt the professor was overlooking her wonderful qualities, such as her kind nature and easy going manner.

"Jane is very nice."

"I'm sure she is. So were the women at Princeton. The

problem is you never knew who they were because they were always trying to present themselves as what you wanted them to be like. You, on the other hand, present yourself the way you are whether it's a flapper, a student, and I have even heard you're a suffragette." At Samantha's surprised look, he added, "Your father told me that last bit."

That surprised Samantha more than Professor Williamson knowing she supported women's rights. It was like he was uncovering her secrets one by one.

"You and my father speak about me?" she asked.

The professor nodded. She doubted that could be a wonderful thing. Her father had a certain view of her life and how she was living it. Not surprisingly, his opinion differed from hers.

"You are my student and his daughter. You are bound to come up in conversation from time to time."

"If you want to know about me, then ask me."

"You are not the reason your father and I sit down to speak, but you do come up in conversation because we have you in common... like the college or cars."

Samantha's eyes widened. "So I'm like a car in your and my father's eyes?"

"Well the way you huffing does resemble the way a car's engine struggles to get up some of these Western Maryland hills."

Samantha was about to yell or hit him, but then she caught the corners of his mouth jerking up, trying to keep from smiling. She took a deep breath.

"I see. Well, professor, perhaps you should be in front of a Vaudeville audience rather than a college class since you consider yourself a comedian. I would warn you, though, you know just as much about comedy as you do cars."

The professor stood up, smiling. "And with that, I'll take my leave. I need to make my way to my next class. I believe it is also yours. May I accompany you?"

Samantha stood up. "Yes, at least I know I won't be late."

Joseph drove slowly down the National Road toward

105

Cumberland. Partly, because he wanted to spend more time driving with Laura. Also, he worried would run off the road because he kept looking over at her classically beautiful face.

The 1922 Studebaker Special roadster's top was down, and the wind was blowing through her blond hair. She tilted her chin up, enjoying the breeze.

He drove to a restaurant on Mechanic Street called Palmer House. He found a parking space across the street from the restaurant. Joseph admired her legs as he helped her out of the car. Laura was wearing a new dress with the higher hemline that was fashionable nowadays. He had encouraged her to buy earlier in the week.

She said she wished that he hadn't spent so much on it, but he could tell she loved it. He knew it was the fanciest thing she owned, and she proably felt like a princess wearing it. Joseph had insisted she buy herself a dress. It wouldn't do for the Eckhart Mines superintendent's date to look shabby.

Joseph had the head waiter seat them at a table he reserved. It looked out over Wills Creek through a bay window. The lighting was dim, and a band played soft music. No jazz for this restaurant.

"I know it's not a big river, but it's larger than anything I've seen in years," Laura said of Wills Creek. They talked about places they wanted to visit. "Matt said the ocean is so large it's unbelievable, but I can't imagine that much water."

Joseph straightened in his chair. "Have you ever thought about taking a trip to the ocean or just leaving Eckhart?" he asked.

"Eckhart's my home. I was born there. I can't imagine leaving. I can't afford to leave. This will be the biggest pleasure trip I'll have for some time."

"I don't know about that. I could take you to the ocean."

"Joey, you already do so much for Jacob and me."

He hesitated and plunged forward with what he wanted to say. "I want to show you I can be a good provider. I can take care of you and Jacob. You'll never want for anything. I want to be better than my father."

He reached out and took her hand in his. He was pleased she

didn't pull away.

"I think you've done all right for yourself," Laura said. "You're running a mine, you live in a big house, you have a maid, and you have money."

He nodded then looked into her eyes and said, "But I don't have you."

He could tell she blushed even in the dim light. "I don't know what my future will be like, but I must provide for myself and Jacob."

"That's what I'm saying. I can create that future for you and Jacob."

If Jacob was the price he had to pay to get Laura, it was well worth it.

"Joey, you are wonderful," Laura said softly, "but don't you want your own family?"

"We can have that. Jacob can have brothers and sisters."

He leaned across the table to kiss her, but she turned away, leaving him leaning across the table and Laura looking out the window at Will Creek. He pressed his lips together in a hard line and settled back in his seat.

"Matt said there are more jobs for women now," Laura said. "The suffrage movement opened doors for us."

Joseph managed not to roll his eyes... just barely. Why did she keep mentioning Matt? Did he mention his previous women? Not that there had been any who could hold a candle to Laura. No, he kept his romances prior to Laura in the past.

"Well, Matt would know about women," Joseph said.

"What do you mean?"

Joseph played innocent. "Matt went overseas in the war. I've heard plenty of stories about how appreciative those European women were with the soldiers. From what I heard, many soldiers left behind a woman and child."

Samantha's eyes widened. "Oh."

"I even heard talk that Matt may have come back to Eckhart to get away from a woman he got pregnant in Baltimore." A complete lie, of course. Joseph hadn't bothered to look into Matt's background. Why should he? He knew Matt from their shared childhood. He couldn't have changed that much.

"I don't believe that," Laura said. "Who would say something like that?"

Joseph would, and now that he thought about it, it might be a good rumor to spread. The problem was, he didn't speak with anyone who would spread that rumor among the miners.

"Oh, I don't know, it's just something I heard. Probably nothing." He took a short breath. "I asked if you would leave Eckhart." He paused then asked, "Have you ever been to New York City?"

"You know I haven't."

"One day, when I move up in the company, I will move there. That's where the Consolidation Coal headquarters is located. When that day comes, Laura, I want you to go with me."

There, he laid his cards on the table. He gave Laura a taste of how much better her life could be with him, and he told her he wanted her with him when he rose through the ranks.

"Joey, I don't know what to say."

"Say yes. I know it can be overwhelming. You needn't be afraid. I'll be there with you."

Laura's brow furrowed. "Are you asking me to marry you?"

Joseph drew back. Marriage? Where did she get that idea? No, the woman he married would be of equal or greater social standing than Joseph. She must be able to aid his rise in authority. Laura couldn't do that. She was a penniless miner's widow.

Not that Joseph could tell Laura that. He also found that he didn't want to hurt her feelings.

He patted her hand. "As enamored as I am with you, I think marriage at this point is rushing things. Don't you agree?"

She nodded. He thought she might have been too quick to agree.

"What I am pro ... offering is a courtship. Let's get to know each other and enjoy each other's company and other things."

"Really?"

"Oh, yes, I want to take my time and get to know every inch of you."

He smiled, but it didn't reach his eyes. No, his eyes were busy taking in every inch of her.

Sidney Bloom paused in front of the door and looked over his shoulder at the guard with him. The man looked intimidating. He had selected the largest of the four guards to accompany him. The man held a Springfield 1903 rifle cradled in his folded arms and wore a Colt .45 automatic pistol holstered on his hip.

"This won't be as easy as the last one," Sidney said.

Sidney began his work of moving or evicting miners living in the company housing. The single men in the company boarding houses didn't want strikebreakers as roommates, so they were told to vacate immediately. They complained loudly, but that was all. It didn't take them long to leave because they had few possessions and didn't own the furniture in their rooms.

The armed guard dissuaded them from taking stealing or destroying any of the furniture. Everything took place indoors, so it didn't create a scene. The miners left the boarding house carrying a suitcase or canvas bag.

Word soon got around town. It would have been foolish to expect otherwise.

By the time Sidney started on the families, a crowd gathered to follow him. They filtered out of their homes and businesses, and there were more of them than usual at an eviction. With none of the miners working, they were free to follow the crowd.

They wanted to see where he would go next. The miners in company housing knew they could be evicted, and more than a few were relieved to see him stop in front of the Spangler home.

Sidney knocked. Scott Spangler opened the door. He was chosen because only he and his wife lived in the house. It involved no children, at least for this eviction.

"Scott, your rent for this house is in arrears," Sidney said. "I have been instructed to order your eviction if you cannot bring your rent up to date today."

Scott sighed and shook his head. "If I do that, I won't have money for food."

"That is not my problem. This house is designated as employee housing for the Consolidation Coal Company, and since you are no longer working for the company, you are no longer entitled to company housing. Mr. McCord has been lenient."

"Lenient?"

"Yes, you can remain in the housing, but to do so, you must keep your rent current. If not, we can use the house for other workers that the company employs."

"What other workers? We're on strike."

"We have new workers arriving tomorrow."

"You mean damned strikebreakers."

"I mean men willing to work for a good wage. If you want to work and earn that same wage, you are welcome to do so. You could then remain in this home."

Scott scowled. "I'd rather live on the street than give in to Joseph McCord."

Sidney shrugged. "That is your choice. You need to leave. We can help you remove your belongings."

Scott looked over his shoulder. Only he and his wife lived in the small house. "Now?"

Sidney nodded. "And we will remain to make sure no damage is done to company property."

Scott stepped over the threshold and lowered his voice as he spoke to Sidney. "We don't have anywhere to go."

"There's the street, which you just said you'd rather sleep on than accept a job from Mr. McCord."

Scott reached out and grabbed Sidney's shirt, but the guard raised his weapon. Scott hesitated for a moment before he let go.

"You're a real bastard," Scott said.

"I gave you three options," Sidney said. "The choice was yours."

The crowd started yelling for Scott to be allowed to stay. Sidney turned to them and shouted, "I have to clear enough room to house the new workers. If he and his wife stay, then someone else must go. Does anyone want to volunteer to leave? Oh, and this won't be the last home I need to visit." The crowd quieted down.

"I thought so."

He turned back to Scott. "You have two hours. After that, you won't be allowed back in the house."

"What if we aren't moved out by then?"

"This man..." He indicated the guard. "... will remove your belongings to the street, and he will do it quickly."

Scott started to say something, but then he turned and went back into the house. Sidney motioned for the guard to follow.

"Make sure they only take their property," he said. "Don't touch anything right now."

The guard nodded and entered the house.

The crowd murmured again. They cursed Sidney and called him a traitor. They closed in around the fenced property.

"Stay outside of the fence or you will be on company property," shouted Sidney.

Someone threw a rock, and it hit him on the shoulder. He yelled and staggered back. The crowd cheered and pressed forward until there wasn't an inch of space along the fence.

Sidney yelled, "Get back. I warned you."

He drew a revolver and fired into the air. The crowd backed off. Some people ran. The guard rushed out of the house with his rifle raised.

Toni rushed up to the gate. "What do you think you're doing, Sidney?"

"I'm protecting company property."

"They don't want to damage the house. They want you to leave. You're making things worse."

"Scott is behind in his rent. We're taking the house back. The company owns it."

"Fine, but give the family time to move their stuff out. You can have the house."

"He needs to be gone today."

"We can help him move out if you stop threatening to shoot people."

Sidney hesitated. Then he lowered the gun and stepped back. "Alright," he said reluctantly, "help them."

111

Toni turned to the crowd. "Form a line. Go into the house. Pick up something and carry it to the church. We have permission to store their things in the basement. Clothes and personal items go to the Burke house. The Spanglers will stay in their extra room for now."

Most of the crowd did as Toni asked, and soon a line of goods was moving out of the house. The men carried the furniture to the church while the women took the personal items to the Burke's.

It wasn't a permanent solution, but it would do for now.

Chapter 11

May 13, 1922

Toni looked around the room at two-dozen women in the Eckhart Junior Mechanics Hall. She had hoped for a larger turnout. The women who didn't show up were the very ones Tony and these women needed to help. Some evicted women and their families had stayed in the church overnight. Consolidation Coal evicted eight families from company housing this week to make room for strikebreakers coming to town.

"Ladies, what are we going to do? We have homeless families in Eckhart," Toni said.

"What are you doing?" Marie Evans asked. "You run a boarding house."

"I have one free room, and I can take in one family for a few weeks, but I am already carrying three miners who haven't paid room and board in weeks."

"You have a larger house than we do. I don't have room."

Toni knew Marie and her husband had an attic room they used just for storage.

"Then where else can they stay?" Toni asked. "These are our friends. If we can't help them, what do we do when the company evicts one of our families?"

"Not you."

"No, Marie, not me. At least the coal company can't evict me. The bank might if my family misses our mortgage payments, which could happen if my boarders can't pay me."

Chastened, Marie shut up.

"What about the school?" Evelyn Parker called out. Eckhart Mines had a small three-room elementary school.

Toni shook her head. "Mr. Wilhide might allow it, but only until the county board finds out. They would surely put a stop to it. Are there empty houses in town that aren't company owned?"

The women murmured, talking amongst themselves and shaking their heads.

"Does anyone have an empty attic?" Toni asked, looking at Marie. "We just need places for these families until the strike ends."

"But how long will that be?" Marie asked.

"I don't know, but since the company is hiring strikebreakers, it looks like they are digging in for a fight."

"Which means this could last months."

Marie crossed her arms over her chest, looking as if she made a brilliant point.

"What about food? Can we feed these families?" Toni asked.

That wasn't as much a problem. Women with more than one cow agreed to send the families milk. Those with plenty of chickens would share their eggs. Most families had extra canned fruits and vegetables set by for hard times. If the strike went on for very long, even those resources would become scarce.

It was slow going, but the women managed to take care of everyone, if it was only temporary. None of the families in town were wealthy enough to support another family indefinitely. Hopefully, either the strike would end soon or the striking miners would find other work. That was doubtful, though. These men were coal miners. It was all they knew.

Toni walked out of the meeting hall feeling proud of what the women in town had accomplished. They banded together to help everyone get through what looked like a long strike.

She walked down the hill toward the business area of town.

She paused to watch the groups of strikebreakers who had arrived on the train escorted through town. They were a motley group of men, most of whom had no experience in a coal mine. So many of them looked too bulky for mine work, which meant they might have been brought in to fight. One group of men were negroes. Toni wondered how well that would go over in the mines, even among the strikebreakers. She thought it would certainly cause problems among the shopkeepers in town.

As the men passed her, some of them smiled and tipped their caps. She ignored them and waited for them to pass. She saw Joseph and his father standing on the porch of the company store watching the men.

When she got back to the boarding house, Myrna was in the dining room setting out the plates for lunch.

"We'll have two more for dinner later," she said.

"Who will that be?" Myrna asked.

"The Pattersons." They were the couple she agreed to take in. She didn't have room for an entire family. "They will be staying in the empty room."

"And will they be paying?" Samuel asked as he poked his head in from the kitchen.

"Who does nowadays?"

"Then we're taking in strays?"

"Everybody has to do their part, Samuel. The Pattersons need a place to stay until all of this gets settled."

"I'd like to see our other guests do their part and try to find some work to tide them over," Myrna said.

Toni nodded. "As would I, but I will not kick them out when they have nowhere else to go. It was a struggle just trying to find places for the families that have been evicted. We didn't even start on the single miners."

"I guess we'll just have to find a way to get by."

Toni looked around. "Where are Matt and Enos?"

"Matt went into Frostburg, probably to see Samantha. I think Enos is still sleeping. He was out late," Myrna said.

"Of course he was," Toni muttered.

115

He'd either been running moonshine or drinking it. What was she going to do about him? Why couldn't he be level headed like his brothers, Samuel or Geno, who had been Matt's father?

Laura walked into Cooper's Ladies Wear. She didn't come here often because she had very little money to spend. The only reason she was in here now was that Joey had given her money to buy another new dress. He said he wanted to take her to a fancy restaurant. This time in Frostburg. She would have been happy with the one she bought for their dinner in Cumberland, but Joey insisted she buy something new.

Her hand patted the folded bills in her dress pocket. She wished she could spend the money on something in silk, trimmed with lace, and a pleated skirt. Not that she wouldn't mind a new dress, but Jacob needed new clothes. He seemed to grow an inch a week.

Joey had suggested shopping at a store in Frostburg. But, she thought if she could find some attractive fabric here, she could sew her own dress and hopefully have enough money left over to outfit Jacob.

The store was small and Mrs. Cooper had a work area in the back where she sewed clothing. You couldn't buy many off-the-rack dresses, but Mrs. Copper offered a wide selection of fabrics. Laura looked at the different fabrics. She saw a green satin that caught her eye, but the price per yard was too expensive.

She heard Mrs. Cooper whispering to another woman behind her. When she glanced over her shoulder, she saw the women staring at her.

"Is there a problem?" Laura asked.

"No problem, Mrs. Spiker." Mrs. Cooper and the other woman turned away.

Laura resumed looking at and feeling the various fabrics, but she could hear the two women murmuring behind her. She caught snatches of their conversation and knew they were talking about her. She heard more and more of this gossip in town, especially since other families had been evicted from their company housing while she kept hers. Some people suggested that she and Joey were more than friends.

She patted the money in her pocket again.

Were they right?

She hadn't been opposed to a courtship, but it hadn't seemed that romantic to her. She had only been a widow for a brief time. She wasn't thinking about getting into another relationship. Who could measure up to Pete? She had loved him. She still did.

Laura considered leaving and heading over to the company store. She could be sure that no one except strikebreakers would be in that store, and they didn't know her. The Eckhart Mines Store catered more to coal miners. Mr. Portnoy offered a poor selection of fabrics. Plus, she didn't like Mr. Portnoy's comments. He barely even tried to conceal what he was saying or meant when she was around. He was worse than the women.

She should just go to Frostburg. No one would say anything about her there.

She turned to head toward the door, and heard one woman behind her say, "Floozy."

Laura didn't look back. She hurried out the door, wiping tears from her eyes.

She went straight home. She was in no mood to go shopping now.

Joey stopped by the house later that evening.

"I saw you heading into Cooper's Store this afternoon," he said. "Did you get your dress? I'd like to see it."

Laura hesitated, wanting to tell him what people were saying about the two of them, but she realized she might not want to see his reaction.

"They didn't have anything I liked," she said. "I'll go into Frostburg tomorrow. The stores there will have a better selection."

"I could drive you, and we could have lunch in town."

Laura dropped into her rocking chair and started it moving back and forth. Joey stared at her.

"Is something wrong?" he asked after a few moments.

"Joey, I enjoy spending time with you. I don't get to talk to many adults since Pete died, but I'm wondering about our relationship."

A short time ago, during their dinner in Cumberland, he made suggestions about their relationship as more than just friendship.

Joey lifted his chin a bit, but he said nothing. He sat down on the worn sofa next to the rocking chair.

"Can't you guess? I thought I was clear," he said finally.

She looked up at him, her eyes shiny with unshed tears.

"We're friends. I know that."

"Is that all you think?" He reached out and took her hands in his. His voice was calm but stern, "Would a friend have violated company policy to allow you to stay in this home? Would a friend have brought you boxes of food and given you money for a new dress?"

She remembered how Matt brought her food and paid her bill at the company store. He also came by to see how she was doing. Not as much as Joey did, but he came. Nobody suspected her and Matt of taking up together, and they had actually been sweethearts once. Why were things different with Joey?

"Joey, it's been less than two months since Pete died. I don't know if I'm ready for a courtship."

He patted her hands and nodded. "I know, and I haven't pressured you to do anything you don't want, have I?"

"No, but I don't know how I feel about you."

"Really?" He remarked, with just a slight edge to his tone.

She started to say something and then shut her mouth. She realized she just wasn't sure how she felt about Joey. He was caring and protective of her. She didn't mind that, but was it love?

Joey leaned over and kissed her. She started to pull away, but then stopped and kissed him back.

Joey sat back, grinning. "I love you."

"Love?" How could he move so quickly from courtship to love when she had just told him she wasn't even sure she could handle a courtship?

"I have since you kissed me at the school dance."

School dance? She didn't remember kissing Joey at a school

dance. They had been friends. That was all. She was not seeing Matt when they were in high school. Then she remembered the dance where she was trying to get back at Matt because he kissed Sallie Harcourt. She kissed a few boys that night, but that was six years ago. Maybe Joey was one of those boys, if he was he never said anything about it before tonight. Laura couldn't even remember whom the boys were she kissed that night. She had just grabbed whoever was closest.

Joey patted her hand and stood up. "I am going to head home now. I'll pick you up at noon tomorrow. We can get lunch in Frostburg, and then I'll go with you to help you find your dress."

She didn't say anything. She simply nodded.

Matt drove Samantha's father's black Nash sedan west from Frostburg along National Highway. He made sure to top off the gas tank since he wasn't sure how available gas was in Garrett County, and he didn't want to run out during the drive.

Samantha sat next to him wearing a designer's version of a sleeveless, loosely fitted red dress decorated with a geometric pattern along the hem. Since it was sleeveless, she draped a shawl over her shoulders. She also wore a cloche hat with a decorative band on it. Unlike many hats, it had no tied ribbon. Sam refused to give into the custom of advertising her relationship status by the use of a ribbon. If it was tied in an arrow style that meant the woman was single but in a relationship, a tight knot meant she was married, and a bow meant she was single and unattached.

"I don't see why I can't drive," she said.

"You don't know where we're going."

"Apparently you don't either. You told me you had never been here before."

"I haven't, but I know the directions. Besides, this is a celebration of your classes ending. You should be chauffeured."

Although it was a Wednesday, Samantha's classes were winding down for the semester, and she had the day off.

"If I was being chauffeured, I would be in the back seat. You just want to drive."

That was true, too, so he didn't argue. He just smiled and said, "Yes, Miss Havencroft."

They drove along the National Road through Grantsville and continued west to Keyser's Ridge. From there, he headed south on dirt roads to McHenry, named for James McHenry. He was one of the Maryland signers of the Declaration of Independence and the Secretary of War under Presidents George Washington and John Adams. McHenry, Maryland, was a valley surrounded by hills and low mountains. They crossed the top of a mountain and started down the other side. He slowed the sedan, searching for a nice overlook. When he found it, he pulled over and stopped. At this time of year, it was beautiful with lots of green from the trees on the mountains. It was also interesting to look at the design of the plowed fields in the valley.

"We're here," Matt announced.

Samantha climbed out of the car and looked around. "We drove two hours for this?"

Matt waved his hand out over the valley. "Do you see that?"

"Yes, it's charming." She sounded a bit annoyed.

"It will be the last time you see it."

"What do you mean?" she said.

Matt shook out a blanket on the ground and sat down on it. He patted a spot beside him and Samantha sat.

"Don't you read the newspapers for anything other than your female pioneers? Next year that will all be gone. It will be underwater," Matt said.

She looked over the farms stretching into the distance.

"What are you talking about?"

"A company in Pennsylvania bought up just about every piece of land down there. When they own it all, they will build dams on the rivers and create a lake."

"A lake big enough to cover all of that?" Matt nodded. "But there are houses and barns and roads down there."

"The company bought all of it. The people are moving out. Next year or maybe the year after, all of it will disappear under water. From what I heard, they won't even tear down the houses and barns. It's too much trouble when millions of gallons of water will just cover it over."

"Why does a Pennsylvania company need a gigantic Maryland lake?"

"They don't need the lake. They need the power that the impounded water can generate. Electricity is the future, Samantha. Each year, more and more of what we use requires electricity. Look at refrigerators. No more ice boxes with their heavy blocks of ice for the cooling. Now, we can plug in a box and electricity will keep things cool."

Samantha frowned. "But all of this land will be destroyed."

"It won't be destroyed. It will be repurposed." He thought for a moment. "They will still be farms, but the crop they produce will be electricity not corn. It will probably even look beautiful. I like lakes. Maryland has no natural lakes from what I read."

Samantha opened the picnic baskets and set out the items that Mrs. Fratelli had packed. A linen napkin covered the delicious cold chicken sandwiches, hard cheese, slaw, and applesauce.

"So why bring me out here?"

"Because this is something unique. Before the war, it might have taken a day or two to reach this point from Eckhart. I would have looked out at the view and said 'nice,' probably not even that because I was a kid then. Now, we got here in two hours, and we are among the last witnesses of these farms. They are dead already and next year they will be gone. You and I," he paused before he continued, "we are among the last to see them."

"That's somber."

Matt shrugged. "A bit, but if you were to bring your father out here in a year or two to see the lake, you could point around and say, underneath there is a two-story farmhouse and under the water there is a bank barn."

"You assume I'll be here in a couple years."

That was the wrong thing to say, and she knew it the moment the words left her mouth. She couldn't take them back, though.

"And where will you be?" Matt asked.

"I don't know, but I doubt it will be here."

"You don't see a reason to stay here?"

She stared at him. "You mean you?"

Matt grinned. "Well, there is that, but I'm not sure if I'll be in the mines for a couple more years. No, I was thinking about you and your goals."

Matt poured himself a glass of water and sipped at it.

Frustrated, Samantha said, "Well, are you going to tell me how you see my life going?"

"Ah, I think you will be a teacher when you graduate, right?"

Samantha nodded. "Yes, and that's why I will need to leave. I have to go where there is a need for teachers."

"Why not teach at the college?"

"They don't hire female professors."

"You could be the first. Then you would be one of the pioneers in your clippings book."

The idea had appeal, but Samantha wasn't sure how much she would enjoy working under her father.

"And how would I do that?" she asked.

"It might be easier for you than you think after all your father is the president of the college. He would probably do it just to keep you near him. You are his only child and he is protective of you."

"I don't want to get a job just because he's my father."

"Why not? Men do it all the time. Besides, he may give you the job, but you will have to keep it by doing a good job," Matt explained. "You could be a wonderful example to the female students at the college."

Could she do it? Would it be possible?

"And if I stayed in Frostburg, would you?" Samantha asked.

"Miss Havencroft, are you proposing?"

She felt herself blush and Matt laughed. Still, she wondered whether she had meant it as a proposal.

Chapter 12

May 18, 1922

John Houck's morning started about five o'clock, when John rolled out of bed to get ready for work in the mine. Amelia fed him before he left for work at six-thirty and trudged up the hill toward the coal mine.

Georges Creek Coal Company was operating with a quarter of its normal number of miners, but they hadn't brought in strikebreakers yet. It was bound to happen if things kept going the way they were. John wasn't sure how he felt about working with scabs. It would put another wall up between him and the coal miners on strike.

He picked up his tools and blasting bag at the tool shed and hung his metal check on the board along with all the other markers of men going into the mine. The board was virtually empty with more hooks without metal disks hanging on them than hooks with disks. The man-trip into the mine was quiet except for the clacking of the wheels of the coal car on the track. No one wanted to talk nowadays. If they were like John, they worried over what their friends thought and providing for their families.

He worked at the face of tunnel no. 6, sweating in the cold air and coughing because it was hard to breathe any air without getting a mouthful of coal dust. By the end of his shift, he had mined three tons, which was a good amount. He could have done more, but with the shortage of miners, it took longer to get a coal car to his tunnel so he could fill it with the coal he mined. Still, three tons was better than nothing.

Even when the Georges Creek Coal Company operated before the strike, John was no Lawrence Finzel. Finzel was a Garrett County boy who had a reputation as the best coal miner in the world. During a typical day, Lawrence could often mine twelve tons of coal. He had even set a record mining 600 tons of coal in a month. He was a coal mining version of John Henry, except Lawrence was a real man. He died in 1919, and his tombstone read "He led the world in coal mining during the World War."

John arrived home bone tired. It was not unusual. Coal mining was exhausting work. He was just happy he could pay his bills and feed his family. Not many miners could say that nowadays.

The miner houses in Barton were not fitted with indoor plumbing yet, but Amelia had a tub of warm water waiting for him. She started with boiling water, but the earlier buckets of water cooled in the tub as she added more and more water.

John waved to James and Beth, and then he walked behind the blanket Amelia hung up to block the kitchen area from the rest of the small house. His children didn't need to see him scrubbing his skin raw to get the dirt and coal dust off his body.

He leaned over and kissed his wife, making sure that only his lips touched hers. He didn't want to get her filthy.

"How was your day?" she asked.

"Dark." This was how he always answered the question unless something interesting happened at the mine. However, today, he added, "And eerie."

"Eerie? How so?"

John nodded. "I'm used to a lot a noise in the mine. Men talking, charges exploding, the clacking of coal cars rolling along the track. With so few of us working, we're spread out, and it makes things quiet. The only person I spoke to was Cooper Haynes when he brought a coal car around."

Amelia wiggled her eyebrows. "John Houck, are you afraid of

the dark?"

He laughed and said, "Careful girl, if I get scared, I may grab onto you."

She threw the rag at him. He laughed again and sunk down into the no. 3 tub filled with a mix of hot and cold water so that the result was a warm bath. He dunked a bar of Lava Soap in the water and tried to create lather, which was difficult.

When the water turned into a dark, muddy soup, and he looked pale white once again, he figured he was clean enough. He stood up, and his wife rinsed him off, dumping a bucket of water over his head. John ran his hands over his body to scrape off what water he could. He reached for the towel.

Amelia turned from the stove. "Just in time. Dinner is just about ready. Tell the kids to set the table when you go into the bedroom."

John toweled himself dry and then dressed himself in a set of clean long johns Amelia set out for him. The ones he wore were already soaking in another tub of water waiting for Amelia to wash them tomorrow.

He stepped around the curtain. Beth was sitting at the dining table doing homework while James laid on the floor reading a book. They both were smart kids, and he hoped they would grow up and find work that had nothing to do with a damn coal mine.

"James, Beth, set the table for dinner. I'll be dressed in a couple minutes. Get it done before I'm back."

"Yes, Papa," they said together.

John walked into the bedroom. It was one of three rooms in the house. He put on a pair of clean jeans. He didn't worry about a shirt. He had no plans to go out this evening.

When he walked out of the bedroom, he saw that his children had set the table and the blanket taken down. He was about to sit down at the table when a rock crashed through one of the front windows, and then another rock shattered a second window. Amelia and the children screamed.

"Get down!" John shouted to his family.

He ran toward Beth, who was the closest to him and pushed her to the ground. He saw his son and wife were on the ground, so he crawled for the bedroom where he kept his rifle.

"Scab! Scab! Scab!" people shouted from outside.

John changed course and crawled to the nearest window. He edged his head up slowly to peek outside. He saw at least a two dozen people surrounding the house. He couldn't tell who they were because they covered the lower half of their faces with kerchiefs. They didn't look like they were armed except with more rocks. He could tell they were all men, but he wasn't sure of hair color because they all wore hats.

John went for his Winchester and checked to make sure it was loaded.

Outside, the crowd had gone quiet. What were they waiting for?

He crawled back to the window. He glanced over his shoulder and saw Amelia holding James and Beth close to her.

John lifted his rifle as he raised his head to the window sill.

The crowd was gone. If not for his broken windows, he would have wondered if they were even here. He saw no one along the road.

"They're gone," he told his family.

They sobbed as they huddled together in a tight circle.

John stood up and walked to another window on the side of the house. He couldn't see anyone outside.

They had been people from Barton most likely, not that anyone in town would identify them. John had gone against the union, and that couldn't be allowed.

Toni stood over a pot on the hot stove, mashing potatoes. Sweat formed on her brow. She grabbed the dish towel on her shoulder and dabbed the sweat away before it fell into the pot.

"You work too hard, Toni."

Antonietta glanced over her shoulder and saw her youngest brother standing at the entrance to the kitchen.

"Someone has to, Enos, since all you healthy young men are sitting around doing nothing."

Enos grinned. Oh, how she loved that smile, even if it usually

126

meant that he was up to no good.

"I'm working, Mother Hen," he said.

"Working at getting drunk at night."

"Only during my off hours."

He reached into his pocket and pulled out a small roll of bills secured by a rubberband.

Toni's eyes widened. "Enos, where did you get that money?"

"I told you. I've been working."

He walked over to his sister and pushed the money into the pocket of her apron.

"What are you doing?" Toni asked.

"I'm helping. That was our deal. You run the house with Myrna, and Samuel and I cover the expenses and upkeep the rents don't. That's for expenses." He patted her hip.

Toni set the masher aside and grabbed the padded pot holders. She slid the five-gallon pot off the burner. Reaching into her pocket, she pulled out money and counted it. Thirty one-dollar bills.

"I used ones to make the roll thicker," Enos said, grinning.

"This is thirty dollars." Many miners couldn't make that much in two weeks.

"I know. I counted it."

"Enos, where did you get this?"

He leaned over, kissed her on the cheek, turned and walked away.

Toni watched him go. She wanted to call him back, but she knew he wouldn't answer. In saying nothing, he answered her question. He'd gotten the money illegally. He'd gone from being a customer of some bootlegging outfit to working for them.

She stared at the money in her hand. She didn't want it, but the family needed it. She might be letting her boarders slide on their rent, but the bank wouldn't be so forgiving. It expected monthly mortgage payments, and so did the electric company and the grocer.

She shook her head. *Kind, generous Enos, why did you have to earn your money this way?*

She had already turned down Matt's money because of where

it came from. Wasn't this worse? At least Matt's money came from a legal, if despicable, source. It was blood money earned from the blood of miners.

Besides, she didn't know exactly where Enos earned this money. He didn't say. He could have found honest work somewhere. If he had, he would have told her. He knew she would have been proud to accept his hard-earned money from any honest work.

But she wouldn't have, would she?

She hadn't taken Matt's money. Enos wasn't a coal company spy, though.

So what was he doing? If she didn't know, she couldn't make a fair judgment on whether or not to take the money, which is just what Enos wanted.

Toni rolled her eyes and slid the money roll back into her pocket. Until she knew for sure, she couldn't afford not to take the money.

She heard Samuel chopping firewood out back. It seemed he was always chopping wood nowadays, although she never saw him dragging logs into the yard to be chopped.

She walked out the back door. Samuel swung his axe and halved a piece of wood. The two pieces fell to the ground. He picked them up, judged them to be the right size and added them to the small pile. In the past, she saw the pile as tall as six feet, but it was usually around four feet tall.

She put her hand to her chin as she realized she never really saw what happened to the wood. She saw no one come to take the pile away, and Samuel didn't have a truck to drive it anywhere.

How could she be so blind as to what was going on in her own backyard?

Samuel wiped the sweat from his forehead with the back of his arm.

"Did you need something, Toni?" he asked.

"I'm worried about Enos."

"When aren't you?"

"This is different." She held up the wad of bills Enos had

128

given her.

Samuel's eyes widened. "Well now, we know he's not chopping wood to earn that kind of money."

"No, he's got to be working for a bootlegger to make this kind of money with a strike going on."

Samuel pulled out a handkerchief and wiped the sweat from his forehead. "He's certainly doing more than I am for the family."

Toni shook her head. "Everyone is struggling right now. It's not a sin, but what he's doing is. Worse, it could land him in jail. You need to talk to him."

"Enos is a grown man, Toni. He knows right from wrong."

She waved the money in the air. "The reason he gets paid so much is because it's dangerous. Those bootleggers have to make it worth his while to risk jail."

Samuel put his hands on his hips. "I don't disagree."

"Well then, talk to him. I've tried. He won't listen to me."

"No more than he will listen to me. Enos is an Ansaro. Sometimes I think that is Italian for mule-headed."

"But..."

Samuel held up his hand. "Toni, you can't change his mind, not with that much money involved. All you can do is watch out for him and help if there's an opportunity. He will have to change his mind on his own."

Toni sighed and shook her head. She knew her brother was right, but she didn't want to hear that. She wanted to hear an idea about how to keep her other brother out of jail.

Toni turned around and walked back into the house. She still had dishes to wash and then lunch to make. Soon, she heard Samuel's axe hacking into wood.

Matt walked into J. J. Carter's Store to buy some milk and cheese for Laura. While she might be willing to go without to save money, she had to think of Jacob. He was a growing boy and needed nutritious food.

He ordered a big block of cheddar and a quart of milk. He also had J. J. throw in a couple cans of baked beans and corn. It was not a lot, but it would help with Laura's immediate needs and maybe allow her to set aside some for storage.

As he waited for J. J. to gather the order, Evelyn Crabtree walked in with Becky Parsons.

"Did you see her in that dress?" Evelyn said. "It was halfway to her knees."

"She might as well be throwing herself at him," Becky said. "They deserve each other."

Why is it that when women gossiped, it seemed a lot more hateful than when men did it? Matt doubted it sounded that way to the women. Maybe that was why he didn't think men's gossip was hateful. He was a man, so it didn't sound that way to him.

"At least Pete is not around to see this," Evelyn said.

Pete? Pete Spiker? Now they had Matt's attention.

"Do you think they were carrying on behind his back?" Becky asked.

"How else do you think they would have gotten together so quickly?" Evelyn told her. "He wasn't dead a week before Joseph was visiting the house, and now they go out to dinner and who knows what else."

Matt gritted his teeth. He wanted to say something, but he doubted it would do any good. It would probably make matters worse because it would call attention to the rumor.

He paid J. J. for the groceries and then carried the box out without even looking at the women because he didn't trust himself not to say something.

He walked over to Laura's house and knocked on the door. She smiled when she opened the door, but the smile fell away when she saw the box of food.

"Not the reaction I expected," Matt said.

Laura opened the door wider and let him in.

"I'm happy to see you, Matt, but you don't have to bring me food every time you see me. I'm not holding you to what you told Pete."

Matt set the box on the kitchen table and started unpacking it.

"And I told you, you're my friend, and I want to help out,

Matt said. "Where's Jacob?"

"Taking a nap."

Laura collapsed onto her sofa, still frowning.

"Don't be upset about this Laura," Matt said. "I know you don't want the help, but you've got to think about Jacob. I imagine keeping him full not easy."

Laura shook her head and sighed. "It's not that."

Matt sat down on one of the kitchen chairs. "Then what's the problem?"

She sighed again, looked way, and then shook her head. "People are talking," she said quickly. "That think I'm seeing Joey because he has money."

Matt nodded slowly. Laura cocked an eyebrow.

"Nothing to add?" she said.

"I have heard some of the talk."

"I'm not sleeping with Joey!" Laura snapped.

Matt held up a hand to calm her. "I didn't say I believed the talk, just that I heard it."

He wasn't sure how he felt about the talk. He wanted to defend hei, but she was seeing Joey even if she wasn't sleeping with him. How could he explain it to her?

"Laura, it doesn't matter whether you're sleeping with Joey. In the minds of people around here, you crossed a line by seeing him, especially now with all the problems the strike is causing everyone."

"Joey's been good to me. Nicer than anyone else in this town has been except for you and your family."

"You've told me he's been good to you before, but do you love him?"

Matt wasn't sure he wanted to hear the answer to that question, but he had asked.

It seemed like it took an hour for her to answer, but it was probably only a few seconds. "No, but I do like him."

"Does he know that?"

Laura shrugged. "I've tried to make things clear to him, but sometimes, I feel confused about it all. Other times, he doesn't

131

seem sure how he feels. I want us to be friends no matter what happens, but now everyone is so suspicious about us."

"With reason."

"It's my life, not theirs. If Joey is my friend… or more, that's my business."

"Is his friendship all you want?"

"What? You think the same thing they do. I only want his attention because of what he buys me." She waved toward the empty box on the table. "You brought me groceries. Why don't they talk about us in that way?"

It was a good question. He had visited her since Pete died, and he had brought her food.

"I'm a miner. I have Samantha. It could be either or both or something else."

Laura shook her head. "No, you're right. I'm sure they can't think of you with me when you have such a beautiful girlfriend."

"Be fair to yourself, Laura. You are beautiful."

She snorted softly. "Maybe among miners' wives who can't afford make-up, but I don't hold a candle to Samantha."

Matt never realized Laura had such poor self-esteem. She hadn't been like this in school. Back then, she had been the girl the boys wanted, and she knew it. Maybe that another reason she liked Joey. He paid attention to her.

"Any luck finding work?" Matt asked. If she could find a job, it might build her confidence up, but it would also give her money so she wasn't dependent on Joey or Matt, for that matter.

"I've asked around town, but people know me. It's good and bad. I guess it's mostly bad since I don't have a job."

"Then try Frostburg."

"Joey talks about taking care of me," Laura said. "Why shouldn't I let him?"

Matt tried not to let his aggravation show. Maybe Joey was genuine with his feelings for her.

"If that's what you want, I guess it's fine," Matt said. "Like you said before, it's your life. Is it what you want?"

Laura hung her head low, and Matt wondered if she was

crying. When she raised it, she said, "I don't want everyday to be a struggle. I want to be happy again."

"You and Pete struggled when he was alive, but you were happy."

"Yes, but we had each other."

"So maybe the struggle part's not the problem. Maybe it's who you are fighting the struggle with."

"Yes. Is that wrong?"

Matt shook his head. "Not at all. Everyone wants to be happy. Will having Joey take care of you make you happy?"

"I don't know."

"You know, if he does that – takes care of you – things will become more serious between the two of you." Laura nodded. "And if that happens, you will be even more separated from people in this town. Jacob will be like Joey was when we were growing up. He'll go to school here, but he won't have many friends because he's the superintendent's son. And most of the friends he does have will be trying to get something from him."

Laura's eyes widened. "I think you're jumping the gun there, Matt."

He didn't think so. If she became involved with Joey, she would be just as isolated as he was. More so, because Joey had the coal company management to support him. Laura would have only Jacob. She might be heading toward a lonely life if she didn't love Joey.

Vernon Houck knocked on the door of his brother's house. Someone inside–it sounded like one child–shouted in surprise.

"Who's there?" It was his brother's voice.

"It's me, John. Vernon."

The door opened a crack, and Vernon saw a rifle poke through the opening. Vernon stepped to the side.

"Don't you believe me?" Vernon asked.

"Are you alone?"

"Yes, I came as soon as I heard about the trouble."

The door opened wider, and John Houck waved Vernon inside.

Amelia and the children cowered on the floor, hugging each other. The boy was holding a toy gun. When Beth saw her uncle, she ran over and hugged him around the waist. He patted her head.

"Have you been on the floor since it happened?" Vernon asked.

"No, but anytime there's a sound, they get down on the floor," John told him.

Vernon looked over and saw the curtains were drawn over the broken windows.

"Is everyone all right?" Vernon asked.

John nodded. "We are. They just busted the windows."

"That's a relief. Did you recognize anyone?"

John shook his head and motioned for his brother to sit down. "No, they were all wearing kerchiefs on their faces, but they were union or at least union sympathizers."

"Not surprising," Vernon said.

"Not surprising? How can you say that?"

"Things like this are happening all over the county, John. Hell, they're happening all over the country since this strike started. Luckily, no one here was hurt."

"That doesn't make it right."

"No, but what the coal companies are doing is not right either. They will bring in strikebreakers soon who will take our jobs. That's how the union men around here see you," Vernon said.

"I'm not taking anyone's job. I'm doing the work I was hired to do. I did it before the strike, and I've kept on doing it."

Vernon scowled. "Yes, but you're working, and they're not. You don't support the union."

"I'm not a member. Besides, the unions have done nothing for us," John said angrily.

Throughout the country, many coal mines had low pay and poor working conditions, but that wasn't the case in Western Maryland. Yes, men always wanted higher wages, but plenty of miners wanted to work in Maryland mines. They saw the conditions in other states. Labor groups tried to unionize Maryland's coal miners without success. They created no goodwill for themselves along the way. During the 1882 strike, the National Knights of Labor, opting to end the greatest strike Cumberland region ever knew. Consequently, the Knights didn't financially support striking miners, which weakened the miners' ability to continue striking. County miners remembered this when the 1894 strike call came and some miners refused to strike because they feared the union wouldn't financially back them.

"I agree," Vernon said. "That's why those unions aren't around any longer, but this is the United Mine Workers and John L. Lewis. He's not letting the coal companies get away with anything. Mark my words. This county will let in the union, eventually. They'll have to."

"Then we just trade a coal company boss for a union boss, or worse, then I guess we'll have to please two bosses."

"But a union boss is on our side," Vernon said. "Where will you be when the union gets into the Allegany County?"

John waved his hand around in a circle. "I'll still be working here."

Vernon shook his head. "Not if you're not union."

"Our grandparents were the first Houcks who came to this county. I won't be the first one to leave."

The family got to their feet. Amelia walked to the kitchen and started washing the dishes. The children sat back down at the table and started reading books they left open when they dove to the floor.

Vernon hugged his older brother.

"I came by to see if you were all right, and you are, so I'll go. Let me know if you want help putting in the new panes," he said, pointing toward the curtained windows.

Vernon left and walked out to Main Street, then into town. He stopped when he saw the group of miners lounging on the porch of Drum's Store. They were sitting in a line along the edge of the porch. Hank Drum, the store owner, stood in the doorway of the store. He wasn't a miner, but he knew where most of his business came from and supported the miners.

"Did you see your brother?" one of them asked.

135

"Yes, and he didn't recognize any of you," Vernon replied.

"We wore the kerchiefs like you said."

Vernon nodded. "And it worked, didn't it?"

"He's going to quit?"

Vernon looked over his shoulder back toward the house, which was too far away to see. "I don't know, but he's worried. He's going to be thinking about his family the next time he thinks about crossing the picket line."

Vernon didn't care whether the attack on his brother's family made him join the union or not. Vernon represented the UMW in this town, and John's refusal to join the union and honor the strike embarrassed him. He was sorry his niece and nephew were frightened, but that was their father's fault, not his.

Vernon had meant it when he said Allegany County would be union. It would happen one way or another. And, he was damn sure going to be part of it.

Chapter 13

May 19, 1922

"Joseph, we need to talk," Matt said as he hobbled into the mine office through the outside door.

Joseph pulled his cigar from his mouth. He wasn't smoking it at the moment. He just enjoyed having it between his teeth "Are you going back to work?"

Matt snorted. "No."

"Then I don't think we have anything to talk about." He put the cigar back in his mouth, turned back to his desk, and started reviewing papers as if he was working. With the mine operating with a minimal crew, he didn't have much work to do. It only took him a couple hours in the morning to get through it all.

Matt leaned on the counter. Joseph could see Matt wanted to walk around it and confront Joseph, but Matt knew that would be too aggressive and trespassing. He wasn't a fool.

"Laura is nice," Matt said.

"She is very nice." Joseph's tone implied more than his words said.

"She's also newly widowed and trying to figure out how to manage life without Pete."

Joseph knew the answer, Laura didn't need Pete; not when she had him.

"I'm trying to help her with that."

"It appears you're trying to help yourself."

Joseph got up from his desk, walked around the counter, and into the store. Matt followed, not getting the message he should just leave.

Joseph grinned. "You sound jealous, Matteo." Matteo had his chance with Laura and messed things up. Now Joseph would show Laura with whom she was destined to be.

"Laura is my friend. I am concerned about her. I don't want to see her hurt... or used."

"Used?"

He poured himself a cup of coffee. Just enough was left in the pot to fill his mug.

"From what I've heard, you are buying her affection."

Now it was Joseph's turn to snort. "Buying? I'm just helping a friend. You've done the same thing from what I've heard."

Matt frowned. Joseph was egging him on, and it was working. Joseph couldn't help it. Matt was always so smug. He'd been so popular in school, but look at him now. He was just another dirty miner.

"Yes, except I'm not trying to sleep with her," Matt said.

Joseph grinned. "Oh, I stopped *trying.*" It might not be true now, but it soon would be. His planted seeds were taking root.

Matt's hand snapped out, and he grabbed Joey's shirt.

"Be careful, Matteo, or you won't have a job."

"Look around, Joey, the mine is closed. You're no one's boss."

"You're wrong. The mine is open."

"With strikebreakers? You can't keep the mine going with them, and they will leave when the strike ends. When they leave, the miners in Eckhart won't think of you kindly."

Joseph smirked. "I don't need them to like me. I need them to work."

Joseph pried Matt's hand from his shirt. Then Joseph smoothed out the creases. "What's the problem? You told me not to try to sleep with her, and I told you I wasn't."

"It was the way you said it."

Joseph hoped he looked innocent, but it was hard to keep from smiling. "I don't know what you mean."

"It sounded like this. I'm *not thinking* about hitting you."

"Let him go, Ansaro," said a voice from behind Joseph.

Matt looked over Joseph's shoulder. Portnoy stood behind him with a raised bat. Matt could have taken the bat from him. He was tempted to because it was Portnoy threatening him with it.

"I never thought you cared much for Joey, or anyone for that matter," Matt said.

Portnoy grunted. "Him? He can go to hell for all I care. I don't want you to destroy my store. If you want to fight, take it outside."

Matt started laughing, in spite of himself. "Doesn't anyone like you?" he said to Joseph.

"Laura does," Joseph replied.

Matt stopped laughing. "She seems to, which I don't understand. If you hurt her, though, I will make you regret it."

Matt turned around and hobbled to the door.

"Sorry if I messed up your store a bit, Mr. Portnoy," he said.

Portnoy just frowned. Matt shook his head and walked out.

"You can't just leave after that, you coward," Joseph called after him.

Matt ignored him. He'd made his point He walked outside and limped his way down the stairs. It was slow going with a cast on his leg.

"You won't get away with threatening and attacking me, Matteo!" Joseph yelled after him. "You'll never work in this mine again."

Matt stopped and turned back. "You already tried firing me once. How did that work out?"

Joseph was pressing his luck because Portnoy wouldn't help him outside of the store.

"You attacked me this time in front of a witnesses," Joseph said.

"Go back inside, Joey. You're making a fool of yourself."

Joseph sputtered and then fell quiet. He looked up and down

the street.

"Lakehurst! Lakehurst, get down here man! You're paid to protect company property and men. That man attacked me!"

Lakehurst? He was in town? Matt saw Joseph pointing at him. He started to turn, searching for Lakehurst when a fist hit him in the jaw. Matt's head snapped around, and his body followed as he spun on his cast. Then he lost his balance and fell to the ground.

Lakehurst tried to stomp on his chest, but Matt rolled away. He got to his feet as Lakehurst came in swinging. They exchanged punches with Matt taking more punches than he usually would in a fight because he couldn't move quickly with the heavy leg cast.

Lakehurst suddenly squatted and kicked Matt's broken leg out from beneath him. Matt hit the ground again with a loud grunt as Lakehurst launched himself into the air, hoping to land on Matt. Matt rolled away, but he wasn't able to get to his feet this time. Lakehurst hit him in the face, knocking him backwards.

Matt landed on his back and swung his cast at Lakehurst. It hit the big man in the knee. Lakehurt grunted in pain and dropped to the ground. Matt tried using his cast as a cudgel against Lakehurst, but the man rolled away and staggered to his feet. At least now, he wouldn't be moving fast.

He moved in close again, hitting Matt in the stomach with a solid blow.

"I know it was you in that alley," Lakehurst said when he was close.

Matt might have slowed down Lakehurst's legs, but he hadn't slowed his fists. Matt had already taken a lot of punches. He blocked some of Lakehurst's blows, but they came too fast. Matt was still dazed from the first sucker punch, and things weren't getting any better.

Lakehurst pounded Matt down to his knees. He couldn't get out of the way. Lakehurst punched him again and again.

Darkness fell.

Matt Ansaro felt the earth collapsing from the roof of the mine tunnel. It must not be true his rational mind told him, but he still

couldn't calm the panic welling up in him.

The ground trembled again. He couldn't remember whether it was the first or third time. It didn't matter. He needed to get out of here. He felt the earth falling upon him like a shower, he opened his mouth and screamed.

Not that anyone could hear him over the sounds of the explosion. Matt heard a timber crack. Something heavy fell on his leg. The crack of his tibia and fibula sounded the same as the timber cracking, but it came with pain.

Overhead, stars appeared as if the mine opened up to the sky. He tried to crawl up the embankment toward them, but he couldn't move forward. Something he couldn't see pinned his broken leg beneath it.

He screamed in pain and panic and reached toward his leg. He had to free himself. He had to get out of here. He had to reach the stars. The stars would lead him to the surface.

Something hit him in the cheek, knocking him onto his back. He blinked the dirt out his eyes and put his hands to his check. What had hit him?

Another explosion. He barely registered it before heat ripped along his neck.

Matt opened his eyes. Well, one eye. The other eye wouldn't open, no matter how hard he tried. It was probably swollen shut. His entire body ached, except, oddly enough, his broken leg.

Aunt Toni wiped his brow with a damp cloth. It was soothing and painful at the same time.

"Idiot," she said when she saw his open eye.

"I didn't start it," Matt said. His jaw was stiff and moving it felt unnatural, but at least he could use it. His voice sounded like his mouth was stuffed with cotton.

"You didn't finish it either. Lucky for you someone came to get Samuel, or you'd still be lying in the street."

Matt tried to sit up in the bed, but every muscle cried out in pain. He collapsed back on the feather mattress.

"What happened?" Toni asked.

"I got beat up."

His aunt cocked an eyebrow at him. "Very funny. You and Joseph have never gotten along. Did you go looking for trouble?"

"Thank you for your confidence in me, Toni. I was arguing with him, yes, but I didn't start a fight with him. I was leaving when Joseph called David Lakehurst down on me."

"You know who that man was?"

Matt sighed and said, "We've had dealings before." Then he told his aunt how Lakehurst had attacked Calista, and Matt had fought Lakehurst in the alley. He also explained how he had convinced Calista to file charges against Lakehurst, but he was out on bail.

"He's not acting too careful for a man out on bail," Toni said when Matt finished.

She was right. Matt would have expected a man facing assault and battery charges to not committ assault and battery. However, he also seemed to be working for Joseph and Consolidation Coal, which would insulate him from the law somewhat.

Matt nodded. "He also seems to know who I am, which means he may know I'm a Pinkerton."

Toni shook her head. "Is this the way it is going to be with you? At least when you were in Europe, I didn't have to see you being hurt."

"It's not something I plan. The job can be dangerous."

She patted his hand. "I know, but it would be nice not to have to worry about what will happen to you next."

Samuel stepped into the Eckhart Mines Store. He didn't come here often. He would come into the office to collect his pay and then walk through the store on his way out. He didn't stop to look around. He knew the items were overpriced. He did his shopping in the other stores in town or wait until the weekend and go to Frostburg to buy things.

Joseph looked up from his desk where he was reading a newspaper.

"What do you want?" he snapped.

"Your man attacked my nephew. I want an explanation."

Joseph stood up and sucked in his stomach as he did when he wanted to look intimidating. He took a few steps closer to Samuel, but still stayed out of the taller man's reach. He didn't want Samuel grabbing him like Matteo.

"I don't owe you anything, but if you and your brother want to keep working at this mine when the strike is over, you better keep your nephew in check."

Samuel's eyes narrowed. "Why is that?"

"I was attacked."

"You weren't attacked, and there are plenty of witnesses to it."

Joseph smirked. "What will they say? What did they see? I'll tell you one thing they didn't see was me lay a finger on Matteo."

Samuel usually spoke in an even tone, but his voice was growing louder. "They saw you sic your company thug on him."

"And they also heard me yelling about why."

Joseph hadn't yelled out of anger. He wanted anyone who was asked what happened to be able to say Joseph said he was being attacked.

"Matt didn't attack you. If he had, you wouldn't have been able to call for help."

Joseph's face reddened.

"Only three people were in the store at the time, Samuel. Matteo, Portnoy, and Me. I think you'll find that Portnoy will agree with what I say... whatever I say."

"And what about that thug the company hired to terrorize people? More than three people saw him go after Matt and start a fight with a sucker punch."

"Then take it up with the company." Joseph held up a finger as if he had just thought of something. "Oh, but they're busy right now with the strike going on. I don't think an employee protecting company property will be high on their list of things to look into except to thank the employee."

"You can't treat us like trash, Joseph. It will come back on you," Samuel said.

"Be lucky I don't press charges against Matteo. Oh, and since

143

the strike is going on, you'll have to pay for any doctor visits and medicine Matteo needs. You aren't on the company payroll now, so you aren't paying for the company doctor's services.

While he was correct, Samuel had seen Dr. Lund, the company doctor, to get painkillers for Matt. Despite what Joseph had said, the doctor hadn't charged him anything. He said he had stocked up on supplies when it was obvious the strike was coming. He could keep treating miners at the company's expense for a few months at least.

"The way I see it, you all have been paying for my services all along. If you need it, who am I to say 'no'?" Dr. Lund said.

Samuel looked around. It was just he and Joseph in the office. He was tempted to hit Joseph, but he held his anger in check. He turned away, ignored Joseph's chuckle, and walked out of the office.

He headed up Store Hill toward the boarding house. Things were much quieter than normal. People were scared. Lakehurst and other Pinkertons were running roughshod over everyone, and the strikebreakers were taking miners' jobs and homes. This wasn't Samuel's Eckhart Mines.

Who was to blame for this? The coal company or the UMW? Samuel was a UMW member, although he told no one but Myrna, and he saw the benefits the UMW could bring to a miner's life. That didn't mean it was perfect. Miners attacked non-union workers just as much as the Pinkertons like Lakehurst attacked the union miners.

He walked into the boarding house and went to Matt's bedroom. Matt and Toni were talking quietly. He was glad to have his nephew back home, but he couldn't have returned at a worse time. Samuel stepped into the room and Toni looked over her shoulder at him.

"Where have you been?" Toni asked. "I sent you for medicine."

Samuel held up the bottle of painkillers from Dr. Lund.

"I got the medicine, but I also stopped by the company store," Samuel said.

Toni frowned. "Samuel, you didn't."

Matt groaned, but it may have been from pain.

144

"I hope you didn't do something stupid like all the men in this family seem prone to do," Toni said.

Samuel walked into the room, shaking his head. "Joey won't take things any further unless we do."

Samuel looked at Matt, who was quiet.

"What are you thinking?" Samuel asked.

"I'm just wondering why I even bothered to come back to Eckhart. I'm not sure I have helped anything," Matt said.

"Helped? Did you think you could change how the world works here?" Samuel asked.

Toni shot a glance at Matt, her eyes widening. Matt squeezed her hand.

"My friend is dead in a mine accident. His wife is now a widow, and his son fatherless. Jenny is in danger. My family is in danger."

"Danger?" Samuel repeated.

Toni said, "He's just tired and in pain. Let me have that medicine."

She reached out and took the bottle from Samuel. He also handed her a spoon he had picked up in the kitchen.

Toni read the directions on the bottle, filled the spoon with the red liquid and held it out to Matt. He raised his head, opened his mouth, and swallowed the painkiller.

"I can understand how things look bleak right now, but they'll get better. After all, you are home with your family," Samuel said. "That's got to count for something."

"It does, Samuel, and I think he will realize that when he's not in so much pain," Toni said.

Samuel nodded. "I'm going to go chop wood. It helps me think."

"What have you got to think about?" Toni asked.

"I think we need to think about our future here in Eckhart if the company will hire thugs like the man who did this to Matt."

"His name is David Lakehurst," Matt said.

Samuel shook his head. "It doesn't matter. He's a thug no matter what he calls himself."

Then he turned and walked out of the room. A few moments

later they heard the back door to the house open and close.

"You should let me tell him," Matt said.

"What good would that do? He's upset."

"Upset? He seemed calm."

"Samuel might not say much, but I've lived with him nearly all my life and most of his. Samuel doesn't like to lose control, but that doesn't mean he doesn't get angry. It just means that when he does get angry, you don't want to be around. If he finds out you are spying on the miners, he might just go over the edge."

"Good. Another example of me hurting the people I want to help."

Toni smacked him on the shoulder and Matt winced.

"Oh, sorry about that. Force of habit."

"So you say," Matt said.

"Matt, you aren't responsible for Pete's death. That was the mine and the Hand of God that did that. It might just as easily have been you killed in the cave-in. You also didn't cause the problems for Jenny. She might be dead if you and your uncles hadn't walked by when you did. She knows that. Why don't you?"

"It just seems like everything I do turns out wrong."

"Well, you didn't cause this strike or hire a thug, as Samuel calls him. I might not like what you're doing, but I understand your motives. You're a good man, Matteo Ansaro, and I, for one, am glad you came home."

She leaned over and hugged him. Matt was glad of that, although the hug caused him some pain in his ribs. He didn't want her to see him cry. Whether it was from the pain or happiness, he couldn't say.

Samantha walked into the house after her classes on Thursday. She hung a sweater on the coat rack next to the door.

"Samantha?" her father called.

She walked down the hallway so she could see her father. He was standing next to the fireplace mantle, and she was surprised to see Professor Williamson seated in an armchair.

"Come in, Samantha," her father said. "You should hear this, too."

Samantha walked into the room as the professor stood.

"Good afternoon, Professor, what brings you here?" Samantha asked.

"I do," her father said. "I decided to meet with my staff individually, to get to know them better. I would rather not have situations like what happened to Professor McTeague surprise me."

"I would venture to say it surprised him, too," Samantha noted.

Her father harrumphed. "Yes, no doubt. I also received some news today that I should share with you."

"What is that?"

"We can talk about it over dinner."

He looked into the dining room. Jenny was setting the table. She stepped back to look at her work and disappeared into the kitchen. Samantha smelled beef cooking.

"It looks like the table is set. Let's go in for dinner," John said.

The men allowed Samantha to enter the dining room first. Professor Williamson pulled back the chair for her. Jenny stepped out of the kitchen and waited.

"We have lemonade, iced tea, and water to drink," she said.

Professor Williamson stared at Jenny, and Samantha realized he knew how Jenny had earned a living before getting this job. Samantha watched his face as Jenny poured him an iced tea. He seemed curious, but it didn't appear he knew her. Jenny glanced at Samantha. She recognized the professor and turned pale as her eyes widened.

Samantha wasn't much for praying, but she prayed now that Professor Williamson wouldn't disclose Jenny's past activities. Her father wouldn't enjoy finding out that he was employing a former prostitute.

"So what is your news, Father?" Samantha asked. She wanted to take Professor Williamson's attention away from Jenny.

"I met with the Board of Regents this afternoon." The Board of Regents was the state-appointed directors for the State Normal School No.2.

A local legislator, John Leake from Vale Summit proposed the school back in 1898. The Town of Frostburg provided the land, and the state provided the funding to build Old Main and its operating expenses. A gymnasium had been built in 1914 and a dormitory in 1919. The two-year course work comprising Latin, mathematics, history, rhetoric and literature, natural and physical sciences, drawing, music, calisthenics, psychology, philosophy of education, philosophy of school management, pedagogy, observation, practice work and primary manual training, graduated more than a dozen teachers each spring.

"News of Frostburg's wildness reached Baltimore and Annapolis, and the regents are worried. The parents who send their children here expect us to not only to educate their children but to keep them safe."

"Which you do," Professor Williamson said.

Her father nodded. "We do our best, but we cannot control every aspect of our students' lives. They are adults after all and have their own minds. Some of our students have frequented speakeasies in the town in violation of the law." He glanced at his daughter but said nothing. "I have heard stories of our students being drunk in the streets of Frostburg."

"I have never been drunk in the streets," Samantha snapped.

"I didn't say it was you," her father replied.

Samantha blushed and looked at her plate. When she looked up, Professor Williamson was smirking.

"While you have not been drunk in the streets or driving through town drunk, your behavior gives me concern. If I cannot get you to obey the law, then how do I get other students?"

Samantha looked up, but would not look at the professor.

"As you said, the students are adults and have their own minds," she told her father.

"Yes, and I said as much to the regents. They agreed but were not moved by the argument. They are watching the situation and may take action."

"What sort of action?" the professor asked.

"They would not say. Perhaps, they haven't decided

148

themselves. Regardless, I want to make sure they don't have to take any such action."

"What can you do?"

"I will make male escorts available to the women who want to go into town. I won't require them to have an escort, but they will be available to discourage any unwelcome attention that the women might get." When no one said anything, he continued. "The college will have a curfew each evening with bed checks. Although it won't stop all illicit activity from the students, it will keep them out of town when the most problems occur."

Samantha wasn't sure how well that would work. Determined students would sneak out.

"Finally," her father continued, "Any student caught with alcohol in violation of the Volstead Act will be expelled."

Samantha wondered if that included her, and if it did, how long it would be before she was expelled from the college.

"That sounds drastic."

"Perhaps, but if they violate the law, it is an honor code violation. I can enforce it."

Dinner didn't go so well after that. Samantha had little to say, and she had lost her appetite. Her father's policy change was a move against her as well as the other students in the college. If the police caught her drinking, she was sure her father would expel to set an example for the rest of the student body.

A ringing bell interrupted the dinner. It startled Samantha because they rarely received phone calls. Not too many people locally had telephones, and among those who did, few needed to call her father.

Jenny walked into the dining, looking even paler than she had earlier.

"Who was on the telephone, Jenny?" John asked.

Jenny said nothing at first. She quivered.

"Are you alright?" Samantha asked.

She blinked and seemed to focus on Samantha. Tears formed in the corners of her eyes.

"Oh, Miss. Samantha... that was Toni Starner calling from a

store in Eckhart. She said… she said a man nearly beat Matt to death. He's unconscious and at the house. She thought you should know."

Samantha felt her chest tighten. This was the mine cave-in all over. She put down her fork and looked over at her father.

"Is Matt a friend of yours?" Professor Williamson said.

Samantha nodded and stood up. "I need to go."

"Samantha, you can't do anything for him. You'll just get in the way of the doctors."

"I want to be there. If his aunt thought it was serious enough to call me, then she obviously wants me there."

"It's not obvious. She was simply informing you of a new situation, and we have company."

Professor Williamson held up his hands in surrender. "Don't let me be the reason you stay, Samantha." He faced John Havencroft. "I agree with your daughter, sir. If this Toni believes Matt's condition is serious enough to call, then she feels Samantha would want to know and be there."

John sighed and shook his head. "Fine. Go, although I'm sure Matt will be fine." He paused. "Wish him my best for a speedy recovery."

"Mine, too, although he doesn't even know me," Professor Williamson said.

Samantha left the table quickly, afraid her father would change his mind and call her back. She picked up her purse near the front door and hurried outside. She trembled as she drove down National Highway to Eckhart Mines.

She parked in front of the boarding house. She knocked on the door, but then opened it and went inside.

"Toni!" she called.

Toni hurried down the hallway from Matt's bedroom. Her eyes were puffy from crying. She saw Samantha and walked over to hug her.

"How's Matt?" Samantha asked.

"He's asleep now. He regained consciousness for a little while and then went to sleep. At least I hope it's just sleep."

"Can I see him?"

Toni nodded and led her back down the hallway to Matt's room. The light was on in his bedroom and Matt lay in his bed with his eyes closed. His face was swollen and bruises were forming.

"The doctor said that he should be fine. He has no additional broken bones," Toni told her.

"What happened to him?"

"A company thug beat him up."

"Company thug? The coal company?"

Toni nodded.

"Why would he do that?" Samantha asked.

Toni grimaced. "They don't need a reason nowadays. Matt's a miner, and the other man works for the coal company. He's been bullying everyone in town."

Samantha sat down in the chair next to the bed and held Matt's hand in hers. She couldn't believe this was happening again. First, the mine, and now this. Was Matt's life always this dangerous? Samantha didn't mind excitement, but this was danger.

"You need to wake up, Matt," she whispered in his ear.

"I will make some tea," Toni said.

The older woman left the room.

Samantha leaned back in the rocking chair still holding Matt's hand. Something needed to be done about all of this. She was paying more attention to all the news in the newspapers since her trip with Matt to Garrett County. It embarrassed her not to know about something so big happening so near her.

Now that she was up on current events. It was almost scary. Miners and company men were fighting. Railroaders and company men were fighting. It was like the war had started again, but instead of a world war overseas, this was a second Civil War happening all across the country.

Samantha looked down and saw Matt's eyes flutter open and stare at her.

Samantha sighed. "Thank God, you're alive."

Matt grinned. "It's not like I was in a coma. I was tired and hurting – still am, actually – and decided to take a nap."

"What happened?"

"David Lakehurst – the man who beat up Jenny – attacked me on the street. I couldn't fight him with this cast on my leg. I just couldn't move around fast enough."

"Why did you even fight him at all?"

"It wasn't my idea. He came at me swinging. He works for the coal company, and Joseph McCord said I was threatening him."

"Why would the coal company hire him? He's a thug."

"He is. I agree. He's not actually a coal company employee, though. He's a Pinkerton Agent."

"I thought the Pinkertons were detectives."

"They are, usually, but they also offer other services."

"What? They hire out thugs?"

"No, I would bet Lakehurst was brought on as a security guard for coal company property. However, if the coal company wants to use them as enforcers, the Pinkertons won't complain."

"You seem to know a lot about the Pinkertons."

This was Matt's chance to tell Samantha the truth. He should admit that he was a Pinkerton agent. He couldn't do it. Right now, she thought so poorly of Pinkertons he doubted she would see it as an improvement over him as a miner.

"Lakehurst is going to be a problem if he stays in town," Matt said.

"He should be in jail."

"He was in jail, but someone bailed him out."

"Then file a complaint against him."

"It won't do any good. Joseph will say I was threatening him, and Lakehurst will say he was protecting company workers and property. Depending on what Joseph says, I could wind up getting in trouble."

"Oh, Matt, trouble seems to keep finding you."

Matt managed a smile. "Just lucky, I guess."

She leaned over and kissed him. She slid her hands behind his head and pulled him closer. He groaned and pulled back. "Ow."

"I'm sorry. Did I hurt you?"

"Lakehurst kicked me in the back of the head."

She let go of his head, and Matt's head fell back on the pillow.

"Ow!"

"Oh, I'm sorry. I didn't mean to hurt you."

She started to straighten up, but Matt reached up and grabbed her by the shoulders to stop her.

"It's all right. It's a good type of Ow."

He pulled her toward him and kissed her.

Chapter 14

May 13, 1922

Matt sat up in bed and swung his legs over the side. He started to stand, but he felt dizzy and plopped back on the bed. He'd taken a lot of kicks to the head. He couldn't remember Lakehurst getting the better of him, which was too bad. He wanted to remember every kick, every punch, and every jab Lakehurst landed on him.

Soon the cast would come off. It wouldn't be there to slow him down. He would be ready to for Lakehurst. Matt had a debt to pay, and he was someone who always paid what he owed.

When the dizziness faded, Matt pushed himself to his feet. He raised his hands over his head, wincing as his muscles screamed. His broken leg actually felt better than the rest of his body. Ignoring the pain throughout his body, he swung his torso to the left and right, stretching.

He'd been bedridden too long. He couldn't keep lying down. He had to get up, he had to move, or he would never regain his strength.

He saw his face in the mirror. It was purple with bruises, but his nose was intact. Lakehurst hadn't wanted to kill him, just injure him, so the brutal man had aimed his kicks for the back of Matt's head. He had half a dozen stitches on the left side of his forehead. It would leave a scar, but few people would notice it because of the much larger war scar on his neck.

His body was a mass of bruises, but he had no broken bones and only the cut on his forehead. That didn't seem possible. Lakehurst was a powerful man, and he had been going after Matt, particularly once he went down. So why had Matt escaped more critical injuries?

Matt ran through the minutes before and during the fight, at least what he could remember. Had Lakehurst held back because he hadn't wanted to get in more trouble with the law? It seemed laughable given how he strutted around town intimidating everyone. The townspeople feared Lakehurst, miners and non-miners alike. Matt heard it was just as bad in other coal towns Lakehurst visited. His beat down of Matt had only made him seem more fearsome.

Matt tried to walk around his room. The cast still slowed him down, but the muscles in his right leg felt knotted.

Matt paused as he thought of another reason Lakehurst hadn't gone too far with the beating. Did Lakehurst know Matt was a Pinkerton agent? If he did, he couldn't be too brutal in the beating, otherwise the agency might come down hard on him. It would also mean that Lakehurst could tell the agency that Matt had attacked him in the alley in February and then pretend to play the innocent.

That might not go too far, though. Lakehurst had been in prison previously, and the home office had to know that by now.

Someone knocked on the closed door to his room.

"Yes?" he said.

"Matt, are you awake?" Toni asked. "There's someone here to see you."

"Give me a second to put my robe on."

He grabbed the flannel robe off the foot of the bed and covered his bare torso. Then he lowered himself back onto the bed in a sitting position.

"Okay," he said.

Toni opened the door. Matt her Jenny put her hand on her mouth to cover a gasp.

"Oh, Matt." Jenny walked into the room to stand closer to him. She reached out a hand to touch his cheek. He didn't pull away.

Matt motioned to the chair next to the bed. "Why don't you sit down?"

Jenny did, never taking her eyes from him. "Samantha told me what happened, and I just had to come see you."

He remembered Samantha was more distraught to see him beat up than she was after his rescue from the mine. She had cried during most of her visit, which had embarrassed her and to some extent him. It didn't matter to Matt now. He chose to remember other things from her visit. Her gentle smile and soft touch.

"I'm getting better," Matt said.

"Really?" Jenny didn't bother hiding her doubt.

"I was just standing a few moments ago."

"If it's not one thing, it's another with you," Jenny said.

"That's what I told him," Toni said.

Matt looked at his aunt and said, "The difference is you are always telling me something like that."

Toni snorted. Then she nodded toward Jenny. "Is this the girl you said he beat up?"

"I'm not much of a girl anymore, Mrs. Starner," Jenny said.

"Well, you're younger than I am."

Matt looked at Jenny and then back to Toni. He nodded.

"Well," said Toni, "you were right to stand up for her. Given what that man did to you, it isn't hard to imagine what he did to poor Jenny."

"She looked worse than I do," Matt said.

Jenny nodded her agreement. "I was in the hospital for days." She turned back to Matt and said, "I feel so guilty about all of this."

"Why?"

"I'm responsible. David Lakehurst hates you because you helped me."

Matt reached out and took her hand. "He doesn't hate me because I helped you that night. I doubt he even knows that. He hates me because I went after him in that alley and beat him. That was my choice to do. Not yours."

"What are you going to do?"

156

Matt raised an eyebrow. "I will get better so I won't be a sitting duck the next time he finds me."

"Next time?" Toni asked.

Matt looked over his shoulder and nodded. "There will be a next time. I don't know when, but this isn't over yet. The trial is coming up."

"Maybe I should just drop the charges," Jenny said.

"No, he deserves to go to jail for what he did to you," Matt said.

Toni nodded. "I doubt you were the first woman he treated that way."

"But you should be careful, Jenny. Not the way you were, too scared to go outside, but be cautious. Watch for him on the street. He's large enough to be obvious. Stay out of the shadows and alleys. Will you do that for me?" Matt asked.

Jenny nodded.

"Then if you stay safe, and I get better, we'll get through this."

They talked a little while longer, but then Jenny left to get to work. When she was gone, Toni came back to Matt's bedroom, and said, "You know that woman's in love with you."

Matt lay back on the bed. He was feeling tired.

"We're friends." He thought about sleeping with her his first night back in Allegany County and amended his comment. "Close friends, but just friends."

Toni shook her head. "You may say it, and she may even say it, but she doesn't act that way. She doesn't look at you like you're a friend."

Matt rolled his eyes. "Toni, she's nearly old enough to be my mother."

"So, it didn't stop you from sleeping with her, did it?"

Matt propped himself up on his elbows. "How did you know that?"

Toni rolled her eyes. "I'm not a fool, Matteo. You said David Lakehurst had beaten up a prostitute, and you said she was the one he beat up. And there is only one way you will get to know a woman like that."

Matt collapsed back on the bed. "Maybe you should be the Pinkerton."

"You don't have to be insulting," she said teasingly, but Matt wondered if she might be serious.

"It was just one time. I thought she was nice, so when I saw her afterwards, I would talk to her. We became friends."

"And you saved her, Matt. Don't forget that. She won't. You're her hero and a friend. It would be hard for her not to fall in love with you."

Matt shook his head. He didn't want to give Jenny the wrong impression. Could she have the wrong idea? After all, she knew he was seeing Samantha.

"What should I do?" Matt asked.

"Nothing. Don't encourage her in that way, not if you don't want a relationship with her. She's not naïve or dumb. She will come to her senses, and you will still be friends."

"And you're not upset she's a prostitute?"

Toni crossed her arms over her bosom. "Do I wish she wasn't? Yes, but she is a kind woman who cares about you. That's a genuine feeling, not something she's playacting about. I don't know her life, so I can't rightly judge her. I've known women who have gone into things like that willingly and some not. Life likes to sneak up on you and surprise you."

Matt nodded. "Don't I know it."

Jenny paused on the porch of the Starner Boarding House and looked around. So this town is where David Lakehurst spent a lot of his time now. What would she do if he saw her right now? What would he do?

Her legs felt weak, and her cheeks tingled as if she was feeling his slaps all over again. She put a hand on a post to steady herself.

She took a deep breath. She couldn't keep doing this. The courts would not send him away. That was obvious. He was out on bail and still terrorizing people, but now it was legal.

She had to end this. No one else was willing to speak against Lakehurst. She asked around, and although Lakehurst had a reputation for being rough and even brutal, no one would say a thing against him, everyone was afraid. Instead, they avoided him when they saw him. It wasn't hard for them because he didn't seem to recall their faces.

He remembered Calista, though, because she had gone against him.

It was time to end it.

The Cumberland and Pennsylvania Special stopped at Eckhart Mines at 10:05 a.m. It brought more strikebreakers to the county. The three passenger cars, engine, and coal car rolled to a stop and company men started to set up empty wooden boxes in front of the doors at the end of the passenger cars. Eckhart Mines wasn't a passenger stop, so it wasn't set up for taking on and discharging passengers. Consolidation Coal Company had hired this train to bring in strikebreakers from Pittsburgh.

Sidney Bloom stood with a clipboard in front of the train, waiting for the men to get off. They filed off, carrying rucksacks on their backs. They steadied themselves against the side of the train as they stepped on the wobbling boxes.

More than one of them looked around the town with a sense of wonder. They came from a big city where they didn't often see trees and mountains. They ranged in age from teenagers to middle-aged men worn down by life so much they looked seventy. Many of them were immigrants who needed work, no matter how dangerous it might be.

Although all the men would work for Consolidation Coal, not all of them would be in Eckhart Mines. The company decided rather than bring the strikebreakers in at the Frostburg Depot, where they couldn't control what happened, they would bring them in at Eckhart. Some trouble was still expected, but nothing as bad as what might happen at Frostburg. This was because most of the Pinkertons in the county were in Eckhart. Their main purpose was to head off any violence and get the strikebreakers to their various mines.

As the men disembarked from the train, Sidney checked their

names off on the list he had and directed them to stand in different groups. The men weren't assigned by name to a specific mine. Sidney had a number designating how many men were supposed to work at each mine. As that number of men came off the train, he assigned a pair of Pinkertons to load them into a truck and drive them to the town where they would stay. Also, Joseph told Sidney if he noticed any men who seemed like they would make good miners to reserve them for Eckhart.

Joseph stood apart from the group, watching things unfold. He kept a particular eye on the crowds gathering at the edge of company property. Lakehurst patrolled the edge of the crowd with his holstered pistol showing as a warning to anyone who got too rowdy. Still, people yelled at the strikebreakers and cursed them. One man threw a rock at a crowd of strikebreakers, and Lakehurst plunged into the crowd, grabbed the man by the shirt and punched him in the nose.

Laura drew the curtain back from her window. She looked down the street to where the rail line crossed Store Hill. She watched the line of men trudge up the street silently as people from town yelled at them. A line of striking miners tried forming a line across the street, blocking the strikebreakers. They linked arms and refused to let the strikebreakers pass. One Pinkertons lifted his rifle and threatened the strikers, but they refused to break the line. The Pinkerton flipped his rifle around and smashed the butt into a miner's stomach. When he doubled over, the Pinkerton knocked him to the ground with a blow to his back. When the miner fell, the miners on either side of him lost their grip on his arms. The Pinkerton waved the strikebreakers through the broken line.

So many new miners were coming into the county. It was amazing so many people had been evicted from their homes to make room for these men. So many families were now living wherever they could find the space.

She still didn't know how she and Jacob had avoided being evicted. It should have happened when Peter had been killed. That was the way of things, but Joey had let her stay on. The company hadn't needed the space back then, though. Now it did. Had some other family been evicted so she and Jacob could stay in their houses?

How could Joey justify letting her stay in their house while evicting families and cramming the boarding house with double the number of people who usually stayed there?

It wasn't right, but what could she do about it? She had nowhere else to go, and no money to spend on rent. She had tried to find a job, but there were none to be had in town. Striking miners had filled anything that had been open.

She was at Joey's mercy. Lucky, he was her friend.

Jacob walked up to her and held his arms up. She lifted him up, and he looked out the window.

"Is Papa coming home?" He asked. The line of workers must have looked like the end of a mining shift to Jacob.

Oh, how she wished he was on his way home. Times were tough when Pete was alive, but at least they were a family. Now she and Jacob were on their own.

She kissed Jacob on the cheek. "No, darling, he's not coming home."

"Not now. Not ever."

Chapter 15

May 24, 1922

Matt sat at his small desk deep in thought and peered down at the street through his bedroom window. He placed his pencil carefully on the desk and picked up the pages he had written. He read over them. It was his first report to the Pinkerton Agency since Lakehurst had beaten him. He wanted to denounce Lakehurst by name, but he knew it would do little good. The company might replace Lakehurst, but it would be with someone similar. He needed to make his bosses understand they were adding to the problem they wanted to avoid.

Matt told the company about the violence going on and that the company men were doing more than protecting company property. They were terrorizing miners and townspeople. Their techniques weren't winning them any support. Those actions only galvanized people against the company and escalated the problems. His suggestion was that the company men take defensive action only and use the police as much as possible, and it would save money. More importantly, it would help keep the company from tarnishing its reputation like the Baldwin-Felts Detective Agency had done in southern West Virginia. The Matewan Massacre resulted in seven detectives, two miners, and three townspeople killed. The Pinkertons and Consolidation Coal

Company didn't want another Matewan, but it sure looked like things were headed that way.

Matt thought he made a convincing argument, but whether or not it had an effect depended upon what the other agents in the county were writing in their reports.

Something had to be done to diffuse things here or Consolidation Coal would wind up with all-out warfare between the company men and coal miners.

He folded the letter and sealed it in an envelope. He addressed it to the office in Cumberland where William Singletary told him to send his mail.

He headed out of the house and walked over to the trolley stop. He couldn't mail the letter in town. Portnoy served as the Eckhart Mines postmaster, and he was too nosy. Matt wouldn't put it past him to steam open letters and read any mail he fancied. Matt couldn't risk it. He mailed them in Frostburg where it wouldn't attract undo attention.

As he walked down the street, he saw Joseph standing on the porch of the company store. The big man watched him approach but said nothing. He just grinned as he watched him pass.

Matt was tempted to launch himself at Joey, but he couldn't risk something happening to his letter. If the wrong people read it, he could be in a hell of a lot of trouble.

Joey would get what was coming to him. He just had too.

Samuel sauntered into J. J. Carter's General Store for a supply of tobacco and rolling papers. He liked J. J. His store supported the miners, and best of all, J. J. didn't gouge the miners. Like nearly all stores, most of the goods were kept on shelves that lined the walls. The counter ran in front of the shelves, leaving a small aisle for the clerk to move back and forth behind the counter. J. J. also set up a few tables in the middle of the store where he stacked work shirts and denim jeans. Normally, at least a dozen customers would pack the store, and now that the mines were closed miners couldn't afford much, so the store was lucky to have any customers.

Samuel heard the bell over the front door jingle as someone

entered. Samuel slid his quarter across the counter to pay for his items. J. J. took the money but stopped before opening his cash register.

Samuel turned about and came face-to-face with Joseph's enforcer. He was a tall, well-dressed bulk of a man, with brawler written all over his beardless face. He was the man who beat Matt into unconsciousness in the middle of the street outside of the company store.

"You're Samuel Ansaro, aren't you?" the man said.

Samuel stepped around him and headed for the door. He wanted to punch this man for what he did to Matt, but Samuel also didn't want to destroy J. J. Carter's store. Like most of the store owners in town, J. J. was not selling to strikebreakers. Samuel didn't want to give him reason to regret that decision.

"Tell your nephew to stay out of my way or the next time, I will break his other leg and both his arms," Lakehurst called out to Samuel's back.

Samuel stopped and turned around. He looked the other man over. They were the same height, but David Lakehurst was ten or twenty pounds heavier than Samuel. Samuel was a peaceful man, but he thought he could take Lakehurst. That might be his vanity talking or maybe his anger at what this man had done to Matt.

Samuel bent his head, then raised it slowly, his eyes staring at Lakehurst coldly. He asked, "Have you ever had a broken bone?"

"Now Samuel..." J. J. cautioned from behind the counter.

"Don't worry, J. J.... but I'll have to owe you for these three pencils," Samuel said.

Samuel scooped three yellow pencils out a box on a shelf and held them up.

"You know," Samuel said. "I've been with men who have broken a bone. Heck, I even broke my arm once. With those real nasty breaks, you can hear the bone snap." With a quick flick of his fists, Samuel broke all three pencils at once. Lakehurst's eyes widened, but he said nothing. "With those breaks, the bone will tear the muscle and ligaments as it pokes through the skin." He walked forward a few paces and held up the jagged edges in front of Lakehurst's eyes. "A break like that is painful. Many a man has lost his arm or leg because of those breaks."

"What's your point?" Lakehurst asked.

"I thought we were talking about broken bones," Samuel said. "It's amazing the damage a break like that does, it can be something simple that causes it. Tripping on a set of stairs. Stumbling and falling while walking along loose rocks. It's just simple bad luck."

Lakehurst shrugged. "Why should I care?"

David put the broken pieces of the pencils in Lakehurst's hands. "A man has to be careful where he walks, Lakehurst, or some bad luck might fall on him."

Samuel turned and walked out of the store.

Dr. Lund kneeled down in front of Matt and rolled up the split leg on Matt's jeans. The plaster cast had once been white, but now it was gray with dirt and coal dust. Dr. Lund rapped on the cast.

"I guess it's ready to hatch," he said, smirking.

"I had an itch for two months that I am ready to scratch," Matt said.

The doctor opened his black bag and pulled out a thin saw blade, a large pair of shears, and a pair of pliers. He looked more like a carpenter in that moment than a doctor.

"OK, I need you to lie on your side on the couch with your broken leg on top," the doctor said.

"It had better not be broken if you're taking the cast off," Matt said.

"From what I hear, I think you are lucky that you didn't break it again." The doctor shook his head. "Fighting with your leg in a cast."

"That's what I told him," Toni said from the dining room. She was warming up water and pouring it in a tub so she could wash his leg when the cast was removed. "Lucky for him his bones are as hard as his head."

Matt rolled his eyes and lay sideways on the couch. Toni set a sheet across the couch to catch the plaster dust and any pieces that broke off.

"I will snip through as much of the plaster as I can with the shears," the doctor said. "If it gets too tight around your leg, I will have to use the saw and pliers."

Matt nodded. "Let's just get this done. I want to walk normally again."

"It still might be awhile before that happens." The doctor fit the shears around the cast and used the leverage of the long handle to force the blades through the plaster. "You will feel off balance at first because you're used to the extra weight from the plaster. Plus, you haven't used those muscles for weeks so they will need to regain their strength."

The doctor used the pliers to break off a piece of the plaster so he could reach further along the leg with the shears. It was slow going, and Matt wanted to smash his leg against something to break the plaster.

Toni came over to watch. She smiled at Matt and patted him on the shoulder. Once the doctor had cut along the entire length of the cast, he pried the ends apart until they snapped in two pieces. Matt tried to lift his leg but found he had no strength in it. He could bend his knee, but his entire leg felt stiff and not part of his body.

Toni waved her hand in front of her nose. "What is that smell?"

"Mostly dead skin, but remember, that leg hasn't been washed for six weeks," the doctor said. "Imagine what you would smell like after six weeks with no bath."

Matt stared at his leg. It was thinner than his right leg and pale. He tried bending it again. He could barely move it.

"Easy," the doctor said. "It may be some time before you get the full range of the knee back again, but it will come."

The doctor examined the leg, running his hands along all sides. He poked at random areas. Matt wasn't sure if it was supposed to hurt, but Matt felt no pain.

"The bones have healed. Now you'll just need to walk daily. Use a cane if you need it for now. Keep trying to bend the knee, but don't force it," the doctor said.

"Let's get him over to the tub so I can wash the leg," Toni said. "I don't want him stinking up the house like a piece of spoiled meat."

Matt sat up, and the doctor helped him to his feet. Matt felt lopsided, but when he leaned to the side, he started to fall over. The doctor helped keep him upright.

"Can the leg take your weight?" he asked.

Matt touched his foot to the floor and tried to take a step. His leg would hold his weight, but the knee still wouldn't bend so the step turned into more of a limping hop.

He made his way across the room and the lowered himself into the chair. He put his leg in the water. The warm water felt soothing on his skin, which he had noticed was itching.

Toni dipped a washcloth in the water and gently rinsed his leg. Then she took a bar of soap and began lathering up.

"Don't use Lava Soap," the doctor said. "His skin is too sensitive for that right now."

"This is the soap that Myrna and I use," Toni said.

She spread the lather along his leg and rubbed it into the skin. Matt leaned back and sighed.

"When you're finished with that leg, you can do the other leg," he said.

She pinched his thigh.

"Ouch!" Matt shouted.

Once Toni thoroughly washed the leg, she rinsed it off. Then she dried it with a towel.

Matt had to admit that his leg already looked better. With the dead skin removed and the massage, the color improved now he needed to get his strength back before Lakehurst came after him again.

Chapter 16

May 25, 1922

Matt and Samuel walked along the side of the National Road as they headed up the hill to Frostburg. They moved slowly because Matt insisted they walk. He wanted to exercise his weak leg.

"We could have attended a meeting in town," Samuel said.

Matt nodded, surprised to find he was out of breath. Before his accident, he had walked to Frostburg with ease.

"All the news about what is happening in the region comes through Frostburg. I am curious about how the national strike is going," Matt said.

"Read the newspaper like everyone else."

"It won't tell the union's side of the talks. This strike has been going on a lot longer than anyone planned, and I want to know why."

Matt wanted to hear the news about what was happening, but he also wanted to see who was at the meetings, and what they might be planning. Violent incidents were increasing against both sides.

Yesterday, announced that several mines along the Creek had restarted limited operations with the Cumberland and Pennsylvania taking out eight cars a day of coal. It wasn't a lot, but no amount would sit well with the striking miners. Matt wanted to hear what the union men would say about it. He guessed it wouldn't sit well with them because it meant they didn't have an iron grip on coal operations in this area.

Matt hoped he might find a way to keep the good men on both sides from getting injured or killed.

Truth be told, Matt also wanted to avoid Lakehurst. They would meet again. That was certain, but Matt wanted to make sure he was ready when they did meet. Lakehurst might show himself at a union meeting in Eckhart to intimidate everyone, but Frostburg was a larger town. It would be easier to stay out of his way.

The streetcar passed, going toward Eckhart Mines, and Matt waved away the cloud of dust it stirred up. It looked empty, which was understandable. People were pinching their pennies. The strike affected more than miners. Many local businesses saw their profits dry up. The miners weren't spending money because they weren't earning money. The businesses where they spent their money also didn't have that income from the miners, and so, the merchants had slowed their spending. It was a vicious circle.

"Where's Enos, anyway?" Matt asked. "He's a union member now. You'd think he would attend these meetings."

Samuel mumbled something under his breath.

"What was that?" Matt asked.

"He's working."

"Working? What is he running shine now and not just drinking it?"

"Yeah."

Matt stopped walking or rather limping. "What? I was joking."

"But you were right."

Matt whistled. "He's just bound and determined to get himself into trouble."

First, Enos joined the UMW, which put his future employment at risk if the coal companies found out. Now, he put his freedom at risk if the police caught Enos running moonshine.

"When did he learn to drive?" Matt asked.

Samuel turned to face him with his arms crossed. "That's your main concern?"

"Not my main concern, but I'm not sure what might be more dangerous. Enos running moonshine or Enos driving."

Samuel's frown turned into a grin. "OK, you have a point."

"I believe Aunt Toni would try to talk him out of it, that is, if she knows. Have you?"

Samuel nodded. "He's as hard-headed as the rest of the family. He loves driving, and now he's getting paid to do it."

They reached the end of Frostburg's Main Street and started walking on the sidewalk. They turned down an alley until they reached First Street and then turned west until they reached the Junior Mechanics Hall.

The meeting hall was standing room only. The out-of-work miners needed money, so they wanted to know when the strike would end and when they would get back to work. Samuel greeted a few people as they walked into the room. Matt found that odd. Samuel rarely left Eckhart, and that was usually to bring Myrna to Frostburg shopping. Matt had no idea Samuel knew miners outside of Eckhart. It seemed rather odd.

They found a spot against the back wall and waited for the meeting to start. Matt noticed people turn to stare at him. They would then whisper to each other. At first, he thought the men were staring at his scar. He was used to that, although people were more circumspect about staring.

Matt said to his uncle, "What's wrong? Is my hair standing straight up or something?" Samuel glanced at the top of his head. "You really aren't so good with sarcasm, are you, Samuel?"

Samuel shrugged.

A man about Matt's age walked up to him. His left eye was black and slightly swollen. He also had a stitched cut along his right cheek.

"Excuse me, are you Matt Ansaro?"

"Yes," Matt said hesitantly.

The man smiled and reached out and shook his head. Then he turned and walked away to be surrounded by men speaking to him. Matt couldn't hear what they said over the general din of the room.

Another man walked up to Matt. This one was older, probably Enos's age. He wore a thick black beard neatly trimmed. He was a few inches shorter than Matt, most likely because he developed a slight hunch many miners got from the low clearances in the mine shafts.

"Matt Ansaro, I'm Brian Kilpatrick, the head of the Frostburg local. Welcome. I'm surprised to see you at our meeting."

For a moment, Matt thought the man might know he was a Pinkerton, but if that were the case, he wouldn't have been welcomed.

"What's going on? Why are people staring at me?" Matt asked.

Brian grinned. "We heard about your run in with one of Consolidation Coal's agitators. They've been intimidating miners at towns along the creek."

"There's more than one?" Matt asked. One David Lakehurst was enough.

"We think there are three. They're damned Pinkertons. They patrol the towns looking for miners causing problems, and when they don't find them, they cause the problems themselves. They've beaten up more miners than the rest of us combined."

He was essentially admitting to the miner attacks on strikebreakers. Matt felt his hair stand up on the back of his neck. These people might kill him if they found out he was a Pinkerton man.

"What's that got to do with me?" he asked.

"Lakehurst is the worst agitator of the lot. He put men in the hospital and knocked more than one out with a single punch. You fought him the longest so far, and you were in a cast, at the time."

"He also nearly killed me."

Brian nodded. "We heard that, too, but you're the closest thing to a victory we've had against the bastards. You'll find more than one person in here who met Lakehurst and backed down. The man who shook your hand earlier tried to stand up to him a few days ago, and you can see where that got him. It's people like you, standing up against the coal company who will lead us to victory."

Matt didn't have the heart to tell Brian that his fight with Lakehurst's nothing to do with the strike.

Brian shook Matt's hand again and walked to the front of the room. Four men sat in chairs behind the podium. Matt guessed which one was the national recruiter for the UMW. He was dressed in a gray pinstripe suit while everyone else wore jeans and shirts.

Brian Kilpatrick stood up. He raised his hands over his head to quiet the room.

"Thanks for coming out for this weekly update. As much as I wish I could say every mine in the county is closed down, I can't. How are we going to show the mining companies that we are united in our goals for more pay and safer conditions, if we can't show solidarity during this strike? I know none of you here are responsible. You are believers in the righteousness of our cause. We must convince the others to walk away from the mines for now."

"How do we do that?" someone called out. "Right now, they're looking smart. They can feed their families."

Brian nodded. "I have news about that, which I will get to in due time. First, about the other miners, those still working. You need to spread the word that no matter who they are, they are not a friend to any miner here tonight" he paused for emphasis, then continued, "or any miner who is on strike. They are selfish men only worried about themselves. They won't stand with us to make things better for everyone. We need to convince them otherwise. Make them see the error of their ways, as the Good Book says."

Brian wasn't coming right out and saying it, but everyone in the room knew he was talking about intimidating the working miners and attacking them, if needed. Matt very often heard news about the attacks. Sometimes, the gangs of miners were just as violent as Lakehurst. Working miners were routinely jeered. Masked miners sometimes attacked and beat single miners. Union men shot buckshot at strikebreakers at the Kalbaugh Coal Company last week. A few men had minor scrapes from that, but everyone was worried that it could have been worse. That happened a few days later when 100 striking miners attacked a small group of miners going to work at the Clair Coal Company in Westernport. Miners had bones broken, cuts, concussions, and eyes swollen shut from that incident. Having been in a similar situation, Matt felt sympathy for them.

"Frostburg announced that the state fireman's convention will be held here this year," Brian continued. "It is an opportunity for some businesses to make back some of their lost money since we miners aren't buying."

It also meant that Enos would be very busy making deliveries because that was why the firemen were coming. Frostburg had a reputation for ignoring Prohibition.

"If the strike is still going on then, we need to make sure that firemen know it," Brian said. "Many of them will support us, and those that don't need to be treated like scabs. If the firemen are discouraged from spending time in Frostburg, then the businesses will continue to feel the same pressure we are.

"As for the scabs in the mines, they are like the stubborn mule that needs to be made to walk in the right direction using both the whip and the carrot. Up to now, we have used only the whip, but tonight I have news about the carrot."

Brian turned and nodded to the union representative, who stood up and replaced Brian at the podium.

"I am Paul Tomlinson, the UMW representative for Maryland and West Virginia. Tonight I wanted to share with you the news that the UMW is setting up a commissary in Frostburg that will provide you and your families with food for the duration of the strike. We stand with you."

Some men cheered. Tomlinson probably thought it would be louder, but while he might stand with the miners, he didn't understand them.

Samuel leaned over and said, "You aren't cheering, Matt."

"Neither are you."

"I suppose it's good news, but not what we want to hear."

Matt nodded. These men didn't want charity, which is undoubtedly how they saw the commissary. They were miners. They wanted to work. They wanted the strike to end. It had lasted eight weeks, so far, with no end in sight. These men were being driven deep into debt.

"This is just going to make people more desperate. Someone will be killed," Matt said.

"Sometimes when people won't listen, they need to be made to listen," Samuel said.

"You approve of the attacks on the miners?"

"Samuel Adams said that the tree of liberty sometimes needed to be fed with the blood of tyrants and patriots."

Enos walked out the back door of the Hotel Gunter and crossed First Street to where he parked his car. He dropped off a case of "scotch" at the speakeasy, and now he had $200 to take back to Vincent Gambrill. He glanced around to make sure no one was watching him. It was hard to tell. The street was dark, which was good for delivering moonshine, but not so good for picking up tails.

A pair of headlights came on. Enos jumped in the car and started the engine. He put the Duesenberg Model A in gear and it jumped forward. The other car followed him.

It might not be the police or revenue agents, but he couldn't take a chance. He had just started on his rounds. He still had fourteen gallons of moonshine hidden in the rear of the car.

He turned right on Mt. Savage Road, which was the opposite direction he wanted to go, but it would be too easy for the police to follow if he headed toward Grantsville. He hit the gas, but he had to hit the brakes almost immediately as he slid into a sharp turn. He sped up and braked again through another turn. He could see the car following behind him. It was gaining on him because he had to limit his speed to make all the hard turns in the road when he wasn't using his headlights.

Enos hit a straightaway and put some distance between himself and the other car. He kept watching for a turnoff he knew, and hoped that the revenuers didn't.

He flicked the lights on, got his bearings, and turned them off. He made a sharp left and then a right. Now he floored the gas pedal.

He saw the break in the trees, hit the brakes as he spun for a hard right-hand turn. He thought for a moment the car would roll as the passenger side wheels came off the ground. When the wheels hit the ground, he shot forward up a dirt trail barely wide enough for the car. It was an old wagon road that went over Big Savage Mountain and came down into Eckhart. Not that he would go there unless it was necessary.

He moved deeper into the woods and then killed the engine. The revenuer's car drove by slowly, searching for some sign of him. Since he used his lights as little as possible, they would wonder if he were still driving along the road with his lights off.

The car moved passed him and continued along the road.

Enos climbed out of the car and walked through the trees until he came to the road. He watched the revenuer's car gain speed along the road and figured they decided that Enos was somewhere still ahead of them.

Enos got back in his car and backed up until he was on Mt. Savage Road again. He glanced over his shoulder to make sure the revenuers were out of sight. Then he turned on his headlights and headed back to Frostburg as fast as he could.

He still had deliveries to make tonight.

Chapter 17

May 26, 1922

Matt knocked on the door to Jenny's house. It was almost a week since Matt had seen her. He wanted to see how she was doing after he warned her about Lakehurst. He suspected he would need to do some shopping to make sure she didn't starve because she was afraid to go outside.

He thought about what he could do if Jenny still felt terrified that Lakehurst would find her. He could understand her fear. He felt it during the war. It was the first time he was ordered to charge into firing rifles and artillery. He watched as machine guns mowed down men and artillery shells blew apart waves of marines. He drew courage from the men around him, and moved forward when they did. As they had fallen, he had continued forward almost as if carried by momentum.

He needed to let Jenny draw on his courage now, until she could move forward under her own momentum. He even had an idea that might help both her and his family. Aunt Toni still had a room to let in her boarding house. If Jenny came to live there, it would take her far enough away from Frostburg where Lakehurst wouldn't expect to find her. Also, she was unlikely to find anyone to ply her trade since the miners had no cash for the extras of life. And if she needed money to pay her board, Matt could supply that and help his family with additional income.

He knocked again, and when no one answered, he called out, "Jenny, it's me, Matt."

The last time he visited her, she came to the door at the sound of his name, but he heard nothing now. Odd. Even if she had gone back to work, she slept for much of the day. Had she worked up the nerve to go out on her own? That would be wonderful.

He knocked once more, and when she didn't answer, he turned away.

Matt decided not to waste his trip to Frostburg. He hobbled over to the other side of town to see if Samantha was home. They could have lunch together. Someone driving through town saw him limping along and offered him a ride, which Matt gladly accepted. He might need the exercise, but he didn't want to spend a couple hours walking across town in his condition.

He knocked on the door to Samantha's house and was startled when Jenny answered. She wore a light blue dress with a white apron across the front. Her hair was pulled into a bun at the back of her head. She looked as surprised as Matt. She recovered first.

"Hello, Matt."

"Jenny, what are you doing here?"

"I work here."

"Really?"

"Yes, I'm the maid."

"That's wonderful. How did it happen?" Matt asked.

He knew she was out and about because she visited him last week, but he hadn't realized she changed so much.

"Samantha heard about my problem and offered to help. By the way, she's not home right now."

Matt nodded. "She wasn't expecting me, but I was in town and thought I would stop in to see her. Actually, I stopped by your house first to check on you."

"Really? That's sweet. I was a mess for a while, as you saw, but Samantha helped me, which is surprising since not too long ago she didn't like me."

That had been when she thought Matt preferred Jenny to her.

He still hadn't told Samantha that he and Jenny had slept together, and now he couldn't because it might cost Jenny her job. Anyway, Samantha was smart. Matt suspected she might already know how Jenny and he were acquainted.

"Will you tell Samantha that I stopped by?" Matt asked.

"Of course." She waved and smiled at Matt, and he could tell a certain weight was lifted from her shoulders.

Joseph heard yelling from the store, but when he got up to look into the store, he only saw Portnoy mumbling to himself as he put some canned goods on the shelf.

He looked back in the office. Nothing was happening. He'd read the newspaper, but it hadn't told him anything that he didn't already know about the strike. He was tempted to call the regional headquarters in Cumberland, but he didn't want to give his father a chance to harangue him over not keeping the strikebreakers working. As if the man could have done any better when he was superintendent of Eckhart Mines.

Joseph picked up a box from the office and walked into the store. He set the box on the counter and started adding canned foods and pasta. He added some smoked meats and cheese.

"What are you doing?" Portnoy asked.

Ignoring the question, Joseph said, "Put it on my account."

"You said not to give credit to anyone who is not paid up."

Joseph scowled as he added raisins, chocolate, and some rock candy to the box. It wouldn't hurt to stay on Jacob's good side.

"What are you talking about?" Joseph asked.

"You haven't paid on your account from the box you gathered last week."

"You know I'm good for it."

"I'm sorry. It's a new policy that has recently gone into effect," Portnoy said, straight-faced.

Joseph took a five-dollar bill from his wallet and slapped it on the counter.

"That should bring me up to date."

Portnoy grinned. "Oh, yes."

He picked up the bill and put it in his cash register. Joseph was surprised he didn't rub it against his cheek or inhale the fragrance of the ink.

"Now ring up this stuff so I can go," Joseph said.

Portnoy took his time. Joseph wanted to throttle him, which was probably why Portnoy moved slowly.

"A lot of food," Portnoy commented.

Joseph said nothing.

"A lot of sweets. You might want to cut back on them, Joseph. You're looking a bit thick."

Joseph growled, but he didn't say anything. He waited until Portnoy tallied the amount and said, "Put it on my account."

Joseph grabbed the box of food and left, trying not to look in a rush.

He set the box on the porch and rolled his sleeves down. He slid his sports coat over his sizeable frame. He straightened his tie and ran his hand through his blond hair to make sure it wasn't sticking up.

Joseph hesitated, considering whether to walk or take his car. Laura's house was only a few homes down the street. He could easily walk that distance, but arriving in his Renault GS was more impressive. He could even talk Laura into taking a drive with him. That would impress her.

The car would attract attention, though. Joseph didn't mind. It was one reason he drove the car the short distance from his home to the mine office each day.

People would talk if they saw his car parked in front of Laura's house. He suspected that they were already talking, judging by Portnoy's comments.

It didn't bother Joseph, but it might Laura. She still mourned Pete. If people started connecting her and Joseph too soon, she might pull back.

He needed to plant the seeds, and wait to see which ones took root. Not everything happened the way he wanted. He had put Pete and Matt in the worst work area in the mine. He hadn't planned on the cave-in, although if he was honest with himself, he had hoped something terrible would happen to them. Pete's death in the cave-in had opened Joseph's way to Laura. The only way things would have worked out better was if the cave-in had killed Matt Ansaro, too, removing a competitor for her love.

Joseph had waited five years for Laura. Sure he could wait a little longer, especially now that he was close to having what, or rather, who he wanted.

Toni left the house and headed for Eckhart Church to meet up with the other women in town. She wanted to see how the displaced families were doing. The strike seemed no closer to being settled, especially now that the scabs were working in the mines. They weren't as good as regular miners, but when the mines were closed, anything was better than nothing.

She wasn't sure what to think about the idle miners in town, though. Another two men had found work in Pennsylvania and were leaving. One was a family man with a wife and infant son. The women in town were caring for them all. Although their leaving would lighten the women's load, it was depriving Eckhart Mines of a family that lived here for two generations. If this slow drain continued, what would Eckhart look like when the strike ended?

She waved to Paul and Dru Barry as they walked in the other direction. She glanced at Dru's stomach almost without thinking. Next year, the town would see a spike in births. With no work to keep them busy, the men in town had found other ways to keep themselves busy. Dru said just last week she suspected she was pregnant, but it was still too early to know for sure. The Barrys already had four children and now a fifth one might be on the way. She had no doubt that Paul wouldn't wait around for the strike to end. They might be the next family to leave.

Toni saw a group of strikebreakers sitting on the porch of the company store playing cards. They must work the second shift because she doubted the company would allow them to be idle otherwise.

They were a scrawny lot of men who didn't seem to bathe

much because they always seemed dirty when she saw them. That might be because she mainly saw them on their way back to their homes after their shift ended.

They looked up as she neared, but Toni made a point of not looking in their direction.

"Hello, pretty lady!" one man called in a thick Italian accent. "Why not come join us? We can entertain each other."

Toni's back stiffened. The men must have noticed because they laughed. They must also be drunk to act in such a manner.

"Don't ignore us!" a different man called. "We have money. More than your man has, I'd wager. We'd be willing to spend some on you even if you are one of the uppity bitches in this town who thinks she's too good to talk to us."

She heard a smack and then a thud. Despite her intentions, she stopped to look over at the group. One man lay in the dirt in front of the porch.

A short dark-haired man stood at the edge of the porch. "I told ye not to talk to women like that, boy-o."

He was thickly muscled, more than any of the other four men.

"What's it matter to you? The women in this town will piss on you here before they'll talk to you. Why should I show them any respect?" the man on the ground shouted.

"Because me dear mother taught me to respect women, and I mean to do just that."

"Don't mean I have to."

The short man jumped to the ground and grabbed the other man by the shirt front and flung him onto the porch.

"I won't have any of you lot disrespecting ladies around me," the Irishman said.

"Ladies? Ha!"

The Irishman's fist shot out, smashing the other man in the face. Blood spurted from his nose. He yelled and grabbed at his face. The Irishman pulled him off the porch and gave him a kick in the backside, sending him staggering away from the group.

"Any of you have something to say?" the Irishman said, turning back to the group.

The other three men shook their heads. One said, "Your deal."

The Irishman turned to Toni, tipped his hat and said, in his best Tipperary accent "Beggin' yer pardon, ma'am."

Toni smiled and shook her head, despite herself. The Irishman grinned and hopped onto the porch. He picked up the deck and shuffled the cards.

Toni watched him for a moment and then continued walking.

David walked down the middle of Store Hill, his shoulders thrown back so he was standing as tall as he could, which was six foot one inch tall. People gave him a wide berth. He towered over anyone who came near. He liked that. Scared people could be controlled, and controlled people made his work easier.

David hadn't seen Matt Ansaro since he had beaten him into the ground. God! That had been satisfying, thrilling even. It was hard to stop. It was nearly as good as sex.

He knew where Ansaro lived. Joseph McCord was more than happy to point out the boarding house. It was private property, though, so David couldn't enter it claiming it was company property and evict the Ansaros.

He passed the company store and turned up Beer Alley. David had no destination in mind. He just wanted people to see him and remember he was around if they should think about damaging company property or attacking company strikebreakers. He made regular patrols of three towns a day and even when he wasn't around, three Pinkerton guards were also on duty in each town watching over the strikebreakers.

He wished he could find the town whore. He was sure Eckhart had to have at least one. The miners couldn't be expected to go into Frostburg every time they wanted to relieve their urges. That took too much time and added to the expense because you needed trolley fare.

His room was still the Hotel Gunter, so he didn't mind finding a Frostburg whore, but sometimes, when he wasn't in Frostburg, he wanted to take a woman out behind a wood shed and have at her.

It had gotten him in trouble from time to time. He still wanted to find Calista and *convince* her to drop the charges against him.

Even if there weren't whores in Eckhart Mines, the town had to have loose women. If he could find them, David would encourage them to spend time with him like he would convince Calista.

He walked along swinging his arms and smoking a Lucky Strike.

Chapter 18

May 27, 1922

Matt stepped out on the back porch of the boarding house. He stretched and savored the warm sunshine wash over him. He stripped off his plaid shirt down to his sleeveless underwear. It felt good to flex his muscles and take deep breaths free from coal dust. He had only been in the coal mines a few months. He couldn't imagine how people like Enos and Samuel did it year after year. Matt grabbed a handsaw and sawed on a log back and forth, in a steady rhythm, until he cut the nine-foot-long log into thirds.

Then he did the Daily Dozen program. The exercises had been part of his Marine Corps training at Parris Island. Although his limp was gone, his left leg was weaker than his right. The sawing motion strengthened his shoulders, but he needed to do more.

Matt bent down and hefted a section of log to his neck. He stood up with a grunt and pushed the log up over his head and let it come down to rest on the back of his neck and shoulders.

Then he started walking. Eventually, he would run with the log on his back, but that was still in the future. One step at a time, so to speak.

He walked out to the front of the boarding house, turned around, and retraced his steps to the backyard. He repeated the exercise until his legs buckled. He threw off the log as he dropped to his knees. Sweat glistened on his forehead and droplets formed on the chest hair exposed from his undershirt. He pulled a handkerchief from his jeans and mopped his face.

That was when he noticed the crowd gathered at the front of the house to watch him. Bored miners made up the bulk of the group, but Matt also saw women and children.

"What in the name of all that's holy are you doing?" asked Bennett Clark, a miner who lived up the street.

"I'm rebuilding the strength in my leg that was broken," Matt said.

"Looks like you nearly broke it again."

"I push myself hard."

"Leave the man alone, Ben. I doubt you could have lifted that log, let alone walk with it on your shoulders," Enos said.

Matt looked around and saw his uncle sitting on the porch sipping at something in a glass.

"Not saying I could have," Bennett said. "I am saying I wouldn't have."

"That's why you look the way you do, Ben, and why Matt looks the way he does," Enos said.

Matt pointed to his uncle's glass. "Is that water?" he asked. He was thirsty and could use something to drink. Maybe he'd be lucky, and the glass wasn't filled with moonshine.

"A part of it is." He held the glass out to Matt.

Matt frowned and shook his head.

"Not enough," Samuel said as he walked up beside Enos. He passed Matt a glass. "This is water."

"Thanks." Matt gulped down the water.

Samuel said to the crowd, "Show's over, folks."

The crowd moved off. Matt's workout had given them a brief diversion. With the mine shut down, anything out of the ordinary was bound to attract an audience.

Samuel walked up on the porch and stood beside his brother.

"What are you going to do when the strike ends?" Samuel asked.

Enos shrugged. "The way things are going you have to wonder

if the strike will end."

"It will. They all do at some point."

"Well, I may not go back. I enjoy seeing the sunlight." Enos held his glass toward the sun.

"Really? You sleep most of the day away," Matt said.

Enos rolled his eyes at his nephew.

"Toni and I are worried about you," Samuel said.

"Why? I'm doing better than I ever have."

"That could change in an instant."

"Can't you say that about anything? Just look at what happened with Matt. First with the mine and then with that thug Pinkerton man."

"What you're doing is illegal, Enos," Matt said. "If you get caught, they'll throw you in jail."

"It wasn't a couple years ago," Enos said. "I'm just delivering a product people are requesting."

"Maybe so, but what you're doing was illegal before Prohibition. Drinking wasn't, but moonshining always has been. It is just more popular now."

Making the legal manufacture of alcohol illegal had only made moonshining more lucrative. While there may have been a still or two in the county three years ago, now there are hundreds.

"I won't get caught," Enos said. "I've got a fast car. I know the shortcuts and back routes, and I'm an excellent driver. You should see me drive, Matt. I can chase the wind and catch it."

Samuel put his hand on his brow and shook his head.

"And the money I'm making! I earn more in a week than I earned for a month in the mines. With that kind of money, I'll have my taxi before long. You should join me. Both of you. Samuel, you would have the money for your hotel in no time. Matt, well, you can save money for whatever you want."

"Even if I wanted to, Myrna would never let me," Samuel said.

Matt thought his uncle sounded almost sad about that his wife wouldn't let him break the law.

Enos grinned. "Then don't tell her, or tell her you got a different job."

Samuel snorted. "She'd know, Enos. Wives are like that. You may think you're fooling them, but they know."

"Then it's your loss, Samuel, and when I get my taxi, I'll be happy to take you and Myrna to Cumberland."

"Be careful, Enos."

"I always am."

Matt almost laughed because he knew taking care was not something Enos was known for.

Samantha poked her head into the kitchen. Mrs. Fratelli was putting the finishing touches on dinner, and Jenny was helping where she could.

"How are things going?" Samantha asked.

"Everything is fine," Jenny said.

Then Jennifer noticed Samantha's dress. It was a short loose-fitting dress like Samantha's typical flapper dresses, but this blue dress was an evening dress. The back opened down to the middle of her back, revealing her smooth, white skin, a large bow pulled in the sides, emphasizing her slim hips. "I hope you told Matt to dress nice," Jenny said.

"He won't wear a suit or anything like that, but he will wear his nice shirt." Samantha shrugged. "It doesn't matter. I'm not planning on going out."

"Really? Dressed like that? I thought you said you were going dancing."

Samantha nodded. "I did."

She went back out into the dining room. Jenny set the table so that Samantha and Matt could sit across from each other on the narrow side of the table rather than on the far ends like she and her father did.

She heard a knock at the door and glanced at the clock. It must be Matt. It was nearly the time she told him to arrive. She checked her lipstick in the mirror, patted her hair, took a turn, and went to the door.

Matt's eyes widened when he saw her. She had been correct. He wore a bright white shirt with a paisley tie and pleated brown trousers that, thankfully, weren't the baggy English style. A few the boys at school wore them because they saw them in England at Oxford University during a visit last summer.

"You look beautiful!" Matt said.

Samantha smiled and turned around so he could see her bare back.

"Wow!" she heard him say.

She looked over her shoulder and winked at him. "Come in."

He poked his head inside and looked around. "Really? I don't think your father will be happy to see me."

Samantha turned back and grabbed him by the arm to pull him inside. As she closed the door, she said, "Father's in Annapolis for meetings with the Board of Regents. He left this morning on the train, and he won't be back until tomorrow evening."

She still didn't understand Matt and her father's relationship. Her father acted like he didn't like Matt, but she could tell he respected Matt. Her father's reaction to Matt always seemed to confuse him, as if Matt expected her father to act a certain way and he never did.

"Where did you want to go to dinner?" Matt asked.

"We are eating here," Samantha told him.

"Here?"

"Yes, how often will we have the opportunity to have a delicious, intimate dinner without my father around causing tension?"

They walked into the dining room. Matt pulled out the chair for Samantha. He knew she didn't like it, but his mother had taught him manners as a boy, and so, it was second nature to him. Samantha had given up arguing with him about it. It was just part of who Matt was.

When they were seated, Jenny walked in carrying a bottle of wine Samantha had hidden in her room. Jenny smiled when she saw Matt.

"Hi, Jenny," Matt said.

"Good evening, Mr. Ansaro," Jenny said.

"It's just me, Jenny. You can call me Matt."

Jenny glanced at Samantha.

"It's all right. My father isn't around," Samantha told her.

Jenny poured the wine. Matt picked up his glass and held it toward the light. It was red with nothing floating in it. Matt smelled it, and his eyes didn't water.

"This looks like real wine and not bathtub gin," Matt said.

"It is."

"How did you find a bottle? It must have cost a fortune."

"It was expensive, but not outrageous. The man who sold it to me likes my legs," Samantha said.

Matt laughed. "I bet he did. Do I have competition for your affection?"

"Always," she said, raising her eyebrows and smiling. "Never think you've got me trapped, Mr. Ansaro."

He raised his glass to her. "Call me Matt, please, Miss Havencroft."

"Then you must call me Samantha."

"Not Sam?"

"Good Lord, no. I am a woman and proud of it. Why would I want a man's name?"

"That's good. I have an Uncle Samuel. I wouldn't want to get the two of you confused."

"Do I look like your Uncle Samuel?"

"Not in that dress, although I have to say I've never seen my uncle in a dress."

Samantha's composure collapsed, and she laughed. Matt seemed to win their game of one upmanship more often than not. She wondered if he practiced lines to find the ones that would make her laugh.

Jenny brought in the meal. It was a chuck roast with potatoes and carrots. Dessert was a chocolate cake. Mrs. Fratelli did an excellent job and both Matt and Samantha told her so.

"Well, I guess since we had dinner here, I'm obligated to take you somewhere to dance unless you would rather go to the moving pictures at the Palace Theater."

Samantha dabbed at her mouth with her napkin. "I do want to

189

go dancing."

"Where?"

Samantha pushed her chair back and stood up. She walked around the table and held out her hand. He took her hand, and she led him to the stairs.

"Where are we going?" he asked.

"Dancing."

They walked upstairs to her bedroom.

"Wow, this is three times the size of my room," Matt said when he stepped inside.

Samantha walked over to her Victrola and put a record on the turntable. Then she spun the handle on the side and lowered the needle to the disk. Fanny Brice started singing "My Man." It was a song she made popular when she rejoined the Ziegfeld Follies, in 1921.

"Here's a slow song. Now let's see what you can do with it," she said.

"I don't know..."

"You don't have your cast as an excuse," she said.

Matt shook his head. She grabbed his hands and pulled him toward her.

"Just do what I do. Don't worry if you mess up. Just keep trying, you will feel the rhythm."

Matt sighed. He staggered around, imitating some of her movements but missing most of them. He took it good naturedly, smiling as they danced.

After they played the record four times, Matt asked, "Can we try another dance?"

"Why? You haven't gotten this one yet."

Matt bobbed his head. "That's why."

She walked over and looked through her records. She pulled out "The Oriental Fox Trot" by Paul Whiteman and His Orchestra. She put it on the Victrola.

"This is more my speed," Matt said.

The two of them started doing a fox trot.

"I thought you couldn't dance," Samantha said.

Matt shook his head. "No, I said, I'm not a great dancer. I like a good fox trot."

"Not as fun as a good two step, though."

"I can think of things that are more fun."

"Such as?"

He leaned forward and kissed her, tentatively.

"Your kissing is nearly as bad as your dancing. You need to practice more," Samantha said with a smile.

He pulled her close enough that she could feel his heart beating, or maybe it was just her heart beating against his chest. They kissed and Samantha felt Matt's rough hands on her bare back. He held her close but didn't force him against her. Their lips met and then their tongues.

She closed her eyes and leaned into him. Her hands wrapped around his back, feeling the tight muscles there.

Matt's hands slid down to her buttocks. When she didn't resist, he pulled her tighter to him. She rubbed her body against him, and like two sticks rubbing together; she felt heat building between the two of them.

Matt moved her backwards, and she felt herself being lowered onto the bed.

Was this happening now? She told herself it was a surprise, but she realized she had built things toward this moment from choosing her dress to bringing Matt up to her bedroom to dance.

He kissed her neck, and she noticed his face was so much smoother than his hands. She felt his muscles tense and a small gasp escaped from her moistened lips. His left hand was on her back, his right hand tugged gently on the shoulder of her dress, she could feel his mouth moving down her chest. She pulled his shirt from his pants when a knock at the door sounded.

Matt pushed himself back and stood up.

"What?" Samantha called.

The door opened and Jenny walked in with a pitcher of tea and two glasses on a tray.

"Sorry to interrupt you, but I thought since the music had stopped you two might have worked up a thirst."

Jenny glanced at their flushed faces and the portion of Matt's shirt that Samantha had pulled from his trousers. Although she gave no hint of it, Samantha knew her housemaid knew what Samantha and Matt were about to do.

Why hadn't she locked the door?

Jenny wouldn't say anything, though. How could she? Jenny had once earned her living doing the same thing. It was nothing new to her.

Jenny set the tray down on Samantha's desk.

"Do you need anything?" Jenny asked, not looking over at Laura and Matt.

"Nothing. Thank you, Jenny," Samantha said more curtly than she had intended.

Jenny left the room, closing the door behind her. Samantha tried to read her expression, but couldn't tell anything.

"She knows what we were going to do," Samantha said.

Matt nodded. "I wouldn't be surprised."

"It doesn't bother you?"

"Jenny won't say anything."

"Can you be sure? What if my father found out?"

"That we were about to make love or that we were going to do it in the house?" Matt tried pulling her close, but her worry overcame her passion. She pulled away.

"Both," she said.

"He'll never hear a bad word against you spoken by me, and I am certain the same holds true for Jenny."

Matt tucked his shirt in.

"What are you doing?" Samantha asked.

"I can tell the mood is broken. You're going to worry over your father finding out."

"I don't know why."

"I'd much rather you worry about me," Matt said.

Samantha deflated. "I meant for this to be a special day."

Matt walked over and kissed her. "It was. I had a wonderful time, and I look forward to more special days to come."

Joseph stepped out of the office through the exterior door. Portnoy had already locked up the company store, including locking the connecting door. Despite living in an apartment above the store that he visited during slow times of the day, Portnoy refused to stay open later than his posted hours. Joseph, on the other hand, was known to work late.

He didn't mind, though. The mines had started producing again as the strikebreakers learned their jobs. Daily tonnage amounts and the names of the men mining now filled the blank blackboard. If he got much busier, Joey would have to start Sidney Bloom working more hours. He was on a half-time schedule for the time being.

The daily tonnage numbers weren't impressive. Even with the strikebreakers in the mine, he was still only working with half of his normal workforce. Not to mention that these strikebreakers weren't as productive as his normal miners.

Still, something was better than nothing.

The numbers increased steadily. That was the important thing.

He locked the door and started toward the front of the store. He had taken to walking home. He thought the exercise would do him good. He wanted to look his best for Laura.

Something, or rather, someone hit him in the chest, knocking him to the ground. Then he heard a shot.

"Stay down!"

It was Matt Ansaro.

Joseph pushed Matt off and sat up. Matt pulled him back down.

"Stay down, you idiot!" Matt yelled. "Didn't you hear the shot?"

Joseph froze. Shot? Then he remembered hearing the sound from a weapon as he fell and something hitting the corner of the store.

He looked up at the store and saw a jagged scar where a bullet had torn away the corner post.

Matt looked around the corner of the store.

"What is going on?" Joseph asked.

193

Matt stood up. "Whoever it was is gone now."

He turned and offered Joseph a hand up. Joseph ignored him. He rolled to his side and then got to his feet.

He started brushing dirt from his suit. "I'll have to have this cleaned now."

"Dirt's easier to get out than blood."

"Who tried to shoot me? And why?" Joseph tried to hide the shakiness in his voice.

"Well, there could be many reasons why?" Matt said. "My guess is because of the strike. I didn't recognize the person. I was walking home from the trolley stop and saw someone sitting on the railroad office porch alone. When you walked out, he stood up and I saw him reach for a gun. That's when I tackled you."

Joseph frowned and tried to hide that fact that he was shaking. He could have been killed. Had the man been trying to do that or just scare him?

Joseph looked over at the railroad office. No one was there. Not that he would have expected the shooter to stay around.

"You miners have pushed this too far," Joseph said.

"Well, don't forget that a miner just saved you."

"I was in no danger. He was probably just a drunk blowing off steam. I doubt he was aiming at me."

"Because you're such a likeable man?"

"Be grateful I don't have you brought up on charges for attacking me."

Matt's eyes widened.

Joey turned and headed toward his house, nearly running.

Matt watched Joseph rush away and shook his head. He looked around to make sure the man didn't step out and take another shot at Joseph's back.

He heard about attacks on miner's and strikebreakers. He even heard of company equipment being burned. This was the worst thing that had happened in Eckhart, but the problems were just getting started.

Matt shook his head and continued up the street toward the

boarding house. He saw Laura coming down the street toward him.

"Matt! I heard a shot and Joey yelling," she said. "Is he all right?"

Matt put his hands on Laura's shoulders. "Everything's fine. Joseph is fine."

Matt explained what had happened to her. She looked panicked, but he kept his hands on her shoulders until she calmed down.

"Has the country gone crazy? We just got out of one war, and now we're in another one," Laura said.

"The sooner they can settle, the better things will be for everyone."

"Thank you for what you did for Joey. I'm sure he appreciated it."

Matt snorted. "I doubt it. He wouldn't want anyone to see him as weak."

"He has a nice side, Matt."

"Not that I've seen."

She put her hands on her hips. "Well, he treats me good. Any girl would like that."

She didn't sound confident of what she was saying, but Matt suspected she wouldn't appreciate him pointing it out.

"Then I'm happy for you," Matt said.

"Are you?"

Matt laid a hand on her shoulder. "I just want to see you happy, Laura."

"Sometimes I wonder if I will ever be happy again." She looked off to the side.

"Of course you will."

"I'm glad you are sure about it."

Matt smiled.

"So where's Jake?" Matt asked.

Laura looked back over her shoulder. "He's with your aunts. I wanted to see how they get along if I find a job."

"A job? That's great news. What will you do?"

Laura held up a hand to stop him. "I don't have a job yet. I thought about doing laundry or sewing, but the women in town can't afford to hire someone to do that work for them. I've asked around at the stores in town, but nobody is hiring. Tomorrow, I'm going into Frostburg and ask at the stores there."

"Do you want me to come with you?"

"Why? I know how to get to Frostburg."

He paused and thought for a moment. "Well, I could treat you to lunch. You'll get hungry walking around town all day," Matt suggested.

Laura smiled. "That's very nice, but it's not needed. However, since you are in Frostburg, a lot to see Samantha if you or she hear about a job, let me know, please."

Matt nodded.

They walked back to the boarding house and sat on the front porch. Laura sat in the straight-back chair and Matt sat on the porch with his back against a post.

They spent the next hour just talking about the things friends talk about. What their old school friends were doing now. Places they used to go. How fast Jake was growing.

Matt even got her to talk about how she met Pete and their dating and wedding. It made Laura sad at first, but then Matt noticed she seemed to drift off as if she was seeing the memories in her head and just describing what she had seen. When she finished talking, Matt said nothing. Laura seemed happy or at least content for the moment and he didn't want to end the moment for her.

Then Jake ran out of the house, squealing with delight. He ran over and hugged Laura. Laura blinked, looked disoriented, then she saw Jake and everything was right. She lifted him onto her lap.

"Did you have fun, Jacob?" she asked.

"Yes, I had cake," the little boy said.

"I hope that was all right," Toni said from the door.

"It's fine," Laura replied.

"I have more if you would like a slice."

"It's chocolate," Jake said.

"Your favorite," Laura told him. She looked over at Toni and said, "Thank you, but we need to go home. How did things go?"

Toni smiled. "He's a little ball of fire, but a joy to have around. I hope you'll let us watch him."

"I guess that depends on how things go tomorrow in Frostburg. I'll bring him by around nine if that's all right."

Toni nodded. "Myrna and I are looking forward to it."

Laura stood up. She took Jake's hand and the two of them headed down the street to their home.

"Do you think she'll find work?" Toni asked Matt when Laura and Jake were too far away to hear.

"I hope so."

"Things were tough on me when Michael died, but at least I had your uncles and Myrna around, and I didn't have a child depending on me. Laura's in a tough spot."

"Well, she has you and Aunt Myrna, and she is looking for a job. All of that will help."

"And she has you."

"I haven't helped her."

Toni snorted. "That's not what I hear."

Matt shook his head. No one needed to know about the help he gave Laura. "People in this town talk too much."

Then he stood up and walked past his aunt into the house.

197

Chapter 19

May 24, 1922

Matt walked up National Road. He passed up riding on the trolley because he wanted to take every opportunity to exercise his weak leg. He newly healed leg seemed to lag a bit behind his good leg, but it grew stronger every day.

He wanted to take Samantha for a walk. Maybe hold her hand, and to somehow remind her of the night in her bedroom. However, as he approached her house, he saw her walking down the street with another man. He was tempted to call after her, but he didn't. He stopped and watched her walk away.

He didn't recognize the man from behind, but he looked about Matt's age, and he was well dressed. Not dressed like a rich man, but certainly not dressed like a coal miner.

Was Samantha seeing someone else? Was the man just another college student walking with her to the campus? Or was he someone else altogether?

He walked up to the house and was getting ready to knock on the front door, but he stopped with his hand in mid-air. What if John Havencroft answered? He wasn't Matt's biggest fan. He might not tell Matt anything about the other man.

Matt walked around to the side of the house and knocked on the kitchen door. Jenny answered.

"Matt, what are you doing here? And at the kitchen door?" she asked.

"I wanted to talk to you about something."

She stepped back and waved him inside. "Come in. It's just me and Mrs. Fratelli right now." Well, that answered his question about whether John was home.

Matt stepped into the kitchen and saw an older woman standing at the table cutting up celery, carrots, and potatoes for a stew. Jenny introduced him to the cook, although Matt had met her on previous visits to the house.

"What did you want to talk about?" Jenny asked.

"When I was coming up, I saw Samantha walking with a man I didn't recognize. Who was he?"

Jenny raised an eyebrow and glanced at Mrs. Fratelli.

"That would be Professor Williamson from the college," Jenny said. "Samantha takes one of his classes."

"So he's just a teacher of hers?"

The women exchanged glances again. How was it women seemed to communicate between themselves without saying a word?

"That's… uncertain right now. Mrs. Fratelli says the professor is being polite and trying to impress Mr. Havencroft since he's the president of the college."

"But you don't think so," Matt guessed.

Jenny looked down. "Well, I have more experience with men, and I think he is interested in her."

"What about her? Is she interested in him?" Matt asked.

Again with the glances.

Jenny shrugged. "Maybe. When it first started happening, I would have said no, but it's changing."

Matt sat down in a chair. He'd lost her. Just like Priscilla. And both times it had been to someone who was a higher social class than he.

"Why hasn't she said anything?" Matt muttered more to himself than anyone.

Was that why she had stopped him from making love to her in

her bedroom?

"Well, she obviously hasn't made up her mind."

"Then I still have a chance?"

Jenny patted his shoulder. "Sure."

"That didn't sound too confident."

"It's just that you and Samantha are two different people from two different backgrounds. Plus, her father doesn't want her married to a coal miner. The temperature in the room drops when they talk about you."

Matt wondered if it would make a difference to John Havencroft if Matt told him he was a Pinkerton detective.

"We've worked out so far."

Jenny nodded. "But you're just enjoying the newness of your relationship. You probably have thought little about the future. When you or she think about how it might be twenty or thirty years down the road, that is when there might be problems. At least, that's what Mr. Havencroft keeps telling Samantha."

Matt hung his head. He had been so excited to see Samantha, and now, she might walk out of his life.

"You can always find another woman, Matt. You're good looking."

Matt's shoulders sagged. "I wasn't looking for Samantha, which is why it was so special."

"You weren't looking for me either." She ran her fingers through his hair.

Matt looked up, remembering Toni's warning. He needed to be careful what he said to her. He didn't want her thinking there was something more than friendship between them.

He took her free hand in his. "No, we've become good friends."

She let go of his hair and turned away. "Friends."

"Aren't we?"

Jenny smiled, but it looked false. "Yes, of course, we're good friends."

Samantha returned home from her classes alone. She wanted to sit down on the back porch, with her copy of *Monday or Tuesday* by Virginia Woolf, and read just for fun the rest of the afternoon. The book was a collection of short stories, and Samantha was reading "A Society," which dismissed and put down the male intellect.

Jenny walked down from the second floor where she must have been cleaning.

"Hi, Jenny, is my father at home?" Samantha asked.

"No, and Mrs. Fratelli is at the market, so let me know if you would like something, and I'll get it for you."

"Nothing right now. I will get my book from my room and read on the back porch. It's a nice day outside."

Samantha started up the stairs.

"Matt was by earlier," Jenny said.

"Oh, did he say what he wanted?"

Jenny shook her head. "No, he just wanted to see you."

Samantha pressed her lips together. In a way–a small way–she was glad she had missed Matt. He put her emotions in turmoil. Here she was wondering whether the two of them had a future together, and she nearly had sex with him. That would have confused her even more and Matt, too.

"Jenny, I'm sorry for what you saw the other day," Samantha said.

"Saw? What do you mean?"

"When you walked in on Matt and me."

Jenny chuckled. "Oh, that. You didn't embarrass me. I've seen a lot more of Matt than him just standing with his shirt out. I'm just sorry I came in when I did. Matt is certainly worth it."

Samantha froze. "What?"

Jenny's eyes widened. "I mean… well, I thought he told you."

"Told me what?" Samantha wasn't sure she wanted to hear the answer.

"Well… that's how we met." Jenny added quickly. "It was just the one time, though."

Samantha felt herself reddening. Matt and Jenny? How could he not have said something about it? Samantha was right when she thought Jenny and Matt were more than friends. Matt lied to her.

Samantha rushed up the stairs to her room. She locked the door and threw herself on the bed and sobbed into her pillow.

Jenny knocked on the door.

"Samantha, I'm sorry. I'm so sorry. I didn't mean to upset you."

"Go away."

"It was before he met you and only the one time. Really."

"Go away, Jenny."

Samantha wasn't sure whether or not Jenny left, but she stopped knocking on the door. Samantha squeezed her pillow tight. All hope of enjoying the rest of the day was forgotten.

Matt walked into the small Frostburg Police Station on Water Street. The front room had three desks. A stove sat in the corner, unlit right now. A door led to the jail cells in the back.

The sole police officer in the room was speaking with another man dressed in a black suit and wearing a fedora.

"We can't help you," the officer said the man. "We are only Frostburg police. The place you are talking about is in Eckhart Mines or at least closer than we are to it."

Matt's ears perked up. What was going on in Eckhart Mines that needed police help? Were they going to try to roust the union men from town? They would need a lot of help because the union would resist.

"I can deputize you to help," the man in the fedora said.

The policeman shook his head. "You need the county deputies. The sheriff should be able to loan you some. The county's been hiring enough of them because of the strike."

All the violence and other problems related to the strike had forced the Allegany County commissioners to hire dozens of extra deputies for the Georges Creek area, which ran along the western border of the count.

"That will take too much time," the man said. "We want to move on it tonight."

"It's just one still?"

A still in Eckhart Mines? The operation Enos worked for?

"It's the largest operation we've seen around Frostburg. If we shut them down, it will cripple illegal operations hereabouts."

The policeman snorted. "Don't kid yourself. It may be a large operation, but there must over 100 stills in this area. Shutting down one large still will barely be felt."

"It will put those other moonshiners on notice."

"What do you have against people drinking?" the policeman asked.

"It's illegal by virtue of the National Prohibition Act of 1919," the man in the fedora said.

"But why?"

"The people voted for it, and Congress approved it. My God, man, they changed the Constitution for it."

"Why go to all that trouble? If someone doesn't want to drink liquor, don't. I don't like buttermilk, so I just don't drink it. I'm not trying to get a law passed to stop everyone from drinking buttermilk."

The man, who Matt assumed was a federal agent, threw his hands in the air and groaned. Then he turned and stormed out past Matt.

"He's not too happy," Matt said.

The police officer chuckled. "He's a new revenuer assigned to this area, and he comes in just about every day wanting us to drop everything and help him with his job. We're supposed to help if it's in town, but we don't have to do a wit if it's outside town borders."

Matt nodded.

"Can I help you with something?" the policeman asked.

"I'm looking for information about the David Lakehurst case," Matt said.

"Why do you want to know?"

"I'm a friend of the plaintiff. I am curious why it is taking so long to go to court."

Matt had decided if Lakehurst would not leave the county, then the best thing was for him to be in jail, since he seemed to be trying to find Jenny.

"I'm surprised your friend hasn't told you," the police officer said.

"Tell me what?"

"The charges were dropped."

"Dropped. Why?"

"You'll have to ask your friend. She came in here a week or so back and said she wanted the whole thing done with."

"But it was a criminal case."

"It was a case the state's attorney can't win if your friend won't testify. When she said she wouldn't testify, he dropped the case."

He was right. Without Jenny testifying, Lakehurst would walk free unless other women could be found whom he beat up, but that had gone nowhere so far, if Jenny had even tried.

Matt thanked the police officer. He walked over to Samantha's house to see Jenny. Hopefully, the Havencrofts would be out since it was mid-day.

He went to the kitchen and knocked on the door. Jenny answered, dressed in her maid's uniform.

"Hi, Matt, Samantha's not here. She was home for a little while, but then she went out again."

Matt nodded. "That alright. I want to talk to you."

Jenny smiled. She was a beautiful woman about Enos' age.

"Come inside and sit down. Do you want something to drink?"

She was taking to her new job very well.

Matt walked inside and sat down at the kitchen table. Jenny brought him a glass of lemonade.

"Jenny, I've just come from the police."

She hesitated and then smiled, "You're not in trouble again, are you?"

"I asked them why it was taking so long for the Lakehurst case to come to trial. Imagine my surprise when they told me you dropped the charges."

Jenny lowered her head but said nothing.

"Why?" Matt asked.

"He was looking for me, Matt. He was looking for me that night in Gunter's, and he threatened to do worse to me than he did the night he beat me."

"That's why he needs to be in jail."

"They wouldn't have done anything to him. He's a respectable man, a Pinkerton agent. I'm just a…"

Matt patted her hand. He had also realized that would be a problem, which is why he would have testified as a Pinkerton agent. It would have been one agent's word against another. No need to tell Jenny that now, though.

"He won't go away, Jenny," Matt said.

"Maybe not, but I won't have to deal with him now. I don't have time for the clubs now, and when I do go, I don't much dress like I did. I'm working now, honest work."

"And if he sees you and recognizes you? What's to stop him from doing something to you again since he got away with it once?"

Jenny sighed and looked away. "I'm sorry, Matt. I just couldn't take the chance and ruin things now that they are going so well for me. A trial might have been in the newspaper. Mr. Havencroft would have read about it and what I used to do."

Matt rubbed his eyes. "Well, what's done is done."

He stood up. "If he does show up, and I'm not saying he will, go to the police or call me."

Jenny nodded. "Thank you for not being mad."

"I just want you to be safe, Jenny."

He hugged her, and then he left through the back door.

When Matt got back to the boarding house, he went to Enos's room, but his uncle was already out, and Matt could guess where. He headed out toward the one still location he knew about on the mountain. This would be where the raid would happen, and Matt wanted to make sure his uncle wasn't there.

The two guards on the trail challenged him as he approached. Both of them carried rifles.

"I'm looking for Enos," Matt said. "Is he here?"

The guard on the left said, "He came by an hour or so ago. I haven't seen him come down."

"I need to talk to him. I was in the police station a little while ago and heard a revenue agent talking about raiding a still in this area. I figure it has to be this one."

The guard nodded. "We know. Word came down about it already, and we're packing up what we can."

Word came down? It seemed the still owner bribes to the local police were paying off.

The guards let Matt pass, and he followed the worn trail through the brush and trees up the mountain. The clearing bustled with activity. Half a dozen men loaded bottles of moonshine into a truck. The liquor was the most-valuable thing in the clearing. Once the moonshine was loaded, the truck rattled down the road. Next, the still was broken down, and the parts loaded into another truck. The mash vats were drained of liquid and then lifted onto the truck. The men worked with precision as if this was not the first time they did this routine.

Matt saw his uncle carrying a copper boiler to a car.

"Enos, you've got to get out of here. The police will be here any time," Matt said.

Enos nodded. "We know. We've got to save what we can. The police are stalling the raid, but this new revenue agent in the county moved without them."

As if on signal, police appeared out of the woods.

"Everyone stop and get on your knees!" the revenue agent from the police station yelled.

A few men did as they were told. Some bolted for the trees. One man raised his pistol, and a police officer shot him.

The revenue agents, a pair of Frostburg Police, and half a dozen Allegany County Sheriff's deputies made up the raiding party. Although Matt had heard the policeman say Frostburg Police must stay within the town boundaries, the revenue agent must have convinced them to take part in the raid.

Enos raised his hands over his head and dropped to his knees. Matt looked around, and searched for a way out.

"Get down, Matt," Enos told him. "It's all right."

"We're about to be arrested."

He was too far away from the woods to make it without being stopped or shot. He might use the car as cover for a few feet, but he would be in the open before he reached the trees.

Enos nodded. "It happens. Vincent Gambrill will bail us out. We got most everything out we could. This would have been the last load."

The agents handcuffed the six men in the clearing. One agent bandaged the wounded moonshiner who had a shoulder wound. Once the moonshiners were all handcuffed, the police marched them down the trail toward Eckhart.

"How do you think they found out?" Enos asked.

"This place is not exactly a secret, Enos. It's been protected in part, because people don't support Prohibition," Matt said.

The moonshiners were taken to the Frostburg jail, which was crowded when eight men were put into two cells. Enos explained to his nephew how Vincent Gambrill wouldn't leave his men in jail, both out of loyalty and caution. He didn't want anyone turning state's evidence against him.

"How is Vincent Gambrill going to know we're in jail?" Matt asked.

Enos rolled his eyes. "We knew the police were coming. When we don't arrive with the last load, what do you think he'll think?"

Matt also realized the moonshiners had known the police were coming, which also meant Vincent knew his men were in jail.

"Why are you doing this, Enos? This may not be the last time you're in jail."

His uncle leaned against the wall. "I didn't plan on doing this. When the strike started, I looked for work. This was a good opportunity, and the money is great. I enjoy being able to help the family with extra money."

"But you're in jail."

"And I'll get out. Besides, I get to drive this beautiful car that goes eighty miles an hour. It's like riding a lightning bolt."

Matt shook his head. It was probably more the car than the money that Enos took the job. His fascination with cars was becoming an obsession.

The cells were so small that with four men in them, Matt couldn't pace. There wasn't enough room for everyone to sit on the bed, so he sat cross-legged on the floor.

They had only been in the cells for an hour when one of the police officers walked back. He unlocked the cell doors.

"Vincent Gambrill posted your bail," the police officer said. "You're all free to go."

The moonshiners filed out, but the police officer put a hand on Matt's chest when he tried to leave.

"Not you," the policeman said. "Gambrill only posted bail for his men."

"But I got caught in the raid, too."

The cop shook his head. "Sorry. Your name wasn't on the list."

Matt sighed and stepped back into the cell. Enos clapped him on the shoulder.

"Don't worry, I'll tell Vincent about you. I'm sure he'll post bail for you soon. I won't leave you here for long, Matt. Toni will kill me as it is."

Matt wasn't so sure. Vincent Gambrill didn't know him. He had no loyalty toward him. Matt also doubted that the family had enough spare money to post bail for him.

The group of moonshiners headed toward the front door. Enos glanced over his shoulder at Matt, and then he also went out front.

Matt lay down on the now empty bunk. Nothing to do now but wait. He napped and dreamed of being rich with a wife, but her face changed between Priscilla, Samantha, Laura, and even Jenny.

A half an hour later, the deputy came back and unlocked the cell door.

"Your bail was posted."

"By Vincent Gambrill?"

The deputy shook his head.

Matt walked down the hall to the front room and saw John Havencroft signing a paper.

"Mr. Havencroft."

"Hello, Matt." He turned to the police officer. "Is that all?"

"Yes, sir," the police officer.

John Havencroft put on his brown homburg. "Then let's go, Matt. I don't want to be here any longer than I must."

They walked onto Water Street and climbed into Havencroft's car.

"Thank you for posting my bail. I want you to know that I did nothing..." Matt said.

John held up his hand. "It doesn't matter. What does matter is that you were in jail. My daughter's name has been associated with yours. How do you think it reflects on her when you were in jail?"

"But..."

"I don't want you to see her, Matt. This was just a minor incident, but look at the whole story."

"What story would that be?"

"I believe you care for Samantha and she for you, but you must see that the two of you aren't suited. Samantha has a future somewhere outside of this county, maybe even somewhere outside of this state. She's smart and destined for success once she settles down."

"I agree."

"Then you must see that her becoming a miner's wife would not be her achieving success."

"It would make her happy, though."

"Happiness can be fleeting, Matt. You know her. Do you really believe that matrimony and motherhood would make her happy?"

Matt couldn't answer that because he knew the answer. No, she wouldn't be happy as a miner's wife.

But he wasn't a miner. He so wanted to tell everyone that, but he couldn't. Maybe, just maybe, it was time to tell Samantha.

Chapter 20

May 24, 1922

Matt stood on the sidewalk and looked up at the Havencroft residence. It was a large three-story Victorian house with a wrap-around porch, a sunroom, and a small yard leading to a carriage house used for guests. All befitting, John Havencroft, President of the Frostburg State Normal School. Although Matt had been to this house before, this was the first time since John Havencroft told him not to see Samantha. Matt felt Samantha needed to know the truth about him, before she decided on whether they had a future together.

Yet, by coming here, he risked John throwing him out. He might actually be able to do it, too. John was a former soldier with war experience. Matt thought they had bonded over their shared experience as military men. Matt kept John's request, though it seemed odd, to not tell anyone about John's prior military experience.

Perhaps they had bonded, but that ended where Samantha was concerned.

And now it might end with Samantha, but she needed to know the truth. He took a deep breath, walked up to the door, hesitated a moment, took another breath, and knocked.

The door opened and Matt saw the woman he had been dating

for a couple months.

"Matt, I didn't know you were coming by today," she said.

"I had to meet with someone over at the hotel and thought I would come by and see if you would like to have lunch," Matt told her.

She glanced at her watch.

"Have you eaten already?" he asked.

"No. Lunch would be lovely."

She took Matt's arm as they left the house and started down the street.

"How is your leg?" she asked.

Matt shrugged. "It's almost back to normal. At least I'm not missing any work with the mine shut down."

"Judging by what I read in the newspaper, it doesn't seem close to being resolved."

"I think you're right."

They walked to Charlie's on Main Street. It was where they had first shared a meal, and it had become a favorite of both of them. Charlie's wife was Italian and cooked authentic Italian dishes, but she made excellent hamburgers and fried chicken. The restaurant was small with only half a dozen tables near the front. The kitchen area was in another room behind a pair of bat-wing doors. The floor was white linoleum, although it was dirty. The exposed-brick walls were decorated with bright, colorful scenes of Italy.

"Matt," Samantha said as they were finishing their meal. "I think it might be better if I came to see you from now on."

"Why?" He wondered if she were ashamed of him.

"It's my father. He doesn't want me to see you."

"That's nothing new. He has said that before," Matt said. He wondered if there was anything he could do to win John's approval other than becoming rich. It wasn't a good way for one veteran to treat another.

"He wants me to marry someone acceptable for a college president's son-in-law."

"What about someone who makes his daughter happy?"

"He thinks an appropriate match will make me happy."

Which meant Matt wouldn't make her happy.

"What do you think? You seem to be accepting his view," Matt said.

Samantha hesitated, which worried Matt. Then she said, "My father and I don't often agree."

Matt thought that was an unusual answer because it didn't answer the question. Should be ask again? Did he want to know the answer?

"Matt, I need to know something, and I'm not sure how to bring it up."

It looked like he wasn't the only one with a hard subject to broach between the two of them.

"Just get it out there," Matt said. "Whatever it is, we can talk it out."

Samantha chewed on her lower lip, and then blurted, "Did you make love to Jenny Washington?"

Matt sucked in air. That hadn't been what he expected her to ask. How had she found out about him and Jenny? He shouldn't be too surprised about it. It was bound to slip out at some point with Jenny working in the Havencroft house.

He looked at Samantha. She wouldn't meet his eyes. She was afraid of how he would answer. She was too afraid for someone who wanted to know whether or not he was still a virgin. He needed to be careful about how he answered, or he would make things worse.

"No, I did not make love to her," he said, "but I don't think that's the question you are getting at."

Her eyes flared. "It's not? Then, please, tell me what I am thinking."

"You want to know whether I had sex with Calista."

Tears formed in the corners of Samantha's eyes. "You're playing word games."

"No, I'm not." Matt took a deep breath. He'd been dreading Samantha finding out about this and given a lot of thought about what he would say to her. "You've seen for yourself that Jenny

212

and Calista are two different people. Jenny's the person you hired. Calista is a role she played. Yes, I had sex with Calista when I first came to Western Maryland. It was before I met you. It was a business transaction, and it was just one time. There was no love involved with it. However, since then, I have gotten to know Jenny because I have seen her in Frostburg. I like Jenny. You do, too. She has been a friend, and I hope I have been her friend."

Samantha closed her eyes and shook her head. "I can't believe you would allow me to have her work in my house."

"Why not? You knew about Calista. You gave her the job, and it solved her problem."

"But I didn't know she was your ex-lover."

Matt shook his head. "No, that's what I'm getting at. Jenny's not my ex-lover. Calista was, and love had nothing to do with it. I had a need that night, and she approached me at the right time."

"But you had sex with her. We haven't, and you say you love me."

"I do."

"But what do you think when you see her in my house? Do you picture her naked? Do you imagine sleeping with her again?" She sounded desperate or afraid of what he might say.

Matt sighed. "No, I see my friend, and I see her happy, and I know she has the woman I love to thank for that."

Samantha balled her fists, and they quivered. "I can't. I can't. I need to think."

She stood up and hurried out of the restaurant, leaving Matt sitting alone.

Joseph wiped his mouth on the linen napkin and laid it on top of the dinner plate. He pushed the plate away and smiled. Everything looked perfect. The dining room was lit with candlelight. A fire burned in the fireplace, warming the room. Laura sat across from him at the dining room table.

He picked up a glass of burgundy and sipped at it. This was one of his reserve bottles. He had stocked up on liquor and wine before Prohibition started. He had tasted moonshine before and had no desire to make a habit of drinking it. He wondered how much money he could get for the liquor collection hidden in his basement.

Laura must enjoy the wine. She was on her third glass. He didn't mind. It made her less nervous.

"Did you enjoy the meal?" Joseph asked.

Laura set her glass on the table. She wore the new dress Joseph had given her the money to buy. It was nice, although not as elegant as Joseph would have hoped. She had picked out a blue-checked dress with a high hemline. Joseph would have preferred to see her in a shimmering flapper dress, but he wasn't with her when she bought it.

Laura dabbed at her mouth. "Everything was delicious."

"I tried to get your favorites. Did I get it right?"

The meal had comprised fried chicken, sweet potatoes, cole slaw, and green peas. It wasn't what Joseph considered a romantic meal, but he had selected foods he heard her mention in the past as favorites.

"Oh, yes, everything was perfect. I can't remember the last time I had a meal with all of my favorite foods," Laura said.

Joseph smiled. So far, things had gone just as he had planned. The setting was perfect. Laura looked lovely. Dinner conversation hadn't touched on any subjects that might derail his plans like her son, her dead husband, or Matteo Ansaro.

He stood up. "And now it is time for dessert."

Laura shook her head. "I don't think I could eat anything else, Joey."

He stepped around to the side of the table where Laura was sitting and held out his hand to her. "It's not that type of dessert." She took his hand, and Joseph helped her stand. "Follow me."

Joseph led her upstairs to his bedroom. He left her standing at the closed door.

"Give me a minute," he said.

"What..."

He put a finger on her lips. "Don't say anything. You'll

214

understand in a minute."

He cracked the door and slipped into the bedroom. He took a box of matches from his pocket and lit a match. He lit a candle on the floor. Then he proceeded around the bedroom lighting two dozen candles on shelves, his bureau, and even the floor. That done, he turned on his Victrola and set the needle on Irving Berlin's "Always."

As the music started playing, he opened the door to his room and saw Laura's eyes widen with wonder. He held out his hand and led her inside the room.

"What is all this?" she asked.

"Dessert."

Joseph kissed her as he swung the bedroom door shut. Then he gently lowered her to his bed.

Laura opened her eyes. Her head throbbed. She had drunk too much last night. She turned her head to the left. Joey was gone. She might have thought she imagined last night, except that this bedroom was much nicer than the one in her house.

She sighed. Well, that had happened. She hadn't expected it. She hadn't thought of Joey in that way, and even if she had, she had only been a widow for two months.

What would happen now?

She sat up in bed, and the blanket slipped to her waist. She pulled it back up, although no one was around to see her nakedness. She saw her dress on the floor where it had fallen after Joey undid the buttons.

She put her dress on and slipped into her shoes. As she straightened up from putting on her shoes, she saw herself in the mirror. Her hair was a mess. She needed to run a hairbrush through it, but didn't see one. She ran her fingers through her hair to get it to lie down.

Laura walked down the stairs, hoping to get out of the house without the housekeeper Maizy Middleton seeing her. The woman already disliked her. She allowed Joey to call her Maizy, but she insisted on Laura calling her Mrs. Middleton, even though the woman wasn't married. Knowing Laura had spent the night with Joey would only give her another reason to do so. She walked carefully, testing the floorboards as she stepped and hoped they wouldn't creak. If she could get to the living room, she might be able to sneak out the front door without Mrs. Middleton seeing her if the housekeeper was in the kitchen.

Then Laura had a thought that froze her in mid-step. Had the housekeeper already looked inside the bedroom and seen Laura sleeping? If so, she already knew. How long would it be before the town knew?

Laura wanted to cry. It had been a mistake. She knew that even as Joey had undressed her last night, but between the wine and her affection for Joey, she had given in. Even then, she hadn't planned on staying the night. She had thought when she and Joey were through, she would get dressed and go back to her house. The sex had released a lot of the tension and stress she'd been feeling since Pete had died. She had relaxed and fallen asleep instead.

Jacob! She'd left her son at the Starner Boarding House all night! No! What must they think of her? She had told Toni and Myrna she would pick up Jacob by ten o'clock.

As she walked into the living room and headed toward the front door, someone called, "Good morning, sleepy head."

Laura turned and saw Joseph sitting at the dining room table. He was dressed and smoking on a cigar as he read the newspaper.

"I had Maizy hold breakfast until you could join me," Joey said. "I'm glad you finally got up. I was getting hungry."

No! Mrs. Middleton knew about her. Joey wouldn't mind. He was an independent person who kept himself above the rest of the town. Laura wasn't like that. She lived among these people, and it would spoil her reputation.

Joey stood up and walked over to her. He kissed her on the cheek and took her by the hand. "Come. Sit down and have breakfast."

Laura shook her head. "I can't, Joey. I left Jacob overnight with Toni and Myrna. They will all be wondering what happened to me. I told them I would be back for him at ten last night."

"I'm sure that Jacob's fine."

216

"Yes, I am, too, but I don't want to impose more than I have to on Toni and Myrna. They aren't charging me to watch him."

Joey frowned. "Well, at least come eat breakfast before you go. You must be hungry after last night."

Laura suddenly felt closed in in this big house. She needed to get out.

"I can't, Joey. I've got to go." She kissed him on the cheek. "I will talk to you later."

She hurried out the door before he could stop her. The sun was out, and it was already getting warm. She walked down the National Road wishing she had worn a dress that wasn't so fancy. She stood out because she was dressed for the evening. She kept her head down and hurried along.

She didn't bother to change. She just wanted to get Jacob, apologize for being so late, and lock herself in her house for the rest of the day.

She knocked on the door to the boarding house. Toni answered it.

"Toni, I'm so sorry to have left Jacob here overnight," Laura blurted out before the older woman could say anything. "I fell asleep and only just now woke up."

Toni looked her up and down. She knew Laura had gone to dinner with Joseph, and her gaze told Laura that Toni knew just what had happened afterwards.

"That's fine. I should thank you. Jacob actually kept Enos home last night. They had fun playing on the floor with some wooden animals Samuel carved. Then we made up the sofa and let Jacob sleep there."

Laura sighed. "Did he cry? Did he miss me?"

"No, Enos tired him out. He's still sleeping. Come inside and see."

Toni stepped back and Laura walked inside. The sofa was on the right, and Jacob was curled into a tight ball under a patchwork quilt.

Laura kneeled down beside him and stroked his hair. Then she kissed him on the forehead.

"Wake up, sleepy head." She froze, realizing she had just called Jacob what Joey had called her earlier.

Jacob stirred, mumbled, and then opened his eyes. When he saw Laura, he smiled.

"Mama!"

"Good morning, baby. Are you ready to go home?"

He reached out and put his arms around her neck. With a slight grunt, she stood up, still holding him.

"Again, I'm so sorry for the trouble I caused," Laura said.

"It's all right. Enos will miss having a playmate."

"I will thank him when I see him, too."

"Aunt Toni, is there coffee ready?" Matt said as he walked into the living room. "Oh," he said when he saw Laura.

He looked her up and down, and she knew he understood what had happened. He frowned. He knew. Matt knew why she was dressed this way so early in the morning. He hated Joey, and he would hate her for this.

"You look very pretty," he said.

Laura looked away, blushing. "Thank you."

"Would you like me to carry Jacob back to the house for you? He doesn't look like he's in the mood to walk."

"I can take care of my son," Laura snapped. She hadn't meant to say it like that. She knew Matt was just trying to help, but Jacob was her son. She could take care of him. She would do what was best for him.

"I'm sorry," Laura said. "I haven't eaten yet this morning."

"Would you like to have breakfast with us? It will be ready soon," Toni offered.

Laura shook her head. "No, I want to get home and relax. Thank you again for watching Jacob for me. I'm sorry it turned out to be a lot longer than I said."

Matt opened the door for her. As Laura walked by him, she tried to read his expression. Was there hate? Pity? Disgust? She knew he hated Joey. What would he be thinking about someone who slept with him?

She kissed the top of Jacob's head. She needed to do what was best for him. He was all that mattered to her. Not Matt's or anyone else's opinion.

Chapter 21

June 9, 1922

Jenny sat at the kitchen table with the Havencroft family silver spread before her. She polished each piece lovingly, and dreamed that someday, maybe someday, she would have her own silver. Of course not as grand as this, when bang! the front door slammed, jolting her out of her reverie. It surprised her because she couldn't remember another time when she heard such a loud noise in the house. The Havencrofts were a quiet family.

She placed the pitcher on the table and tip-toed to the dining room doorway, and poked her head through the half open door. Mr. Havencroft stomped across the floor with his fists clenched against his sides. He threw his head up and spotted her, his eyes blazing.

"Jenny! Come out here!" he shouted.

That didn't bode well. She hesitantly stepped into the dining room.

"Yes, Mr. Havencroft?"

"Did you think I wouldn't find out?"

"Find out what?" Although she knew what he meant. Only one thing would cause such anger from him.

"Your… work before you came to this house." He was red in the face and looked as if he could barely keep from yelling again.

"I didn't try to hide it from you, Mr. Havencroft."

John Havencroft snorted. "Hide it? You most certainly did."

"No, sir. Miss. Havencroft knew…"

"Don't bring Samantha into this! I do not want you associating with her. I do not want her associating with you. She is a respectable young lady."

"Yes, sir, I just meant…"

He held up a finger. "No, no. It doesn't matter what you just meant. Your services are no longer required here." He pointed to the front door.

Jenny gasped.

"But sir, I've done a good job for you," she said.

"It doesn't matter. I can't have a whore working in my home. What would people say? I am president of the college. I need to set an example for my students to follow, and what sort of example do I set if I allow," he was sputtering now, "you to stay?"

"But sir, I didn't do… I mean since you hired me I haven't…" she started to say.

"It doesn't matter. People know you. People have seen you coming into this house; people who know what you are." He took a deep breath and tried to calm himself. "You need to leave. You need to leave now."

What she was? Was she only what she did for work and work she no longer did? If that was true, was she not seen as a wife, as a daughter? Long before resorting to selling herself, she was a wife, and she was still a daughter.

Jenny started crying. She fled into the kitchen. Mrs. Fratelli saw her and put an arm around her shoulders.

"I have to go, Mrs. Fratelli," Jenny told her.

"I know, dear. I heard."

"Then you know about me?"

"I've known for awhile. It was no secret really. I've seen you around town. Like I said when you first started, as long as you were a good worker and did your share, I would not condemn you. Life takes people to different places."

Jenny hugged the older woman and headed up the servants'

stairs to the room in the attic where she lived. The bed, desk, chair, and bureau were not fancy, but they were better quality than those in the house where she had been living. She packed her clothes and personal items. It all fit in two suitcases.

She walked downstairs. Mrs. Fratelli handed her a bag filled with food.

"I couldn't think of anything else to do for you," she said. "At least you won't need to worry about a few meals."

Tears ran down Jenny's cheeks. "Thank you."

"Take care of yourself."

Jenny nodded and left through the back door. She walked along the street in a daze, not sure of where to go or what to do. She made her way back to her house before she realized it was no longer her house.

When she did, she dropped her suitcases and sat down on the ground, sobbing.

Never had it seemed so dirty, so small, like her life. What was she going to do now? Go back to a life she had started thinking she had escaped?

Matt started up the walk to the front door of Samantha's house. He needed to work things out with Samantha. He had to get her to understand he didn't love Jenny. He loved her.

He hesitated as he raised his hand to knock. What if Samantha's father answered? He told Matt he didn't want him to see his daughter.

He walked around to the kitchen door and knocked lightly. Mrs. Fratelli answered.

"Is Samantha home?"

She glanced over her shoulder. "No sir, I don't quite know where she's at, and Mr. Havencroft, he's in a state. You probably don't want him seeing you right now."

"Why's that?" Matt asked, figuring it had something to do with him.

She lowered her voice to a near whisper. "Well, he found out something about Jenny Washington, and he fired her."

"Jenny? What? What did he find out?"

Though there could only be one thing about Jenny that would make John Havencroft feel he needed to fire her.

"It's not for me to say, sir. I don't want to be spreading rumors about that poor woman. She's going to be facing enough problems now without a job. Do you want me to tell Miss Samantha you were here?"

Matt shook his head. "No, I'll find another time to talk to her."

He left the Havencrofts and headed straight to Jenny's old house. He didn't think she would be there, but it was the only place he could think to look for her. She would be upset about what had happened. He knew somehow John had found out about Jenny's work as Calista. Given how John had reacted to Matt's moonshining arrest, his reaction to Jenny's past would not have been calm, to say the least.

Matt found Jenny sitting on the ground along Water Street. He walked up and sat down next to her. She looked at him and then leaned her head against his shoulder.

"I heard," Matt said.

He wondered how John had found out about her, but then, how had he known Matt had been arrested?

"No surprise. It had to come out sometime." Her voice was slurred. Had she been drinking? He didn't see a bottle, but she wouldn't keep it out in the open.

"Not necessarily. I wonder how he found out."

"Samantha."

"You think it was her, really?" The thought had crossed his mind, but Matt wasn't so sure. It didn't seem like something she would do.

"Of course it was her. She found out about what we did, and this happens."

It could be a coincidence, but it just didn't ring true.

"It's not her like her to be sneaky like that," Matt said.

Jenny shrugged. "I don't know. Maybe it wasn't her. It doesn't matter either way. I don't have a job anymore."

"Will Mr. Havencroft give you a reference?"

"He fired me, Matt. He's not going to give me a reference," Jenny said.

"What about Samantha then?"

"Not if she's the one who told him. You know I liked it. I enjoyed being in that house. The work was something I could do that was respectable. I didn't have to worry about the way people looked at me."

"Maybe you need to get out of town at least for a little while and pull yourself together."

"And go where? I can't go back to my family in Pennsylvania. I'm not even sure they're still there. I will have to go back to what I was doing in the evenings. Most of the time it wasn't too bad. There were things about it I enjoyed, but no job's perfect, right?" She gave a short laugh that abruptly cut off.

"Is that what you want to do?" Matt asked.

"Does anybody really want to do that?"

He'd never thought much about it. "I don't know. If a guy could get paid for having sex, he might."

"It depends on who he was having sex with, you know what I mean? I've got to do something though. I don't even have that shack I was living in."

Matt saw an opportunity. He had put aside his idea concerning Jenny when she had gotten work with the Havencrofts. Now she no longer had the job.

"I have an idea. I've been trying to help my family with expenses because of the strike. We don't have much in the way of money coming in, but my aunt won't accept my money."

"Why not?"

"I can't say. Let's just say she looks at where that money comes from, the way Mr. Havencroft looked at the way you used to earn your money. If you were to move into our empty room, I could pay your room and board. You'd be living free, and my family would get money."

The family Toni had taken in that been displaced by strikebreakers had pulled up their roots and moved to Cumberland a week ago because the husband had found work in the Kelly tire plant.

"But you can't keep doing that. You can't keep paying my expenses. What happens when the strike ends, and you won't need to be sending extra money to your family?" He knew this would be a short-term solution, but it was one that helped everyone.

"I don't know. I only know they need the money now, and this is a way around my aunt's objection, and it gives you a chance to get out of Frostburg where people know your face. You can get a fresh start."

"I doubt there's much call for maids in Eckhart."

"No, you're right about that, but maybe you can get a job in Cumberland and take the trolley to work. It just gives you time to think through things. Sometimes you have to go one step at a time."

Jenny fell backwards, so she was lying on the ground.

"Are you sure you can get me in?" she asked.

"Yes, we can go down now and make arrangements."

Jenny hesitated and then nodded. Matt helped her to her feet and picked up her suitcases.

"Let's grab the trolley, so you can get moved in."

They caught the trolley near the Hotel Gunter. On the trip to Eckhart, Matt described the house and the household routine. He also gave her enough money to pay for her first week's rent.

When they walked in the front door, Matt called out, "Aunt Toni!"

"I'm in the kitchen, Matt, you don't need to yell." She walked into the living room, wiping her hands on her apron.

"Aunt Toni, do you remember my friend Jenny Washington? She needs a place to stay."

Toni shook Jenny's hand. "I remember when she came to see you after you got yourself beaten up. What happened to where you were staying, Jenny?"

Jenny glanced at Matt. "My roommate got married and moved out. I couldn't afford the place where we were living on my own."

Matt was surprised at how easily Jenny lied, but then, she used to create a whole separate life when she worked as a prostitute.

"Well, I have a room to let, but you will be living with miners," Toni said.

Jenny nodded. "Matt explained that to me, but you and your sister-in-law also live here, so I won't be the only woman."

Toni smiled. "No, but we are related to some of these men. You aren't. There's also the question of your... other work."

Jenny blushed. "You don't need to worry, ma'am. I'm not doing that anymore. I was working as a maid before I was let go."

Toni nodded but still looked skeptical.

"I have the money to pay." Jenny dug into her purse and pulled out the money that Matt had given her on the trolley.

Toni counted out the money and said, "That will cover it. Let me take you up to see your room. Welcome to the household."

As Toni and Jenny walked up the stairs, Jenny glanced over her shoulder and smiled at Matt.

Laura walked into her house and was struck by its small size. She had never felt like she was struggling as much as she did now that Joey had showed her an easier and grander life. Was it worth it?

She was tempted to fall over and take a nap, but things still needed doing around the house. She had supper to cook, laundry to wash, and a child to bathe. That boy could get dirty standing still in a church. She also needed to pick him up from the Starner Boarding House.

For now, she just needed a few minutes to rest. She had walked up and down Main Street in Frostburg for the second time in a week. This time, she had even included the side streets as she looked for a business that was hiring. She had already asked around Eckhart three times over and even expanded her search to Lonaconing and Midland. She could reach them on the trolley, although it would make her workday longer. The problem was it didn't look like she would have a workday. No one was hiring. Even the laundries and seamstresses, which needed a lot of help, didn't need it because their work demand had fallen off with the coal strike. Miners, who couldn't work in the mines, had taken all the other open jobs in town. It was not the time to be looking for work.

The front door flew open, Jacob came running in.

"Mama!" he shouted as he jumped onto the sofa and hugged her. She hugged him back and kissed him on the top of his head.

Myrna Ansaro came hurrying in behind him. She sat in a chair and tried to catch her breath.

"Tell me how a boy with short legs can outrace me so easily," she asked.

"Your legs may be twice as long, but he moves his five times faster. I know from experience. I hope he wasn't any trouble."

Myrna shook her head. "No trouble. He's a delight. He's so curious about everything. He helped me with the wash, and he helped Toni in the kitchen."

"We made cookies, and walked to the stores, and Miss Myrna read me stories," Jacob said quickly.

"Thank you for watching him, and thank Toni, too."

"We enjoy it. He makes the day go by quickly." Myrna stood up and rubbed Jacob's hair. "He even helps where he can. Just let us know anytime you need someone to watch him." She paused. "Any luck today?"

Laura shook her head. "Anything that was open a month ago has long been filled by an out-of-work miner."

Myrna nodded. "Sitting around with no work is driving Samuel crazy. He can only chop so much firewood for people."

"Right now, I'd settle for chopping firewood," Laura said, half seriously. Although she couldn't handle a lot of wood chopping, she needed to find work. Her savings, what little she had, were nearly gone.

Myrna waved good-bye and left. Jacob got out his toy soldiers and spread them on the floor to begin his imaginary war game. Laura sat on the sofa weary from an unsuccessful day. She heard a knock on the door, but couldn't bring herself to get up. Her feet had stopped throbbing, but she just didn't feel like walking right now.

"Jacob, please answer the door for Mama?" she asked.

The toddler walked over to the door and pulled it open. Joseph was standing outside. He looked down and saw Jacob.

"Come in, Joey," Laura said.

"I saw you come home and thought I would stop by."

"I was out looking for a job in Frostburg."

He stepped into the house and closed the door behind him.

"Why are you looking for a job?" he asked.

"I need money, of course. I can't stay here. My money is running out. I need a job, but there doesn't seem to be any around here."

Joseph sat down next to her on the sofa. "You look exhausted."

"I am. I walked to and from Frostburg and all around the town talking to business owners about jobs. I didn't eat lunch, so I could have some money."

"Turn to the side," Joseph said.

She did as he asked, and he started rubbing her shoulders. It felt relaxing, although it was her feet that ached, not her shoulders. It eased some tension from her, though. She felt like taking a nap.

"If you are worried about food and rent, why not move in with me?"

Laura stiffened and turned to face him.

"What?"

"Move in with me. I have plenty of room in the house. It's just my housekeeper and me. Jacob can have his own bedroom, and it will be bigger than the one you two share now."

It was so tempting, but would he expect her to be his lover? Was she ready for that?

"I couldn't impose on you, Joseph."

"You wouldn't be. You know how I feel about you. I would love it. It would help you. You wouldn't have to worry about rent or food. You wouldn't even have to do cooking and cleaning because the housekeeper does it. If you still want to look for a job, you can, but there's no rush. And the truth is, I can use this house to put up some of the workers we're getting."

Laura hesitated. It was a generous offer, but it didn't seem right. She would be living with a man she didn't love. That wasn't fair to him. However, she knew her pantry was virtually empty, and she had little money to restock it. She wouldn't allow herself to go back into debt to Mr. Portnoy. Wouldn't she be going into debt to Joey, though?

He was doing her a favor, but what was he getting out of it? He was taking on a family without being a husband or father.

She watched Jacob playing. He was already so thin. He was growing quickly, and she couldn't afford new clothes for him, let alone food to keep him from feeling hungry.

Laura said, "Okay, Joey, I'll move in with you."

Chapter 22

June 12, 1922

Toni left the Eckhart Church where she met with the women of Eckhart, so they could update each other about the displaced families in town. Two more families had left Eckhart Mines seeking jobs out of the area. It spread the burden of the other families in town to house and feed them, but Toni wondered what the town would be like when the strike ended. Once the strikebreakers left and with the families leaving town, Eckhart would look like an Old West ghost town.

It was a shame. Eckhart wasn't a perfect town by any standard, but it was a community. The people watched out for each other and cared. That was changing now. Strikebreakers made up a third of the town now. They were single men, and many of them didn't speak English. It didn't do much to create a sense of community between them and the town.

The businesses in town couldn't support the miners without getting in trouble with Consolidation Coal Company's enforcer. He used intimidation to force pro-union store owners to do business with the strikebreakers. He patrolled the streets and viciously protected the strikebreakers and coal company property. Toni hated the man for what he had done to Matt.

Toni saw a man leave the ice cream parlor licking an ice cream cone. Louis Chabot did a busy side business during the warm days selling homemade ice cream.

She didn't recognize the man, which meant he was probably a strikebreaker.

"Good afternoon, Mrs. Starner," he said with a heavy Irish accent, as he touched the brim of his hat with two fingers in a jaunty salute.

"Good morning," she said automatically. Then she stopped. "Excuse me, have we met?"

"Not officially." He spoke hesitantly, as if English wasn't his native language. More likely, he was trying to speak clearly and minimize his accent.

He was a light-skinned man with blond hair that was almost white. He had an erect posture, which marked him as military in her mind, because she had seen other former soldiers with the same bearing.

"I was with the group of miners who bothered you when you walked by the other week." He didn't meet her eyes as he spoke.

Toni remembered the incident and stiffened. Then she remembered this man. "You were the one who tried to stop them and got into a fight."

He gave her a quick nod. "Yes, ma'am. I didn't like what they were saying to a lady like yourself." Lady. He said it like it was her station in life, not her sex.

"How do you know my name?" Toni asked.

"I asked. You are well liked in town."

Toni didn't know about that, but it was nice to hear. She was curious why this man needed to know her name.

"Well, thank you for defending me, Mr...." she said.

"Kennedy, Paul Kennedy."

"Thank you, Mr. Kennedy."

"May I walk you back to your home?"

Toni froze. She stared at Paul.

"Oh, no, I don't think so," she said.

Paul nodded. "Yes, I understand. I am a worker for Consolidation Coal Company, and you don't like strikebreakers."

"Well, yes, you could say that is true."

"It can be hard to deal with bias."

"Bias?" Toni repeated, raising her eyebrows and implying a question.

"Yes, that is the correct word, isn't it?" Paul asked. "You have decided you don't like strikebreakers without knowing all of them. It is like hating Jewish people or Italians or even my people early last century."

That stung. Toni didn't consider herself biased, although it she certainly looked that way to this man.

"But I do know all strikebreakers, or at least I know the reason I don't like all strikebreakers. You are all taking a job from a union worker."

Paul held up a finger. "No, ma'am, I must disagree with you about that. We don't take a job from a union worker. The jobs are open because the union miners walked away. We are hired, knowing our work will not be for long. We are hired to fill an open job until the strike is settled. When the union miners return, we leave, so you see we are not taking a job from anyone who wants one. If anything, the union miners are taking jobs from us because we are fired to make room for them."

"But you make it harder for the union to win a strike."

"I have nothing against the union. It is not for me, but I have nothing against the union or anyone who joins one. I must work, though. I must eat. When the work is available, I take it," Paul explained.

Toni started to walk away.

"I am sorry I have offended you. I did not mean to do so," Paul said.

"You haven't. I just don't see the point of this conversation," Toni told him.

The Irishman smiled. "No? I thought it was obvious. I wanted to get to know you."

"Why?"

"You are a beautiful woman, but beauty fades, although yours has not yet. I wanted to see if the person you are is as interesting as the person you appear."

Toni felt herself blushing despite her best effort not to. How long had it been since a man had complimented her or looked at her considering her beautiful? His Irish accent was lilting and, she must admit, charming.

"I'm sorry, Mr. Kennedy. I can't offer you what you seem to want."

"Conversation? You have already done that."

"A relationship."

Toni forced herself to walk away before Kennedy could find a way to extend the conversation any longer. She was surprised she had spoken to him as long as she had. She hadn't said more than a word or two to any strikebreaker.

As she approached the house, she saw Enos sitting on the front porch with Matt's friend, Jenny. She was a friendly woman, but bringing her into the same house as Matt could be a problem since Jenny loved him.

Enos waved when he saw Toni.

"What are you two doing out here?" Toni asked.

"We are enjoying the day, and I am telling Jenny about the strike."

"What about the strike?"

"There are a lot of problems going on with both sides. Men are getting beaten. A few have been shot. Two houses have been set on fire and a coal tipple, and that's just in Allegany County. It's just as bad or worse in other places."

That was no surprise. Matt had been beaten here in town. Luckily, no one had been shot, although she wasn't sure how long that would last with David Lakehurst walking around with a pistol on his hip.

"How do you know all that?" Toni asked.

Enos grinned. "I do more than drive, Toni. I talk to the people I meet."

"Enos said he would take me on a ride in his car and show me how fast it goes," Jenny said.

"His car?" Toni asked.

Enos smirked and shrugged. "It's the car I drive, so in a way,

233

it's my car."

Toni rolled her eyes and shook her head.

"Toni, you and Jenny share something in common. Did you know you both are widows?"

Toni looked at Jenny. The woman still appeared young, unlike Toni who had married late.

"I'm sorry to hear that," Toni said.

"He was a wonderful man. He was a coal miner, but he died in the war. He is buried in France somewhere. I have never seen his grave. We had a memorial service for him here, but it wasn't the same. It doesn't feel like he's actually dead because I never saw the body."

"We nearly lost Matt in the war, and we didn't even know about it until he came home."

"I know." She patted her neck, showing she knew where the scar came from.

"You and Matt talk about a lot it seems. How did you meet him?"

Jenny hesitated and then answered, "We met at a previous job I had. I worked as a maid before I was let go."

It was a lie, but Toni was glad that Jenny was trying to protect Matt's reputation.

"Is that why you keep trying to clean the house for me?" Toni asked.

Jenny shrugged. "I just want to feel useful."

That was more than any of the men in the household were doing. They treated the strike like a vacation except for Enos, oddly enough. He was the only one in the house still working, even if it was illegal work.

Toni smiled, "While I appreciate it, you don't need to do that. You pay for you room and board."

"Maybe she thinks it's fun," Enos said.

"Only a man would say that, Enos," his sister told him.

Toni went inside the house. Dinner still needed to be prepared, and Myrna would need help.

Chapter 23

June 17, 1922

It was dinnertime when David Lakehurst entered the boarding house for single miners. He knew he would find all the men living here at this time. They wouldn't miss a meal they were already paying for out of their wages. Joseph McCord had crammed so many men into the house that an extra table had been added in the living room to feed everyone at once. Fourteen strikebreakers lived in a house where seven miners usually lived.

The men looked up at him when he walked into the room, but they didn't stop eating or talking amongst themselves. Smoke filled the room with a gray haze.

He looked over the group. It was a mix of men from different cities and countries. They all looked different, but he was looking for a particular type of man. He looked at their faces, in particular their eyes and noses. Did they have a hard stare? Had their noses been broken in the past? Then he looked at their hands. Were their knuckles scarred?

He found three men who fit the bill and told them to meet him out on the porch of the house.

"After dinner," one man said as he reached for a cob of corn.

David drew his pistol and stuck the barrel in the man's ear. The man froze with his arm stretched out across the table. All the conversation stopped as everyone waited to see what would happen next.

"Do you know who I am?" David asked in a quiet, menacing voice.

"I've seen you around town," the man gulped.

He slowly pulled his arm back and rested it on the table.

"Then you know I don't tolerate backtalk, ever. So if you want there to be an after dinner for you, I would get out on the porch, now."

The man nodded and stood up. He and the other two men hurried out onto the porch. David holstered his pistol and followed them out, as the remaining men at the table resumed eating. Two of the men he had chosen were as large as he. The third man was small, but he had a hard look in his eyes that couldn't be ignored.

"You three are employees of Consolidation Coal Company, and I have company business. I need your help. Meet me at nine o'clock tonight in front of the company store. Don't be late because I wouldn't want to have to come find you. Don't talk about this with anyone. I wouldn't want to have to explain to you the error of your ways. Do I make myself clear?"

The men nodded.

"Fine. Then go eat. I will see you in a few hours."

A nine o'clock, David drove a company truck up to the Eckhart Mines Store and saw six miners waiting for him—the three from the boarding house and three others he had found at the mine earlier in the day.

He let the engine run as he climbed out of the cab and walked over to the strikebreakers.

"We have company business to do tonight," David said. "The reason I chose you is because you look like men who have nerve and can handle yourselves in a fight."

"Is there going to be a fight?" one man asked.

"Maybe. My goal is to get in and do what needs doing and get out. No one should recognize you where we're going, but we don't want to bring the deputies down on us just the same."

The county had hired extra deputies to keep the peace between the miners and company men. Some rural towns even had a deputy assigned to the town.

"When we get where we need to go, I'll let you know what needs doing. Then you're on your own until you finish. Now get in."

The men climbed into the truck bed. Lakehurst drove south along the Georges Creek Road until he reached Carlos, one of the tiny coal towns along Georges Creek. David stopped the truck outside of the town because he didn't want to alert anyone in town they were coming.

Carlos was a strong union town, although the miners weren't union members. The miners had shut down the mine in town, and unlike the mines in Eckhart, this one hadn't reopened. The strikers had been causing trouble for Consolidation Coal, and David meant to break them up.

"There's a union meeting in the school tonight. I want that meeting disrupted and stopped," David explained.

The Pinkerton office had sent David the information, which he assumed came from one of the undercover detectives in the area.

"They'll just meet somewhere else another day," one strikebreaker said.

David nodded. "I know, but I want them nervous that something like what we're about to do will happen wherever they meet... and it may."

David explained what he wanted the men to do. The men picked up the buckets of rocks in the truck bed and carried them with them. David led the group to the small school in town. Light shown through the windows, and all the miners could be seen clearly. The strikebreakers surrounded the school and waited.

David gathered brush onto the porch in front of the door. He took a bottle of gasoline from his pocket and poured the few ounces of gasoline on the brush. Then he lit a match and tossed it into the pile.

Flames shot up as David ran off to hide behind the nearest building.

The strikebreakers saw the flames and started throwing the

rocks in their buckets through the windows. The glass shattered as rocks flew into the classroom from both sides. The miners inside yelled and cursed. They ran for the door, opened it and saw the flames covering their exit. This caused the miners in front of the group to turn back while the miners at the back still pushed forward, adding to the chaos and confusion.

The rocks continued flying into the classroom, some striking the miners who were now clustered near the doors. Smoke from the fire filled the room. It wasn't much because the broken windows allowed it to escape.

The strikebreakers ran out of rocks and ran back to the truck. The miners surged toward the door again.

David drew his pistol and fired into the school above their heads. The miners shouted and dropped to the floor. David emptied his pistol and ran for the truck.

This would be a meeting those miners would never forget.

Matt opened his eyes and lay still in his bed.

What had awakened him?

Then he heard his door open slowly so as not to make much noise. He looked in that direction, but it was too dark to see anything clearly. He could only see shifting blackness, and he wasn't even sure whether it was the door or a person causing it.

He slowly moved his hand up under his pillow and grabbed the pistol he kept there. As a Pinkerton detective, he could never be sure of who might come for him.

"Matt?" a voice whispered.

"Jenny?" he said.

She hurried to his bed and climbed under the sheets with him while he was still trying to figure out what she was doing in his bedroom. She grabbed his face and started kissing him.

He felt a moment of enjoyment before he pushed her back.

"What are you doing?" Matt asked.

"Enjoying myself." She tried to kiss him again, but he pulled away, which wasn't easy to do with her lying on top of him.

"No," he said.

"Why not? It's not like we haven't done it before."

"I'm seeing Samantha. You know that."

"You said she broke up with you."

"I didn't say that. I said we had a fight. She's angry with me. We'll patch things up," Matt said.

Jenny ran her fingers over his lips. "Then why am I here?"

"In my bed? I'm wondering that myself."

She shook her head. "No, why did you bring me to your house and pay for my room and board?"

"To help you. I didn't want you to have to go back to being a prostitute or risk Lakehurst finding you alone. He still might want to hurt you even though you dropped the charges. I saw what you were like when you thought he might come after you."

Jenny threw back the blankets and stood up beside the bed.

"Then you don't want to have sex?" she asked.

She was nude. How had Matt not noticed that? It was distracting. And how had she gotten out of her robe and into his bed so quickly? She bent down and pick up her robe and slip into it.

Matt sighed. "You are pretty and... tempting."

She leaned over the bed. The robe draped open giving him a view of her round breasts. The paleness of her skin gleamed in the pale moonlight that shone through the windows.

"The night we had together was wonderful, but I thought we were past that. We didn't even know each other then. Now we're friends," he said.

"And now that you know me, you don't want to have sex with me?" Jenny asked as she closed her robe and cinched it. "I'm just a whore to you, aren't I?"

Matt sat up. He reached out to take her hands, but it was Jenny who pulled away this time. He knew he needed to be careful about what he said now.

"Even if you were, and, just to be clear, you aren't just a whore, but even if you were, it doesn't mean you should be treated poorly or unkindly. That would make me no better than Lakehurst."

"Then why? Why treat me like I'm special? Why make me

love you?" Jenny's shaky voice sounded as if she were on the verge of crying.

Love him? Toni was right. What had he done to make her feel that way? Was someone offering her kindness so foreign to her she mistook it for love?

"Jenny, honestly, I can't say why I treat you the way I do. Yes, you are a nice person, but there are lots of nice people out there. I think... I think it has to do with that night in the alley. I saw you beat and hurt, and it made me angry that someone would do that to you. You didn't deserve it. I think I decided then to watch out for you. I wanted to protect you because no one else does."

"Protect me? I've been on my own since my husband was killed. I am an independent woman. I got along before you came to town, and I will continue to get along after you and Samantha go off and get married."

He and Samantha married. Was that even possible now? He wanted to smile, but he needed to focus on the conversation.

"I know you are an independent woman, but even an independent woman can't handle Lakehurst. Hell, I'm not even sure I can handle him after what he did to me in the street." He paused and stared at Jenny. He was glad it was dark because he wasn't sure he could handle looking her in the eyes. "Are you mad at me now?"

"How can I be? You didn't do anything wrong. I made the mistake."

"Jenny, that's all it was, a mistake. I don't want you sleeping with me because you feel like I paid for you. I didn't. I wanted to help you because I like you... you and who you are, not what you can do for me."

"What if I wanted to sleep with you? What if I would have done it even if you hadn't paid for my room and board?"

"Then I would be a lucky man, but there's still Samantha."

Jenny nodded. "I guess I'll move back to Frostburg in the morning."

"Why?"

She waved her arms around the room. "Well, because of

this…"

"You don't need to move back. You are still helping me here. I didn't lie to you about that."

"Really?"

He reached out, and this time, she let him hold her hands. "You've met my aunt? What do you think?"

"I think you have a wonderful family, Matt. Toni is kind, and Enos sat with me on the porch this afternoon and had me laughing."

"Then stay, Jenny. Please, help me."

Jenny smiled and nodded.

Chapter 24

June 19, 1922

Laura laid Jacob on the feather mattress. He squirmed as he nestled into the softness of it.

"Mama, I want Miss Toni and Miss Myrna," he said.

She brushed his brown hair out of his eyes. He had played all morning, and his hair was sticking out in all directions.

"They're not here, honey," Laura told him.

"Can we go to their house?"

"Maybe, but we don't need their help anymore. Don't you like our new house and your nice big room and Mrs. Middleton?"

Their move to Joey's house was surprisingly easy. Joey had sent four strikebreakers to her house. They had carried all of her things out of the small house, through town, and up the hill to Joey's house. While she had no worries about the move, she still felt she needed to watch the men carry boxes of clothes and food to their new home. They didn't carry her furniture, though. Joey had told her to leave them because she wouldn't need them in his house. She saw people walk outside their homes to watch the procession of her boxes go from her house into Joey's house. Then they had turned and saw Laura.

Laura felt their stares on her and with it, their disapproval. It had been a mistake to move through town like that, but it was done, and she and Jacob were in their new place and they would, by God, start their new lives.

Joey had purchased rubber balls, toy trucks, and wooden blocks to decorate one of his guest rooms for Jacob, but it still looked like an adult's room. The bookshelves held books Jacob couldn't read. The bed was far too large for a child. The furniture looked too nice for Jacob to touch. It wasn't an inviting room.

"I miss Miss Toni and Miss Myrna," Jacob said.

Laura kissed her son on the forehead. She tucked him into the bed and walked into the hallway of Joey's house. True, she lived here now, but it didn't feel like her house, and she wondered if it ever would. She couldn't even display her and Pete's wedding picture because it made Joey uncomfortable. She kept it in her hope chest and showed it to Jacob when Joey wasn't around so her son wouldn't forget his father.

At least she didn't have to worry about having enough food to feed Jacob.

She looked at the pictures of people she didn't know hanging on the walls. They wore nice clothing, not expensive, but of good quality. Laura didn't have a dress she hadn't repaired multiple times. Or rather, she didn't have a dress from before Pete had died that she hadn't repaired multiple times. Those dresses were in the trash now. Joey had promised her a new wardrobe. The floor was covered in colorful carpets, not the rag rug she had left in her small house. The furniture was well built and sturdy. It looked elegant, which was something of which she was unaccustomed.

Laura walked past the kitchen and saw Mrs. Middleton preparing dinner. Laura had tried to help her when she first moved in, but the older woman had spurned Laura's efforts to be friendly. At least the housekeeper was kind to Jacob.

Laura paused in the living room and looked out the window. The house sat high on Big Savage Mountain and overlooked the Eckhart Mines. She could see her old house. Of course, it wasn't her house any longer. It now had four strikebreakers living in it.

The day was warm, but she didn't want to go outside. When she went into town nowadays, people stared and pointed at her.

They talked about her when she passed by. By now, everyone knew she had moved in with Joey. Even if they didn't know for sure, they had to suspect that she and Joey were lovers. People hated her for that. They thought she was betraying miners because she was sleeping with the mine superintendent. Others thought she was betraying the memory of her dead husband by taking up with someone else so soon.

This was the only way she could get by. She had no choice. She had tried to find work. What was she supposed to do? Prostitute herself?

But wasn't she doing that in a way? Instead of trading sex for money, she was trading it for home and food.

Why did Pete have to die? He had been such a sweet and gentle man. A wonderful husband and father. He worked hard to provide for his family, but most miners had trouble making ends meet. It hadn't been his fault that they never seemed to save enough. If Pete were alive, she would not be in this situation. She would be poor, but she'd be happy.

What would Matt think about her situation? He must have heard about it by now. He'd hate her or at least hate that she got herself into this. He might be her friend, but he hated Joey.

She walked over to Joey's hidden liquor cabinet. He had had recessed shelves installed behind a landscape painting of the Western Maryland mountains. The painting swung out on hinges, revealing three shelves filled with bottles of various liquors. Joey hid his wines in a hidden room in the basement. She still wasn't sure where that one was because she hadn't ventured into the basement.

Laura grabbed the closest bottle and walked across the room. She went into the kitchen and took a glass from the cabinet. Mrs. Middleton watched her with a scowl on her face. Laura tried to ignore her. Carrying the glass, she hurried back into the living room and filled it. The liquor turned out to be vodka. She assumed it was good. Joey wouldn't keep less than the best liquor. She didn't care much for the taste, although it seemed to be growing on her.

After a few drinks, the self consciousness disappeared, and she felt at ease and happy. It was always good to be happy when Joseph came home. He wanted her to be smiling when she came to his bed.

Was this wrong? It felt wrong.

Luckily, when she felt that way, all she had to do was take a drink.

Chapter 25

June 20, 1922

Enos walked along Parkersburg Road, headed into Eckhart from the east. He finished up his nightly deliveries an hour ago, but he stayed in the clearing to sample the newest batch for himself. Now it was four in the morning, and he had to concentrate on walking in a straight line as he headed home.

He might have overindulged the sampling a bit, but he was celebrating. Business was good in Western Maryland, and Vincent Gambrill said he was planning on adding a second car to help on the nightly runs. He wanted Enos to help him pick out the make of car to buy. Enos would spend next few days visiting car dealers and test driving cars with his boss. Thus far, he had only driven the Duesenberg, but he was eager to try out other models on the market.

He hummed the "Three O'clock in the Morning" waltz, now so popular on the radio, as he strolled along, He was feeling very content as he enjoyed the pleasant pre-dawn morning. Everyone was asleep, and all was quiet. Even the tension of the strike was temporarily missing. The lights in the homes were off, and he could see the stars still shining in the sky. He appreciated starlight and moonlight. He considered them his friends. Some nights they were the only things with him, helping him navigate the roads as he avoided police and revenue agents.

Dawn wouldn't start brightening things up for another couple hours, but by then, he hoped to be asleep.

He swung his arms in wide circles to stretch out, but in his current state it nearly knocked him off balance. He staggered a few steps to the left before catching himself.

Enos smelled the smoke before he saw it as a black cloud against the night sky. When he turned the corner onto Store Hill, he saw flames eating away at the front porch of the boarding house. It was spread across the floor in splotches and had started up some posts.

He was instantly sober. Since he didn't see anyone outside, he knew no one had discovered the fire yet.

"Fire, Fire!" he screamed as he ran toward the house.

He couldn't get in the front door with flames spread across it. He ran around to the back door and dashed inside, still yelling, "Fire! Fire!"

Toni hurried out of her room, tying her robe shut around the waist.

"Enos, you had better not be drunk," she said.

Enos pointed to the front of the house. They saw flames in the front window, and the front door was smoldering.

"Oh my God! Fire!" Toni yelled. "Everybody get up! Enos, run upstairs and wake everyone!"

Toni sprinted back down the hallway and pounded on Matt's door. "Matteo, fire, get out!"

His door opened as he pulled his suspenders up with his free hand. "I heard you. I was putting on my pants."

Toni nodded and ran into her bedroom. She started taking pictures off the wall and tossing them onto the bed. Then she stuffed the pictures into a pillowcase to carry outside.

Matt wasn't a heavy sleeper, and Enos' shouts had awakened him. He had wondered if Enos was drunk at first, but then Matt smelled smoke. By the time Toni had banged on his door, he was ready to run out and help.

He could hear other people yelling outside. Hopefully, they

were forming a bucket brigade and not just standing around gawking at the fire.

Matt ran into the living room in his bare feet, but he at least he had his pants on. Smoke filled the room. Flames caused the window to break, and the flames caught the curtains on fire.

He ran into the kitchen and grabbed a pot off the counter. He turned on the water and filled it. Then he threw the water on the living room fire, only to hear it sizzle and do little to douse the fire. Now the sofa was on fire.

Jenny and the other boarders came scurrying downstairs.

"Fill pots from the kitchen!" Matt yelled. "We've got to get this fire put out before it spreads!"

"It's no use," Isaac Thompson said. "The flames went up the wall. They were coming into my room."

Matt threw the pot across the room. This couldn't be happening. Not now. His family needed this house for income.

"Get outside where it's safe," he said.

The miners headed for the back door. Jenny headed in his direction, but he pointed to the back door.

Enos came downstairs carrying two jugs of moonshine.

"Enos, how can you think of that now?" Matt yelled.

Enos looked at the jugs and then at Matt. "I wanted to get them away from the flames. Fire loves this stuff more than I do."

"Where's Samuel and Myrna?"

Enos glanced over his shoulder. "They were right behind me."

Matt waved his uncle toward the back door. "I'll find them. Go ahead out."

Matt coughed from the smoke. He ran upstairs to the second floor. The hallway was dark and filled with smoke. Samuel and Myrna lived in a room on the third floor. He felt his way down the hall with a hand on the wall until he found the bannister leading upstairs.

"Samuel! Myrna!" Matt called.

He heard a cough and Samuel said, "Over here, Matt."

Matt walked toward the sound of his uncle's voice because he couldn't see anything. Then he saw Samuel struggling to carry

Myrna, who was passed out.

"The smoke was too much for her," Samuel said.

It was almost too much for Matt. He could barely breathe in without coughing more air out.

"Here, let me carry her. You look like you're about ready to pass out yourself."

Matt took Myrna from Samuel and slung her over his shoulder. It wasn't the most-dignified position, but it allowed Matt freer movement.

Samuel started down the stairs, and Matt followed him. He was careful where he placed his feet since he didn't know if fire had compromised the staircase yet.

"Use the back door," Matt said.

They went through the kitchen and out the door. Matt laid Myrna on the ground, away from the heat and smoke. He laid his head against his aunt's chest to see if he could hear a heartbeat.

"Is she going to be all right?" Samuel asked.

Matt leaned close to his aunt. He could feel her breath on his cheek.

"She's breathing. That's a good sign. She probably just needs to get all that smoke out of her lungs."

"What happened? How did the fire start?"

Matt shook his head. "I don't know. Maybe Enos saw what happened. His yelling woke me up."

The fire had started creeping around the sides of the house. Matt saw occasional flames poke out from around the corners.

Myrna coughed. Samuel dropped to the ground beside her. He lifted her head and rested it in his lap.

"Myrna, we're out of the house," Samuel told her. "You're going to be all right."

Matt put a hand on his uncle's shoulder. "I'm going out front to help the others try to put out the fire."

Samuel waved him off. "Go, go."

Matt ran around to the front of the boarding house. A line of men and women had formed at the well to the house next door to the boarding house, and buckets of water were being passed along.

"Did someone call the fire department?" Matt asked.

"I did. They're on their way." Matt was surprised to see it was Portnoy who answered him. The older man was also on the bucket line.

If the fire department didn't get here soon, the house would be lost. It had already progressed in the brief time that Matt had run out of the house. The front door was burning, as well as the front porch. He could also see flames on the second floor.

Samuel walked around from the back of the house. He was holding Myrna by the waist. She looked like she would fall over if Samuel had let go. She was coughing, but she was conscious and on her feet.

Samuel looked at the fire and said, "This isn't a natural fire."

"How do you know?" Matt asked as he stared at the flames.

"Look at it. It started on the porch. What started it? We didn't have any flames burning on the porch. No electrical lines are on there that could spark. Someone set this fire."

Matt looked at the flames. It was possible. He had been hearing stories about mining company equipment being set on fire. Was it possible the company decided turnabout was fair play and set a non-company miner's home on fire?

"Myrna could have been killed," Samuel said. "If I find out who did this, he'll have to answer to me."

Matt patted his uncle on the arm. "She's all right, though, Samuel. Be thankful for that."

Matt heard the wailing siren of the approaching fire truck. Eckhart Mines didn't have a fire company, but it was close enough to Frostburg that its fire company covered calls in Eckhart. The Eckhart men also served in the Frostburg fire company.

The crowd around the boarding house parted as the fire truck approached. It was a new Ahrens-Fox pumper easily recognizable by its chrome appointed gear. It stopped in front of the boarding house, and the firemen scrambled off the sides. They wore metal helmets that looked like something a European field marshal might wear and heavy fire-resistant coats.

Orders were shouted back and forth, as the firemen struggled

250

to be heard over the shouts of the crowd and the crackling fire. One man connected the end of the hose to the forty-gallon tank while two more started unraveling the hose and pulling it closer to the fire. Another pair went to get a hose in a well so that additional water could be pumped onto the fire. The chief ordered one group of men to work to keep the tank filled while he barked commands at the men he wanted manning the line.

The bucket line broke up as people moved to get out of the way of the firefighters. Some men on the bucket line were volunteers with Frostburg Fire Company and started working with them, although they weren't wearing protective gear.

The men grabbed onto the hose as the pump was turned on. Water surged through the hose, and the firefighters aimed the stream into the burning boarding house. It appeared to do little good as the flames remained undiminished.

When Matt turned away from the fire, he saw David Lakehurst sitting on a porch step of a house across the street. When the big man saw Matt, he just laughed. He patted a pail standing next to him. Then he lit a match, tossed it into the street and imitated an explosion, puffing out his cheeks, blowing out the air in a whoosh sound and throwing up his arms. Then suddenly he turned his laugh to a sneer, and said loud enough for Matt to hear "You got to be careful if you play with fire, Matt. You might get burned."

"Did you have something to do with this?" Matt shouted.

Would Lakehurst have gone so far as to set the house on fire just because he hated Matt? Wasn't beating him enough?

"This is a company town. If you aren't helping the company, then you are causing a problem."

Eckhart Mines was far from a company town, and it certainly wasn't Lakehurst's town to decide who belonged or not.

"Did he start the fire?" Samuel asked, stepping up beside Matt. "He needs to be stopped now. This has gone too far."

Samuel started forward, but Matt grabbed him by the arm. Samuel might beat Lakehurst. They were both the same size. It wasn't his problem, though. Lakehurst was Matt's problem.

"No, Samuel. It's my fight."

Matt walked across the street and Lakehurst stood up from the porch.

"Better be careful, Matt. You wouldn't want to fall and break your leg again."

"What's in the pail?" Matt demanded.

Lakehurst looked at the pail as if seeing it for the first time. "This? Why, it's empty. See for yourself."

He tossed the pail at Matt's feet. It was empty, but Matt could smell gasoline. He bent over and picked it up. It hadn't been empty recently. It was still damp inside.

This man had tried to kill Matt, his family, and other innocent people in their sleep. Why? Because Matt had beaten him in a fight? Because Jenny had pressed charges against him? He'd gone too far for simple revenge.

Matt threw the bucket at Lakehurst. It hit the larger man in the head. Lakehurst staggered back until he hit the porch and sat down on it. Then he yelled and charged Matt. Matt braced himself and at the last moment, threw an uppercut, hitting Lakehurst on the chin. He staggered and went to his knees. Then he was on his feet again and ready to fight.

Matt was slightly surprised. He expected Lakehurst to at least be fazed from the upper cut. He had hit him hard, so hard Matt's fist ached.

Lakehurst swung at him. Matt ducked and hammered at the larger man's stomach with a left-right combination before ducking around behind him.

Lakehurst laughed. "This might actually be a bit of a challenge this time."

They moved in close and hammered at each other with quick jabs. Matt's blood raced. He felt the heat of battle. The pain faded as he took blow after blow from this man who was willing to kill his family.

No one hurt his family.

No one.

Lakehurst dove at Matt, and they both fell to the ground. With

252

Lakehurst's greater weight, he could pin Matt to the ground. He reached up, grabbing Matt's head and then tried to drive his thumbs into Matt's eyes.

Matt tried to arch his head back, but the ground blocked him from getting far enough away. He shook his head back and forth, keeping Lakehurst from getting a grip on his face. Then he saw or rather felt an opportunity as he moved his head. One of Lakehurst's fingers brushed across his lips. Matt bit it.

Lakehurst yelped and pulled his hand away. It shifted his weight and allowed Matt to push the larger man off him. Matt rolled to his feet and stood up.

The firefighters were still spraying the boarding house, but many people had stopped watching the fire and had formed a ring around Matt and Lakehurst to watch the two of them fight. Most of them had unpleasant experiences with Lakehurst, so they were cheering Matt on.

Matt tried to catch his breath and felt a sharp pain in his side. He guessed it was a cracked rib. He would have to try to keep his left side away from Lakehurst. He also realized he was unconsciously still fighting as if he needed to protect a broken leg that was no longer broken. He focused on protecting his side rather than his leg and moved it, exchanging blows with Lakehurst.

It was tiring, and his muscles started aching from powering punches into Lakehurst's hard body. Sweat dripped into his eyes and stung.

At one point, he thought he heard Jenny and Laura calling his name. The one voice he knew he heard was Toni's.

"Fight, Matt, fight," she called. He knew it was his aunt, although it wasn't something he expected to hear from her.

Then he heard Samuel. "You can do this, Matt."

Matt couldn't risk looking for his family in the crowd because Lakehurst would have taken advantage of the distraction to attack him. Matt was already having to deal with the larger man's longer reach.

Matt ducked and dodged, moving in ways he hadn't been able to do when he wore a cast.

Matt saw an opening and punched Lakehurst in the mouth. Feeling one of Lakehurst's teeth breaking gave Matt a moment of satisfaction. However, it threw Lakehurst into a frenzy. He grabbed Matt in a bear hug and head butted him. Matt yelled as he saw stars.

He hooked his legs around Lakehurst's and tripped the larger man. They rolled around on the ground, hitting each other with huge, swinging punches.

When Matt got on top, he struck out hard, smashing Lakehurst's nose. Blood spurted and Lakehurst thrashed. Matt hit him in the face again and again. He moved faster and faster. He felt a bone break, probably Lakehurst's jaw. He hit again. He couldn't give Lakehurst a chance to fight back now. He had to maintain his momentum.

Lakehurst drew a pistol. Matt saw it coming up on his left side. He grabbed Lakehurst's left wrist with both hands, rolled his body so that his back was on Lakehurst's chest. Then he let go with his right hand and smashed an elbow into the man's stomach. Then he snapped his fist upward, hitting Lakehurst in his already broken nose.

Hands grabbed Matt and pulled him back off Lakehurst.

"No! Let me go!" He struggled to break free, never taking his eyes off the larger man.

"Matt, stop!" It was Samuel and Enos. They were holding him back.

"You knocked him out."

Matt stopped struggling. Lakehurst was indeed unconscious. He lay still in the dirt.

Matt picked up the gasoline pail. He walked to the pump between the two houses and filled the pail with a little water. Then he walked back and dumped the water on Lakehurst's head. Lakehurst shook his head back and forth. Then he opened his eyes and yelled.

"Owww! That's gasoline."

The bucket had still had the remnants of gasoline in it, but now water diluted it.

"Can I get a match, Samuel?"

His uncle eyed him suspiciously.

"Don't worry," Matt assured him.

Samuel reached into his pocket and pulled out his box of matches. He tossed them to Matt.

Matt walked over to Lakehurst. "I guess that bucket wasn't as empty as you thought. Smell that? It's gasoline."

Matt took a match out of the box and struck it against the side of the box. He waved it around over Lakehurst, watching the man's swollen eyes follow the flame's path. Then the match went out.

Matt tossed it aside and saw Lakehurst flinch. Then he took another match, lit it and looked at the flame.

"I wonder what would happen if I dropped this onto you?"

Lakehurst said nothing.

"Would you catch on fire?" Matt asked.

"You wouldn't," Lakehurst said. His lips were swollen, and he couldn't form the words properly.

Matt dropped the match next to him and Lakehurst rolled away with a screech. Matt followed him and lit another match.

"Listen to me closely, Lakehurst. You are going to get out of this town. I won't say you have to leave the county, but once word of this gets out, you won't be so terrifying to people anymore. Your worth to the coal company here is worthless. In fact, I would guess if they found out you started this fire along with the charges from beating that woman up, you might not even have a job. Understand me?"

Lakehurst glared at him, but he nodded.

"Then get out of here before I change my mind."

Lakehurst groaned as he rolled over and pushed himself to his hands and knees. He leaned back and slowly rose to his feet.

Matt turned back to the house. It was fully engulfed now. The best the firemen could do was to keep it from spreading to the neighboring houses.

He saw Toni crying and walked over to hug her.

"We can rebuild it, Aunt Toni."

She punched him in the stomach. "You fool! Do you think I was worried about the house when you could have been killed in that fight? The man had a gun."

Matt looked over at Jenny who was hugging her robe around herself and crying. She saw Matt looking at her and mouthed, "Thank you."

"The man had a lot to answer for, Aunt Toni." He hugged her. "Thanks for worrying about me, but I think I went easy on him compared to what you could have done."

She smiled and patted his chest. Then she leaned her head against his chest as he hugged her.

Chapter 26

June 21, 1922

Antonietta walked through the remnants of the burned house, trying not to cry. The fire had gutted the structure. Most of the wood was charred. Large sections of the second and third floors were missing; either burned away or collapsed. Most of the front side of the house was missing. What was left of the house wasn't enough to save. At least the fire company had kept it from jumping to a neighboring house.

What the fire hadn't destroyed, the water had. The place smelled of smoke, and wisps of it still drifted up from the ruins, to let people know the fire may still be smoldering despite the tons of water poured on the flaming house. She stood amid the remnants of her bedroom and looked around to see if they might salvage something. Thankfully, she had saved the pictures and the family Bible. Everything else could be replaced... but at what cost?

Some cookware was saved and some clothing from the third floor, although it would have to be thrown away because the pieces would never be rid of the smoke smell.

She walked out what was the back door. It was now just an open space. The shed and animals were fine. They would have to be cared for until the family could figure out what to do next.

She walked around to the front of the house. Matt, Enos, and

Samuel were loading up a truck that Enos borrowed from a friend. Myrna walked over and hugged her.

"What will we do now?" Myrna asked.

"That's what we have to decide," Toni told her.

Toni watched Joseph McCord walk up the street holding hands with Laura Spiker. How could they be together? That made little sense to Toni. Yes, Laura was lovely, but she had a son, and Joseph didn't strike Toni as a man who would want to raise another man's son.

The men stopped loading the truck and turned to watch Laura and Joseph. Laura lifted her hand in a brief wave to Matt as she passed. Toni didn't think Matt saw because he was focused on Joseph. He looked like he might attack the man.

Lakehurst might have been a company employee, but Joseph had controlled him.

Joseph and Laura stopped in front of Toni.

"I'm sorry this happened, Toni," Laura said.

Joseph frowned and chewed on his lip. Then he said, "I am too."

"Especially since it may have been a company employee who did this," Toni added.

Joseph's face flushed. "That hasn't been proven." He paused. "However, the company will pay to rebuild your house and refurnish it."

Toni's eyes narrowed. "Why, if, as you say, it hasn't been proven that a company employee did this?"

Joseph straightened up. "This is a small town, and we are neighbors. We should support each other in a time of need."

He had never shown much of an inclination to do such a thing before. Toni knew Joseph must have an ulterior motive for his generosity. She just didn't know what it was. She also wasn't in a position to reject his offer. If he was willing to rebuild the house, it would be a blessing for the family.

"Thank you," she said.

Joey nodded.

Laura walked over and hugged her. "If you need anything,

please let me know."

Toni smelled alcohol on Laura's breath. She didn't realize that Laura was much of a drinker, but then she hadn't realized Joseph and Laura were so close.

"Are you responsible for Joseph doing this?" Toni whispered so Joseph couldn't hear.

Laura shook her head and mouthed "no."

While Laura and Antonietta were talking, Joseph walked over to stand next to Matt. They both stood in silence for a few moments.

Joseph leaned toward Matt's ear and said softly, "This cancels my debt to you."

Joseph would not stay indebted to Matteo. Joseph owed Matt his life, but that ended once he rebuilt the house. The sooner, the better.

A construction crew made up of his strikebreakers, showed up at the site and started tearing down the burned-out boarding house that day.

Matt used his own money to put his family and Jenny up in the St. Cloud Hotel. Toni grumbled about taking his money, but he knew she didn't have a choice. There was nowhere to stay in Eckhart. She had been the person who helped the families displaced because of the strike find places to stay. Now it was Toni's turn to accept help, something she didn't like, at all.

Matt chose not to stay in the Hotel Gunter because he thought Lakehurst might still be staying there. He was registered at the hotel, but Matt hadn't seen him. Besides, the St. Cloud was closer to Eckhart.

The house burning was just another symptom of how bad the strike was getting, and he didn't expect it to get better anytime soon.

Toni went to the house every day to watch how things progressed. Neighbors brought her food and clothing when they saw her.

Samantha showed up at the hotel one day. She and Matt walked away to talk.

***

David pushed himself into a sitting position in his bed. His side ached, and he wondered if he had a broken rib. He slowly stood, wincing as he straightened up.

He was done here. Ansaro had seen to that. David had been a symbol of the coal company's power in Western Maryland. With his defeat, the miners would be energized in their efforts to defeat the coal company.

How could a smaller man have beaten him?

He was certain that the chief of police in Frostburg would be looking for him again. He had talked his way out of beating up one whore since Calista's charges had been dropped, but he suspected the other whores he had been rough with might be willing to come forward. One of them had already gone to the police. They weren't afraid of him any longer, which meant there was a chance the others would come forward and tell their stories to the police. David was heading to jail if he ever went to court.

He walked over to the desk and sat down. He pulled a sheet of stationary from the drawer and started writing a letter.

Ansaro might have uncovered David's secret, but Ansaro had secrets of his own. David wondered how the UMW recruiter would react when David told him that Ansaro was an undercover Pinkerton.

David smiled as started writing his letter.

Author's Note

I originally planned the Black Fire Trilogy to be a single book, but when I mapped the story out, it stretched into three books. I am already working on the third novel, *Frostburg Burning.*

Although historical novels are fiction, they involve a lot of research, sometimes into minutiae that is hard to find. Forgive any inaccuracies that have made their way into the story. I tried my best to keep it as accurate as I could, but sometimes certain details just weren't available or couldn't be found. In these cases, I tried to find something similar that occurred nearby and failing that, I made an educated guess based on available information.

I wanted to add more detail to a couple things noted in this novel.

The scene where Matt and Samantha drive to McHenry to look over the valley before it becomes a lake is something that actually happened. The lake, not the drive.

The project was announced on November 21, 1923, and at that point, the Army Corps of Engineers had been planning how to make the lake a reality for eighteen months. The Youghiogheny River Power Company and the Youghiogheny Water and Electric Company planned to generate 100,000 horsepower of hydroelectric power by building a controlled water power dam and tunnel.

To create the lake, a 70-foot-tall, 1,200-foot-wide dam was

constructed to impound the water from streams in the area. The lake began flooding the valley in March 1925, and it filled in just a few months. The result was the 1.5-mile-long Deep Creek Lake filled with 7.7 million cubic feet of water 2,340 feet above sea level. It's a beautiful place to vacation if you are looking for ideas.

Another thing I wanted to point out was how poorly Prohibition was enforced in Frostburg. The town was notorious for ignoring the law, and local police generally only took action when the federal agents forced them.

Things got so bad in the town that it experienced a water shortage in the fall of 1922. The town was using three times the amount of water a town that size typically used. The difference was blamed on moonshiners and the 100 stills that were estimated to be operating within the town's boundaries. The town government published a flyer calling on citizens to conserve water and moonshiners, specifically, to stop making moonshine until the town had more water.

Finally, I'd like to thank my new editor, Rosemary Hutchison. You did a great job!

James Rada, Jr.
April 5, 2020

About the Author

James Rada, Jr. has written many works of historical fiction and non-fiction history. They include the popular books *Saving Shallmar: Christmas Spirit in a Coal Town, Canawlers,* and *Battlefield Angels: The Daughters of Charity Work as Civil War Nurses.*

He lives in Gettysburg, Pa., where he works as a freelance writer. James has received numerous awards from the Maryland-Delaware-DC Press Association, Associated Press, Maryland State Teachers Association, Society of Professional Journalists, and Community Newspapers Holdings, Inc. for his newspaper writing.

If you would like to be kept up to date on new books being published by James or ask him questions, he can be reached by e-mail at *jimrada@yahoo.com.*

To see James' other books or to order copies on-line, go to *www.jamesrada.com.*

PLEASE LEAVE A REVIEW
If you enjoyed this book, please help other readers find it. Reviews help the author get more exposure for his books. Please take a few minutes to review this book at *Amazon.com* or *Goodreads.com*. Thank you, and if you sign up for my mailing list at *jamesrada.com*, you can get FREE ebooks.

If you enjoyed
Strike the Fuse,
try these __FREE__ novels by James Rada, Jr.

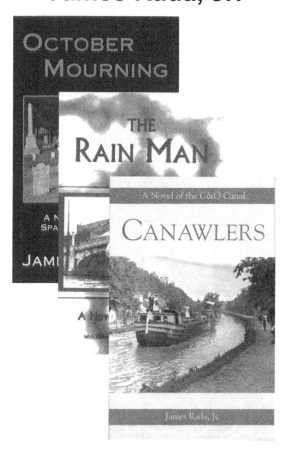